THE GENTLEMAN

A NOVEL

BY

NATASHA POWELL

NAPOW INC. PUBLISHING

First paperback edition April 2014

Cover Art © by Natasha Powell Cover Design. All rights reserved.
Layout and Design by Finish the Story www.finish-the-story.com

Publishing History
First Edition, 2014
Print ISBN: 978-0615990378
Published in the United States of America

THE
GENTLEMAN

"There is nothing like suspense and anxiety for barricading a human's mind against the Enemy. He wants men to be concerned with what they do; our business is to keep them thinking about what will happen to them."

— C.S. Lewis: The Screwtape Letters

ACT I: JAMES

CHAPTER 1
STORM OF THE CENTURY

It was 1981, and a year since James Greene's deal with The Gentleman. Days ago, he'd fled from the terrors in South Carolina for the Florida Keys. He intended to reach the Keys before the sun rose, but the storm that put cannon-sized dents into his truck in the wee hours of the morning spoiled his plan. Worst of all, the feeling of someone watching and following him had heightened after he'd entered Florida.

When the droplets of rain became tiny atom bombs exploding on the windshield, he'd swerved around potholes and driven slower than the speed limit to avoid driving his 1959 pickup into a muddy quicksand. The condensation on the windshield formed faster than his wipers could clear it off. As the rain fell harder, gallons of it flooded the inside of his truck by way of the rolled down window on the passenger's side.

"Damn it! I had only one hundred miles left." He slammed his fist into the steering wheel. The impact left knuckle marks in the plastic and bent the frame. After taking a deep breath and a swig of rum, he looked on either side of the road for a place to hole-up until the storm died.

Only dreary trees lined the sides of the road. Then, finally, a sign for The Hotel Love Nest blinked on and off beside the road as he drove past. James mashed the brakes to the floor, turned his truck around, and drove back in the direction of the hotel.

His bag splashed onto his floorboard, into the swimming pool that grew with each passing minute. As his tires screeched, they pushed slushy mud up and sprayed rocks in every direction.

He parked his truck, more crooked than usual, in front of a rundown hotel. It had all the makings of a bad-side-of-town look. As the rain increased its frenzy and cascaded harder from sky, he rolled the passenger window up to prevent more from pouring inside.

"Okay, one, two, three!"

On three, he opened his door and battered through the storm, until his boots landed in a large puddle outside the main office. He ignored it and continued toward the door. The rain confused his sense of perception, and he overshot the distance to the handle, causing him to open the door with his shoulder, shoving his way inside where he collapsed onto the floor.

Once the door shut, reducing the sounds of the raging thunderstorm, he stood and wiped the rain from his face. With clearer vision, he saw a man with stringy hair, coke-bottle glasses, and greasy clothes sitting dangerously close to a black and white TV behind the desk.

"Hey," James said and waved his hand to the guy.

The man paid him no mind and watched a woman on the tube scream as a monster slashed her throat.

James moved his hand to his side with stealth and unsheathed his knife.

"No," he whispered, squeezed his eyes shut, shook his head, and snapped closed the button to the knife's casing. "Hey buddy, I need a fuckin' room." James smashed his hand on the bell that sat on the desk.

The man moved around to face him. "Ten dollars." He turned back to the TV.

James ripped out his wallet and put the soggy bills on the counter.

After the man had removed the key from the wall, he slid it over to James. "Room four," he said while gawking at the TV where a townsman was dragging the monster from its hole. He stuffed more donuts into his cavity-corroded mouth.

"*Thanks*," James said and ran back to his truck for his soaked bag.

The rain pelted his skin; the gusts slapping his face and slowing him to a fast walk. Because of the hurricane force winds, the truck's door weighed a thousand pounds, and he had to dig his feet into the mud to yank it open. After removing his bag and shotgun, he hustled to the sidewalk, but not before grabbing the two sets of dog tags that hung around the rearview mirror. As he stepped onto the sidewalk, the hotel roof finally provided relief from the storm.

He reached into his pocket for the key and accidently snagged a drenched flyer with a fisherman on the front along with it. The wind tossed the paper in the air, and he captured it before it disappeared into the downpour. He held it to the moonlight, scanning it before returning it to his soaked pants.

"Soon, I'll be James, the fisherman. Just one night and that's it." He strolled to room number four and paused before entering. "Something doesn't feel right."

The wind swirled, pulling him back toward the rain. He forced his feet forward and focused on the lock. The sounds of the hotel building settling resembled the hair-raising screams from a serial killer's basement. Something, he was sure of it, called his name.

"It's not real." He stabbed the key into the lock. A swift jerk and shake of the door caused the room number to fling free of the bent nails that held it up as the door swung open. Without looking back, he darted into the dark room and closing the door, leaned his back against the door as it closed out the howls of Hurricane Nightmare. Rain dripped off his wet body and streaked down the doorframe.

"Okay, I made it. It'll take him a while to catch me now." After standing up from the ground, he turned on the lights and marveled at the disaster of a room. The walls resembled the pocked surface of the dark side of the moon. The bathroom, covered in mildew and mold, had no door. Cracks similar to the ones in the Sahara desert appeared on the ceiling, and cancerous black spots filled the corner. The only positives were a bed, a desk and chair, and a TV.

"This is the worst of the worst. No wonder it was ten dollars."

Not wasting a minute, he dropped his duffle bag on the floor and unzipped it. After pulling out a velvet pouch, he spread soot at the inside of the door. The smell of burnt leather drifted up to his nose, and a small haze rose from the material. He burned sage in the window seals and set fire to a hard material that he laid in the middle of the room. As the hard substance burned, a smell worse than the room lingered. But once it evaporated, the muggy smell of a dead man's anus withered away.

Now to get out of these. He wiped away some of the water from his face as he reached down, unlaced his boots, removed his wet socks, peeled off his shirt and pants, and tossed them onto the ground. From his bag, he retrieved a dry pair of socks and pants and put them on.

After unsheathing his knife, he felt the groves and tic marks engraved along the handle and placed it on the table. There were thirty-four marks etched in the wooden handle.

When he'd finished, he rested his short-barreled shotgun against the table where he relaxed and pulled out his Florida State game-winning baseball from college. He tossed the ball into the air, launching it higher and higher. It hit the ceiling and pieces of plaster fell on his head.

"Fuck!"

Once he stood, he brushed the fragments from his matted hair and shoulders onto the stained carpet and stopped the baseball from rolling under the bed with his foot. The ball still had pieces of plaster on it, and he brushed them off then tossed it into his bag. His bag contained another treasure of his—rum. He removed a new bottle and uncapped it, sucking down the spicy juice through his dehydrated lips.

"Huh." He wiped what spilled off his face and recapped the bottle.

Sitting at the table, he flattened the torn flyer and spread it across the broken and splintered top. While shutting his eyes, he pictured the sea, the way it smelled, and the way it felt against his skin. The whales collided with the boat, and he heaved and hoed with the dozen or so other men that worked along with him on the large vessel. The ropes burned his hands and blood mixed with the salty water. No one knew if they'd die by the whale's hand or the storm. Nevertheless that was all right by him. There was no one around hounding and harassing him, taking away his sleep and ability to think. No one threatening his life, family, or conscience. It was him and the sea. James and his thoughts.

"I can't wait." He smiled and interlaced his fingers behind his head.

A violent bang at the door erased the peaceful vision. James fell from his seat onto the floor, whacking his head along the way. When he rose, he dashed to the light switch and flicked it off.

The thing outside beat and hammered on the door. With his back pressed against the wall and breathing as little as possible, he shook each time the door thumped. Sweat raced down his chest and forehead. His nostrils flared as lilac seeped into the room, and he resisted the urge to gag.

"No," he whispered.

The thing scratched and chattered on the other side of the door, and multiple voices talked simultaneously. It raged and laughed, and the windows vibrated; little cracks spread across the glass.

James squeezed his eyes shut and prayed to God, any God that happened to hear him. He prayed until his mouth was too dry to open. Then he prayed in his head.

The commotion ended, and the ominous presence left. He lifted his trembling hand to the newly cracked window, pushed the curtain away, and saw nothing. After turning on the lights, he sat at the edge of the bed with his head in his hands.

"Only one more day. I've had one hundred fucking miles, and now this." He drove his fist into the wall beside the bed. The pain caused him to wave his hand.

"It's one of the hallucinations. You haven't slept in what, three days? It's like the time in Macon." He rubbed his head.

A letter swished into his room from under the door and floated beside him onto the tattered covers. James leapt from it. His eyes widened at the sight of the handwriting.

"It's just paper," he muttered. Mustering the courage, he seized the letter. It shook in his unsteady hands as he read the words.

I WANT MY SOUL, AND SINCE I'M SUCH A NICE GUY, I'LL GIVE YOU UNTIL DECEMBER 22 AT 1:30 AM. I KNOW WHERE YOU'RE AT. NO NEED TO RUN, IT'LL ONLY MAKE THINGS WORSE. OH, AND CLEAN UP.
FROM THE GENTLEMAN, WITH LOVE

James' thoughts spun. He looked around the room for something, anything, to help him stand upright, but instead landed on the bed. The words raced through his mind, smashing the good memories aside.

"I can't *leave*?" He tugged at his hair and wiped the sweat from his face. What he'd spent the last several months planning was all for nothing. A deep emptiness filled his soul. Not even the burning of the rum could fill it. He curled into a ball and wept himself to sleep.

CHAPTER 2
KNOCK, KNOCK

James slept through the morning and most of the afternoon. He awoke to silence and the sunlight peeking through the curtain. Before that night, he hadn't slept for three days and before that, a week.

He rose from the bed then wiped the dirt from his face and the crust from his eyes. Standing caused his bones to crack and pop. To his dismay and fright, the letter was still in his hand, and he flung it from his fingers. How it got there was a better question. The thing attracted to him like a magnet. The image of the paper ignited the empty feeling, the deepening hole inside him, and he grabbed the rum to smother it.

After going for his bag, he pulled out a small journal with a black background and white spots, and sat in the chair, pondering his next escape. He ran his finger along his laundry list of anti-demon spells and doodads he'd picked up from voodoo folks and witches. The underground of the real world. The ones that hid in the shadows of the regular people and came out when someone summoned them.

"Wormwood, demon wood," James said in a tired voice.

"I did the soot shit, I did the necklace crap." He tore out page upon page of the journal. The pages contained illegible scribbles, crude boob drawings, and notes written all over—not following the lines on the paper. He had written most of this while drunk, without sleep, in dire straits, or all of the above.

"I can't leave, I'm stuck here." After reviewing each page,

he crumpled it up and tossed the paper onto the floor. The room soon resembled the floor of a writer.

Once the journal was bare bones, James turned to his bottle. He sat drinking, leaning over in his chair, and glaring at his shotgun until the moon sat high in the sky.

"A bullet hole straight through my mouth and out the back of my head, no pain, no more running, no more games."

Memories of The Gentleman's torture the year before melded with his discussion to pull the trigger.

He put the bottle of rum to his mouth. He thought of the time The Gentleman forced him to shoot an elderly woman in the head. He put the bottle of rum to his mouth. The smell of the pistol, the blood from her head, the way her body twitched when she fell—the images were as vivid in his mind as the day they happened.

"I shot that fucking old bag in the head."

He put the bottle of rum to his mouth, and then pulled it away to catch his breath.

"I, I put my hands, and I...Oh, God." As he widened his eyes, the opening of the bottle went to his lips.

The things he had done for The Gentleman, the gruesome things that had changed him from who he was into a hardened criminal, echoed inside of him. In a weird way, he enjoyed this new emotion--guilt. For a long time, during his stint as The Gentleman's hit man, that feeling remained absent, and only the desire to kill had invaded his conscience.

The last act before he lost his soul involved his daughter. She stood on the ledge of a building in Charleston, South Carolina, wearing her Sunday best, with her arms spread for flight. All because he didn't want to play any more games. His daughter became part of the wager. The Gentleman gave him an offer he couldn't refuse. Him or his daughter, James or Jenni. That choice was easy, and he made it without thought. And because he didn't want to play the games, the fine print read, *The Gentleman keeps your soul.*

"Then he...I tried to stop it. I said I was done." James stared at the swirling liquid inside the glass he tipped from one side to the other.

"Look, Daddy, I can fly. ' Me or Jenni,' he said. My little girl." He wiped the sweat from his face, and then poured more rum into his crusted mouth.

"Your whore of a mother didn't want me to name you Jenni; she wanted to name you Stacey." James held his bottle up to the sky. "Fuck her," he said and put the bottle to his mouth again.

He drank and drank until he became a drunken fool. Bantering, laughing at inappropriate times, and crying in the next moment. Anyone who walked by his room would have guessed someone else was inside with him, given the way he carried on.

"Rum, the best woman…I never had. Always…listened and made me feel…better when I needed you the most," he slurred and took the biggest swig yet.

During his travel down memory lane, James spilled the contents of his duffle on the table and inventoried his belongings one by one. He sprayed them out and fell over the table as he stumbled to position them in the order of his precedence.

He picked up the ring from the table, twirled the thing in his hands, and slipped it on his left ring finger—it fell off.

"Why did I even take this thing with me? Damn ring doesn't fit anymo'." Looking down at it spinning on the ground, he took a drink and spat some of the alcohol on it. "Good riddance."

While running his hands over the table with his treasures, James picked up a picture of himself and an older man out in the woods. He turned it over and read the back.

JIMMY AND DAD'S FIRST DEER.

"Give me a sign, old man," he said to the photo. After rubbing his thumb over his father's face, he put the picture on the table. He didn't have his father's dimples; he only had his deep ocean blue eyes and dark brown hair. To his disgust, he had his mother's smile and hated when folks that knew her reminded him of that fact.

The note from The Gentleman found its way to his hands. It flapped against his fingers like a paper stuck on the back of a fan.

"You can't have me." He removed the paper from his hand and held it before his face. He struck his lighter on the corner and watched as the blue and sapphire flames engulfed the writing. The fire flickered in his eyes. James released what was left of the paper from his hand before the flames touched his fingers. The ashes fluttered like butterflies in the room. The letters *'Mine'* shined with a lavender glow before melding with the smoke from the sage burning on the windowsill.

He turned his head away from the letters and focused on the shotgun. "I can't wait. The longer I wait…" He took five deep breaths and slapped his face.

"All right this is it, no more games, it's now or never." Positioning the barrel of the gun in his mouth, he leaned over. His dog tags draped from his damp neck.

Once he closed his tired eyes, he squeezed the trigger in slow motion.

His face scrunched, and he breathed heavily in anticipation.

Snot, sweat, and tears covered his face, hands, and the gun.

Tick tock.

Squeeze, sweat, snot.

Tick tock, squeeze…

Thump, thump, from his chest. The sounds heightened with each passing second as he continued to apply pressure on the trigger.

Click.

He flinched as the loud sound ricocheted through the room.

After opening his eyes, he let out a deep sigh at the sight of all the rounds on the table. As he removed his finger from the trigger well, someone banged on his hotel's door.

"Delivery for James Greene," a muffled voice shouted.

"Delivery?" he asked with the barrel still in his mouth. *At this hour?*

He stumbled from his chair, fell to the ground, and pulled on the curtain for assistance standing. Walking was harder after finishing a fifth of rum.

Out the window, he watched the deliveryman set the package down and walk away from the door.

"It's not him."

But knowing the man at the door wasn't The Gentleman wasn't enough. As a precaution, his feet followed an invisible tightrope to his shotgun, and he took it with him to the door. When he opened the door, a strong gust pushed in the cold of the night. The wind bit his face and blew back his hair.

"What's this?" His teeth chattered. He stepped over the line of sulfur and soot by the doorstep to retrieve the package. "Who the hell knew I'd be here?" He scratched his shallow beard.

A muscular woman, with emerald green eyes, wearing a blonde wig and a prostitute's startup kit, followed a stocky man into the room to the left of James. She pulled on the man's jacket and placed soft kisses on his neck. While the man opened the door, she waved and blew James a kiss.

"Ew." James closed his door; his big toe's print divided the line.

"Lola...L-o-l-a, Lola." He mustered up a snicker.

"I haven't laughed in weeks." Using the burning sage from the window, he purified the door and waved the sage over the package, eliminating any essence of the demon.

"Just in case." Then, he brought the package to his nose.

"Doesn't smell like that son of a slut, though." He pulled out his knife and carefully opened the package, revealing a letter inside.

"What the hell is this?"

Meet me at the return address. You'll be able to get rid of him once and for all.

He tossed the paper aside, blew hard through his nose, and kicked the splintery table.

"Stop messing with me."

The baseball rolled out of his bag, and he picked it up, rotated it in his hand, rubbing off pieces of plaster that remained on it from the day before.

With a marker he fished out of his bag, he drew a large X on the wall. The smell of the ball reminded him of college, the women, the drinking, the parties, and his best friend Jeff. He held onto the memories. And after pushing a pile of wet clothes together from the floor, he placed his foot on top of it and used it as a mound.

"Greene at the mound looks at his catcher and shakes his head." As James leaned forward, he twirled the ball behind his back in his left hand. "The count is three-two. The catcher signals again, Greene shakes his head. He can't hear the crowd chanting because of the pressure." He positioned three fingers on top of the ball, and then stood up and eyed his hand. During his reenactment of his perfect game, he had forgotten about his missing ring finger on his left hand.

"No change up anymore." The Gentleman had robbed him of throwing the winning pitch from college. He needed three fingers for that. He put his two fingers along the red seams of the ball for the perfect fastball instead.

"He winds up and releases."

The ball spiraled out of his grasp. It banged on the black X at 80 miles an hour, and clumps of plaster fell to the ground along with it.

Someone hit the wall in the room to James' right.

"You fucker. Stop hitting the wall, asshole!" a man screamed.

The man's words didn't reach his ears, he picked the ball up muttering, "Jimmy's perfect game," and placed it back in his bag.

He glanced at the door. "Where are you, you piece of shit?"

Suicide was still a way out, it seemed, and as the time passed, he wrestled with the reality of parting with the world.

He reached inside his bag and found a picture that had belonged to his father. It was a photo of James' grandfather, whom he had never met. But the stories his father told created an image of a WWI Vet, a simple man with family values and unafraid to spare the rod. In the age-spotted, black and white picture, a tall man stood holding a pregnant woman outside a white plantation home. They exuded happiness, they appeared new; they seemed dreamy, as if they had it all, and nothing in the world could take that away from them.

"This was your old man? I wish I would've known you better, Dad. I wish I was there. I should've been there, but I chose to deploy again..." He stood the photo on the table. To know the man who raised his father would have been an honor. He wanted to thank him for doing a hell of a job.

After he turned on the TV, he opened a new bottle and let the warm liquid slide down his throat. He walked around the room with the bottle up to his mouth until he needed to breathe. Moving in front of the mirror, he beamed at his scars, some from the war and others from The Gentleman. He grazed his four fingers over them.

"Get rid of him, huh?" he asked and fell flat on the bed.

A black and white TV blared reruns of old sitcoms that mixed with the knocking of the bed from the other room against the wall near his head.

"Oh, Jimmy," a deep voice called.

But he lay staring into the darkness.

The sounds around him became background noise. "Get rid of him? That'll be the day," he mumbled.

***

Morning came with another deafening pounding on the door. Sweat shot from his body as he rose. He'd had that dream again. The dream where he chased his daughter down a corridor, and at the end of it, there was The Gentleman holding his mouth to hers. In this dream, she was eighteen, maybe twenty, and fully developed. The Gentleman rubbed his hands up and down her curves, and she didn't fight him. The more James ran, the slower his movements became. He could only watch as his worst fear unfolded in front of him.

He slapped his head several times and said, "It's just a

dream."

But the knocking didn't cease.

James put on his shirt, picked up a grayish colored powered from the table, and looked through the peephole.

"A letter for Mister Greene," a man said. He peeked around the corner as James opened the door.

After tossing the substance onto the man's shirt, James relaxed when there was no sizzling, bubbling, or smoke. The man simply looked at the powder James hit him with and forced a smile.

"Leave it on the floor and leave." James gave no apology for his actions. The demon had taken his gratitude and sense of decency long ago.

"Yes, sir, and have a great day." The man nodded and left.

James waited until he was no longer in view before opening the door completely. As he bent over to get the letter, he paused at the sight of the divided line. Using his unsteady hand, he spread soot over the space.

The room next to him opened, and the woman he'd seen the night before trampled outside with a half-naked man. James winced at her new appearance; she wasn't wearing her wig, she wore smeared makeup, and her voice dropped to a baritone. Something was familiar about her green eyes, but James couldn't figure out what. He damn sure never slept with her; that he was sure of.

The man pushed the woman onto the wet gravel with his stubby hands, and he tossed her clothes beside her. "You didn't tell me yous had a dick!"

"You still owe me," the woman said and held out her hand.

"Get the fucks outta here!" The man pulled out wads of cash and threw the bills into the air.

"You didn't mind it when I was suckin' your tiny dick, and you were fuckin' my ass!" She picked up the money. "You'll get yours tonight, *pojke*." She gave the man the finger and wobbled away on the wet sidewalk.

The man cuffed his hands around his mouth and yelled to her, "Bag yah face, honey, bag yah face." His voice carried in the spacious lot.

James watched the spectacle, leaning on his doorframe. The creak from his door caught the man's attention.

"What the fuck yous looking at, cock sucker?"

James shook his head and slipped back into his room.

He slapped the envelope against the palm of his hand. "The same address." He put the package close to his nose. "And it smells like peaches." He flipped it on both sides. "Who the hell is this?"

"Meet him at one-thirty or meet the barrel?" He debated and chewed away at his fingernails before ruffling his tangled hair. He laid the envelope on the table and scooted his chair closer to the bed behind him. He slid a pair of pliers and a c-clamp to the other side of the table as he sat peering at the envelope. A possible escape from him was one thing. But killing him? James could hardly control the excitement that burgeoned inside of him.

"Get rid of him?" He rushed to the envelope and ripped the packaging to shreds.

YOUR TIME IS RUNNING OUT. IF YOU WANT TO BE DONE WITH HIM, NOW'S THE CHANCE. YOU CAN'T ESCAPE HIM AT 1:30, NOT EVEN IN DEATH. HE WON'T STOP UNTIL YOU'RE HIS.

"What do I do?" James clutched the letter and sat back in the chair. The note scraped away the idea of suicide that callused on his brain.

"It is about time I shave this." He rubbed his thumb and index finger against the wiry hair on his face as he lumbered into the bathroom and switched on the light.

When the lights came on, hundreds of roaches scattered in different directions inside the sink and into the walls. He flicked the ones that crawled on his body onto the floor and smashed the others on the sink. He stood in front of a mirror covered with crust and mold and touched his sunken cheekbones, drug his fingers across his stubby beard, and felt the grooves of time written under his eyes.

"Who are you?" He reached inside his wallet for a picture of himself and held it up against his reflection. The two men only shared the same ocean-blue eyes. It was a picture of him when he was twenty-two in 1971, a time when he'd had it all. The girl, the best friend, and his dad. The Gentleman's torment didn't exist, and only joy filled him inside. Now at thirty-four, James looked as if he had lived through the civil war and the turn of the century.

"Jeff...I'm glad you can't see me now." He clasped the two sets of dog tags that hung around his neck.

When he turned on the faucet, brown-yellow water and the smell of sewage slushed out of its opening. But after some time, light-yellow tinted water flowed, steam rose, and the smell of sewage decreased and he placed his hand under the water.

"Ah, God dammit, it's either too hot or ice cold." The hot water burned, and he hobbled around in response to the pain.

"Ice cold water it is." He turned on the opposite dial and positioned his hands underneath. As he stroked the blades against his wet face, pieces of his hair twirled down the drain.

"Not bad, not bad. ' Clean up,' he says. 'Meet me there,' he says." He knocked hair from his razor into the sink.

"Fuck you, I say."

"Ah!" After nicking his neck, he placed pieces of toilet paper on the cut; they did little to stop the bleeding. The second he looked up, another man's face grinned to him from inside the mirror. The man wore a bowler hat that was darker than the shadows in the room. His grin caused James to shiver, and the creases in the man's smile pressed through his black-inked beard.

"No, you bag of dicks." He lifted his hand and curled his fingers to form a fist. He pushed all the rage in the world, seven years of pain, and one hundred and fifty pounds of skin and bones, into the mirror. The glass shattered and covered the floor. He turned his body to the emptiness behind him, and when he turned back to the mirror, he only saw twenty different images of his frightened face. His fist, unclenched, rested at his side, and blood rolled from his fingertips to the bathroom floor.

He swallowed the trepidation that wedged in his throat and charged into the bedroom. Wrapping his hand with an old shirt, he sat shaking and cowering in his chair. Right when he felt he came to a point when he could relax, The Gentleman's image appeared and drove James back to the bottle.

He paced in his room for hours, twirling his knife in his wounded hand, and he topped-off the second bottle with the other. Oh, how he wished he could stop time, but the clock marched on, and time sped up.

"I won't let that fucker have me, not this time." Panic inched its way into his stomach. He picked up the rifle and scrutinized the chamber. It was fully loaded. He cocked the rifle and sat in his chair, his eyes fixed on the clock. The scenery from the other day played out, him in the room with a gun in his mouth. However, this time, the bullets were in the chamber.

His breath fogged the metal, and his hands shook the weapon against his teeth. He bit down hard on the end of the barrel and closed his eyes. After he slipped his finger in the trigger well, he began to squeeze the trigger.

Then, the radio came on. *Ain't wastin' No Mo' Time* by the Allman Brothers played. The picture on the table tipped over. The glass of the frame shattered. His gun fell from his hands, and he gravitated to the broken frame.

His feet crushed some of the shards of glass surrounding the frame, and he bled onto the floor, but his blood didn't show on the already soiled carpet. In an effort to remove the pieces of glass from the picture, he blew across it and the image drifted.

He grabbed the downward-facing picture and raised an eyebrow at the words written on the back.

THE GREENE'S DEC 1917. FIXED THE FAMILY'S
HOME ON EVEREST RD. HERE'S TO YOU, WILLIAM!

"What?" He went to the box and compared the two addresses. "This is the same street." After he ejected the rounds, he fell into his seat.

"I guess that's my sign, old man. You always had good timing."

"My last one," he said as he grasped a new bottle of rum from his bag. Then, after twisting off the top, he raised it to the sky.

***

The time read six p.m. when James packed his belongings in his duffle bag. "I got time. I got time. I can get there before he comes. I can get there," he said and departed from the room into the dusk.

However, the further he ventured out of the hotel room, the more he deduced that his chances of killing The Gentleman were as slim as Boston winning the pennant. How could anyone stop that demon? His jog decreased to a stride, and his stride became a dead stop.

"What am I doing? I don't even know who this is or if this is my family's place." He ran back to the hotel room.

"This is so crazy. All of it." He rubbed his eyes as he came to the door.

In the corner of his eye, he noticed that the door next to his lay wide open. As he turned his head to get a glimpse of the room, a small girl skipped across parking lot and dashed into the room.

"Jenni?" he asked as he motioned to run.

"Jenni!"

With his bag slapping his back, James galloped to the entrance of the door.

Despite what common sense told him, he felt compelled to enter. James gave the open door one tired push, and it opened completely.

He stepped inside and turned on the lights.

The room smelled of sex and bourbon. Lilac melded with the aroma. He scanned the room, looking for the little girl, but only found the man spiraled across the bed with his throat slashed. He continued to walk into the room.

"Jenni...," he whispered. The sheets on the bed bore leopard spots of blood. Someone had sliced off the man's cock and stuffed it in his mouth. Blood gushed out from where the man's penis had once been.

"Ew." James put his forearm over his nose to diminish the smell. A note with a knife driven through it lay on the nightstand. His face tensed when he read the words, *"You're next."*

Stumbling, James walked backwards to the exit. After getting out of the room, he fled at the speed of sound to his truck. He spiraled his bag inside and threw himself into the driver's side. The keys fumbled in his hands, and he dropped them in a puddle on the floor several times.

"Come on." He used both hands to steady the keys and find the hole. The engine roared. The lilac smog traveled from the room and threatened to suffocate him.

"Not this time." He pounded the gas, and the truck accelerated away from the hotel for the highway, traveling the same direction in which he'd come. In the rearview mirror's reflection, the structure of the hotel crumbled to ash, and a man in a suit stood in the place where it had been.

CHAPTER 3
BAT OUTTA HELL

With the exception of filling up his tank, James drove miles nonstop and used piss bottles to relieve himself. Although it was fifty degrees outside, he left the windows down to allow the breeze to cool him off and aid with drying out the ocean at his feet. A fog settled in, and his truck barreled through it as he sped down the bleak Florida Highway. As he forced the truck to go faster and faster, the engine knocked as if it would shake itself loose from the blocks.

He winced at the sign on the side of the road that read Ocala 12 miles. It was close to where Jeff's family lived.

"I'm sorry Jeff. I should've seen them after you died. I should've said I was sorry, something. Anything," he said and placed his hands on the dog tags around his neck.

He grabbed his warm piss bottle, filled to the brim with pieces of pubic hair and blood floating at the top of the plastic container. Freeing his hands to open it, he used his knees to steer the truck. When he put his hand out of the window to empty it, the wind snatched the bottle from his hands. Warm liquid splattered on the pavement, and some hit his face.

"Shit!" He screamed and rubbed it from his eyes, reluctantly tasting the salty liquid as it hit his lips. "Gross." Using rum, he washed his mouth out and spit what he could out the window.

"Music will take my mind off it." As he flipped through the stations, each song spoke of waterfalls, and each advertisement told him to drink their refreshing product. The sounds of beer pouring into a glass echoed in others. His legs trembled, and he gripped his crotch, pinching off the hose. The water at the bottom of his truck slushed and gulped, and James weaved all over the road.

"I can't wait any longer. I'm pulling over."

He parked near a line of trees that disguised his truck and flung himself into the open. His feet crunched the grass as he walked to a large bush not far from where he parked. Up ahead, he heard voices. Before unzipping his pants, James snuck around the corner, deeper into the wooded area. With his hand shadowing the knife in his sheath, he crept around brush and dipped under hanging branches. Then, 50 meters in front of him, he saw two men arguing and hid behind the tallest brush near him, hiding his face from the light of the full moon. Although the full moon touched most of the area, the shadow that the building on top of the hill cast, hid the men's appearance. He couldn't tell if The Gentleman was one of them. He inched closer, and the voices became clearer. One deep, commanding, and one shaky and desperate.

"Come on you know I'm good for it?" a shaky voice called. James could tell which man spoke. It was the scrawny son-of-a-slut wearing a thick jacket, rubbing his hands up and down his arms, but not from the cold.

"You said that last week…I know what you can do for me," a large man said.

The light from the moon revealed he had a mullet, which meant no bowler hat.

It's not him, just a drug deal. James snuck away from his hiding area and went back to where he parked.

James decided to take a piss on the other side of his truck away from the hedgerow.

Pushing his shoulders back, he reclined his neck and exhaled, unzipped his pants, and let it rip. The warm liquid ignited the ground as it hit the cold, wet grass.

"Jeff, remember when we said we'd open that sports bar not far from UF? We said it'll be better than any of them." He lifted the corner of his mouth. As he looked at the dog tags around his neck, he read what he could from in the light of the moon.

"AB negative, just like me. I wish the last time I saw you wasn't the only memory that sits in my head Jeff, I wish—"

Something large rustled in the brush, and without urinating on his boots, he veered in to see what it was. He placed his hand over his knife.

A large beast, with the speed of a banshee, galloped in his direction and rippled the fog as it advanced.

The loud sound of its hooves beating the ground left James in a daze. He collapsed to his knees with his pants unzipped, and his eyes focused on nothing. This was his first flashback in months.

Flying over the jungles of Vietnam in his Chinook, James, then Captain Greene, looked ahead at FSB (Fire Support Base) Ripcord. From his height, the bunkers and tents looked like monopoly house pieces. In another ten minutes, they'd be able to land and finish the massive operation that followed the salvo on the base. More importantly, this was their last flight to FSB Ripcord before returning to Evans.

"Hey, Black Moomba!" James said through his headset.

"Yo, crackerjack," Jeff responded.

"I think something's going wrong with the engine, let's try to safely land this thing in the LZ." James signaled to the other copilots and the gunners, and they adjusted with the orders given by him.

"What's that over there?" Jeff asked. The Chinook was within meters of their landing zone.

"I don't know. I can't see," James said and focused on the area. "Over there? Oh, shit. Are those anti-aircraft guns? Shit!"

"We gotta go. We need backup; I say again, we need back up. Over!" James radioed their position to the TOC.

The gunners in the window fired fifty caliber rounds at the enemy's location, and the rounds pelted the dirt and flashed over the vegetation. The force lifted three of them from the ground. As the gunners reloaded, two NVAs exposed themselves from behind a brush, one with an AK-47, and one with an anti-aircraft weapon. One fired a round at the Chinook.

The blast from the weapon knocked the NVA to the ground. The fire from the Chinook pierced their bodies twenty times, and their blood emptied onto the lush grass. The missile the NVA's shot, sailed close to the plane and danced among the clouds before clipping the bird.

"Oh, shit! Ah great, they hit us!" James said, "We have to evacuate!"

All the co-pilots began evacuations procedures.

The plane descended faster to the base than James could prepare for. He pulled and yanked on the level to tip the nose of the bird, but it broke, and a large metal object ripped flesh from his thigh.

The Chinook crash-landed into the howitzers, destroying two of them. Rounds set off from the blast, and fifty caliber rounds began to cook inside. As they went off, the rounds exploded into every direction.

"Jeff!" James reached for Jeff, but the thing on his leg restricted his movements.

He attempted to pull his right leg out from under objects that fell on it.

"Ahhhhhhh!" he wailed.

After freeing himself, he limped to Jeff and almost slipped on the blood that pooled under Jeff's seat.

"Jeff!" James touched the large gash on the side of Jeff's body, and his eyes widened. Jeff struggled to keep his eyes open and twitched each time James touched his side. Outside, the rounds cooked and hit the windshield, and James protected Jeff's body from the glass that sprayed inside the plane. Oil and gas continued to drop onto the ground from the engine and spread to the fire that ignited two feet away. Racing against time, James broke the seat belt with his razor-tipped knife, eased Jeff from his seat, and carried him out of the gunner door of the Chinook.

The rounds flew and zipped past his face, but he ignored them all and only heard a loud buzzing noise, his heartbeat, and

Jeff's fading breath. He positioned Jeff near a wall of sandbags, away from the crash site, and performed first aid.

As James attempted to stop the warm blood from pouring out of Jeff's body, Jeff opened his eyes. He smiled and moved his lips.

"Jeff, I can't hear you, buddy. Don't fuckin' die on me!" James dropped the tourniquet and gauze from the pack.

Jeff grabbed James' blood covered hand. "Remember you still owe me that game, we haven't seen the Braves play live man. We gotta go to a game. You promised. The sports bar we were supposed to open. We were going to hike the Appalachia."

Salty tears cleaned the gunpowder and dirt from James cheeks. "Okay, Jeff' let's play a game. The dead hooker game. So you parachute and land near the highway. As you walk..." James stopped each time Jeff shuttered, attempting to breathe. With his shaky hands, he continued pulling out the gauze from Jeff's first responder pack and pressing it on Jeff's side. The blood flowed from the wound, and James placed gauze after gauze but the blood wouldn't stop. He even used the gauze from his own pack.

"You're...my...brother. I love you." Jeff's mouth formed these words but the wind carried away the sound. "Don't-t...trust," he swallowed, "the flower man." Then Jeff's eyes focused on something behind James.

James stopped from patching Jeff's side and pulled Jeff's body close to him. "What, what's that mean? Jeff, stay with me. What flower man?"

Jeff's eyes closed; his pulse faded, and his breathing shorted. When his chest fell for the last time, his head fell to the side, and his body became limp in James' arms.

"Jeff, wake up man. No...no...," James said as he slapped Jeff. He held on to Jeff until someone pulled them apart. When James looked up, he saw a face blended in the smoke from the fires that erupted on the camp. It was dark, and soon, a full body emerged. A deep purple flame burned around the body of the dark being. A man appeared out of place amongst the chaos that surrounded James. Shifting his head to see if anyone else

noticed the man appear, James forgot medics were pulling him away from Jeff's body. No one looked in the man's direction and some ran past the figure without stopping to look at the man floating in the smoke. The men pulled him further away from Jeff's body, and James' heels drug over the tan soil and left long steaks in the ground.

As he blinked to focus, the face became clearer. He released a loathsome breath when he saw the deep creases in the man's smile, and James' eyes widened when he felt the lust that seeped from the man's stare. But worst of all, the musk from the man was unbearable; it smelled of rotten flowers, maybe dying lilac. The more James gazed at him, the stronger it got. Once he began to dry heave from the smell, the men holding James arms almost dropped him on the ground. He turned his face way and the nauseous feeling decreased.

Then he looked up. The face was gone, and all the darkness left with the mysterious man. This was a face, in due time, that he would know all too well.

CHAPTER 4
WHO IS JEFF?

"Boy, who the hell is Jeff?" An officer questioned him and shined his flashlight into James' face.

James shielded his eyes from the light, the warzone faded into the background, and the potbelly of a stubby man replaced Jeff's face. He read the nametag on the man's shirt. 'P. Dansk.'

"What the hell?" James looked down at his open fly.

As he struggled to zip his pants, the cop raised his voice. "Don't you move, druggy. Stand, with your hands up!"

"What-what's going on? I—" For a moment, he was the old himself again.

"Said stand up now, boy!"

James stood and zipped his pants in the process before raising his hands.

"Turn around, sissy boy, then get on your knees, I know that's whatcha like."

James followed his instructions without hesitation.

Cars he hadn't seen before sped from the area for the highway and police cars followed them. A hand full of cops trailed the runners, penning the men and women down in the cold grass. Although a dozen cops chased after them, some escaped the area. James noticed the appearance of some, pale and shaking, not from the cold, but from something else. They looked the same as the scrawny man he saw deep in the woods before he took a piss. One man that James watched, a dark man no taller than five foot one, broke the hold of three cops, and he jetted from the scene down into a decline surrounded by trees.

"Officer, what's going on?" With his hands behind his head, he looked up at the officer.

"I ask the questions, boy, you_sit!" The officer put cuffs on James hands and pulled them tight enough to leave marks on his wrist. His sausage fingers molested James' back pocket searching for his wallet, and James couldn't hide the rising anger from his face.

Insert knife, then twist.

Pull trigger, then kick in teeth.

Snap the neck, then drop body from the building.

Smother with pillow.

Purge head into water, boiling water.

It'll take me thirty seconds top to do it and get away with the other cars.

After a pen dropped from the cop's clipboard, near James hands, James shook his head and let the desire for murder fall from his train of thought.

No, if I do that, all of Florida and Georgia will be after me, and that's what he wants.

"Johnny Walker, from Florida. Oh, here's your Boeing employee card, huh?" the officer said and continued rummaging through the moleskin wallet.

"Oh, looky here, a military ID." The officer mocked, paid no mind to the name on it, spat dip next to James' hand, and tossed the card on top of the tar-colored goo.

Out of breath, the robust man knelt and spoke softly in James' ear. "I don't know what kind of druggy you are, but this ain't 'Nam, boy. You shoot up; you go to jail."

While the officer whispered sweet nothings, James fondled the plastic casing of the pen, removed the ink cartridge. Using his shoe and his nails, he bent it, shaping it into a hook.

An older officer approached them, pointing his flashlight on James as he radioed in the calamity. James read the name 'Lt. Carol' on his nametag. "Dansk, what we got here?"

Dansk walked in front of James and handed Carol a card.

"Edgar Alan Poe, aye." Carol squinted at James, who sat

with his sweaty hair in his eyes and his mouth pressed tight.

"Whatcha doin' in this area, this a far aways from Alachua county? ' Bout a hundred miles or so, I'd reckon, said the raven." Carol tilted his head toward James.

"I...I'm driving to Athens. Went to take a piss and fell, nevermore." James had always been good with the comebacks, even when he found himself in a quagmire.

Jiggling the lock to the cuffs, he stopped once he heard a click and the tingling sensation in his hands disappeared. The sounds of a door slamming encouraged him to look in the direction of his truck, but after examining it, he only saw fog develop on the window. Nothing appeared out of place, and he remained on the ground calculating the right time to knock out the officers and escape for the highway.

"Yeah, he fell all right... Fell on his knees, screaming...what's his name—oh yeah, JEFF! Is that your drug dealer? You didn't have the cash, so you wanted to pay for it this way?" Dansk grabbed his stomach and laughed as he pressed his boot into James' back.

"That's enough Dansk," Carol said and touched Dansk's shoulder. A twig broke, and all three men turned to the sound of someone coming toward them.

"Carol, we gonna take these down to the station. You need one of my boys to stay and help with this one?" A lanky man asked as he came near James. Since he addressed Carol without his rank, James guessed they were equals. He shined his light into James face and smiled at him in a mocking manner.

"Hey, Kevin. I think we got this one. He hasn't given us any trouble so far," Carol said and walked in front of James.

"I can handle this boney druggy," Dansk said and spit more tar from his mouth.

"How many of y'all here still? Thought most had left by now," Carol asked as he walked away from James and closer to Kevin.

"Not many. Most of 'em left already and there's only my small team and two of your guys here still."

"We did good tonight," Carol said and shook Kevin's hand.

"All right y'all. See yah at the station. We gonna celebrate O'Brian's new baby boy," Kevin said and walked away from them.

"Cigars all around," Carol said and began to turn but stopped after looking at his arm.

"Gosh, darn it. Forgot my watch. What time is it Kevin?" Carol asked, Kevin turned around and placed his watch in the light of the moon.

"Ten twenty…," Kevin said and Carol nodded as Kevin continued walking around James truck and on the other side of the wooded area.

James eyes widened.

If I stay too long…

Carol walked back to James and touched Dansk on the shoulder.

"I'll get the car and bring it round. It won't take me long. You okay with him?"

"I got it. Just let him try something." Dansk rounded and came in front of James smiling and adjusting his tight britches.

To James left, he observed as police car after police car drove off and headed for the highway. The last car in the convoy drove around the hanging branches where James' truck sat and pulled next to it.

"You gonna be taken in son. One night in the joint will detox you. One night without, *JEFF*." Dansk laughed and held his hand on his hat as he dipped down to tease James. The door slammed and Carol walked out. "Should we take this one in? Before Kevin left, he told me the cells were packed."

"One more won't hurt." Dansk laughed and shoved James shoulder.

"I can watch him personally if you need me too."

"No need." Carol walked back to his car.

"I'll radio it in," Carol said as he looked over his shoulder.

Now.

James picked himself off the wet-cold ground and spun around to face the fat son-of-a-slut.

"My friend, I advise you to release me or somethin' bad's

gonna happen to you and your lieutenant over there."

"You threatening me?" Dansk squinted at James and took two steps forward.

A large black nightstick appeared in Dansk's hands, and he launched himself at James. After removing his hands from behind his back, James dangled the cuffs on one finger.

Frozen, Dansk's eyes narrowed. His lips shook as he pushed out words that lodged in his throat. James tossed the cuffs into the grass, and his free hand played with the hilt of his knife.

"You let me go, and we don't have any problems. Otherwise…" James said as he took three steps toward Dansk.

"Boy, you under arrest for assaulting an officer. You know that, you yellow-belly cock suc—"

Dansk's words stopped short when James' knife struck him under his chin and drove into his brain.

He twisted the blade until Dansk's eyes shut. When James removed his knife, blood and guts fountained from the hole. Dansk's limp body dropped to the ground, landing on his mountain of a belly.

With his jacket out of the way, Lieutenant Carol moved his hands to retrieve his .45 caliber from his right hip.

Taking two steps, James tossed his knife and struck Carol in the throat, severing the jugular. The officer's handgun flew from his hands, and his body floated to the grass. Blood streamed around the body as James took his knife out of the man's throat.

Images of laughing families, smiling children, birthdays, and celebrations glinted across James' mind. He saw Dansk taking his daughter to the prom, and peered at the images of Carol getting his promotion.

"Stop it!" He yelled and rubbed his fingers over his temple as if he was putting out a cigarette butt. He smelled the candles burning and smelled the sweetness of the perfume from Carol's wife on their wedding day. He saw their wives, mothers, happy and sad moments, flash across his mind in no real order.

Within seconds, the animalistic thirst for blood in James'

veins became bewilderment. After the memories of the two men faded from his mind, James starred at their dead bodies that lay before him.

"Fuck, fuck, fuck!" He pulled at his hair and wiped the blood from his face. The loudness of his heartbeat drummed in his ears; it was louder than the radio traffic coming from the cop's car.

"Calm down, no one probably saw. Remember all the cops left," he said and bucked to his truck and crushed a needle that lay within inches of the passenger side.

As he rounded the corner, he almost fell on the icy grass, and he held on to the side while he opened the door. His nervous hands shoved the key into the ignition and brought the pickup back to life. He backed out of the area and pressed for the highway toward his destination.

He peeled his shirt from his chest and changed into a new one. Using the bloody shirt, he rubbed his hands, face, and then let the wind swallow the garment. It fluttered and flapped before entangling in a large tree. His head shifted back and forth, searching for lights from cops, looking for birds in the sky.

The exploit did take his mind of The Gentleman, for a spell. With the amount of adrenaline racing through his veins, he found it difficult to concentrate on driving, and ran over the reflectors in the middle of the road.

"I'm not him. I'm not who I used to be," he said as both hands gripped the steering wheel.

"I'm not him!" He convinced himself and stared at his image in the rear-view mirror. His imagination transformed his sunken face to a mischievous one, one full of evil and yearning for murder and sin.

"I'm not YOU!" he screamed. "I'm not…you."

"They would've stopped me." James made up excuses for why he killed the cops. But he knew the true answer, it was easy.

He did a double take to the rounded figure under several of his blankets, on the floor of the truck on the passenger's side, and stopped staring at the never-ending white stripes on the road.

Crinkles formed in his forehead as his trembling hand lingered over the massive blankets. Something was breathing in and out heavily.

"What the…" James said and snatched the covers off, revealing a slender man shaking on the floor.

"What the hell?" James stared at a man wearing a sleeveless Grateful Dead shirt, tight pants, and a mullet meant for the King of moonshining. As James sat looking at the stranger, the man remained on the ground vibrating like a paint mixer. Now, the fog he saw in his truck and the door slamming back there made sense. It was from the guy sitting next to James. This needle poker slipped into his truck while the cops interrogated him.

"Please don't kill me," the man said as tears streamed down his cheek. The needle poker got up from the ground and sulked into the seat with his hands held over his face.

James relaxed somewhat and placed his gaze on the road.

"Get out of my truck now," James said and his foot weighed down on the gas pedal.

The man looked out of the window, then back at James. His eyes stretched as he placed his hand on the handle of the passenger's door. His hand knocked against the handle as he gripped it.

Without speaking, James clenched his teeth and looked at the needle poker as he reluctantly held on to the door's handle. After the needle poker gave James a sorrow-filled expression, James shook his head and pulled out his knife.

"Out…," James said.

James passed a speed sign that read fifty mph as his speedometer read ninety. When he looked in his rear view mirror, he saw red, white, and blue lights flickering behind him.

"Shit," James said.

The needle poker took his hand off the handle and turned around to see the cop trailing them. How could James explain a man flying out of his truck?

I'm stuck with this needle poker.

"I'm a floor it," he said and the needle on the speedometer

went from ninety to one hundred. The truck began to vibrate wilder than before.

James' head slammed into the steering wheel after the tires dipped into a large pothole. The truck jumped.

His increased speed didn't deter the cop, who continued pursuit.

The jerking of the truck caused the paper sitting under his bag to fly from underneath it. The wind beat the paper against the radio. After removing it, he glanced at the bright calculator numbers that flashed 001.

"Only one cop. I'll take the ticket and move on. If he tries something..." He touched a small gun stashed close to his right leg, a .22 peashooter, the just-in-case gun. In his peripheral, James noticed the needle poker staring at his hands as he touched his pistol and James looked over at him. The needle poker turned his head away and began to play with his fingers.

James decelerated and pulled over to the side of the road. The cop followed close and parked behind him.

After smelling his breath, James looked at the bottle of rum that fell from the bag when the truck hit a dip in the road.

"Switch with me," James said and turned around. The cop's head was down.

The needle poker lowered his eyes and opened his mouth as he gave James a slight shake of the head.

"Switch. Now," James said and raised his knife. He looked back at the cop; his head was still down.

As the two changed positions, James grabbed his bag. He touched the sticky and damp skin of the needle poker and smelled the rancid breath that came from the needle poker's mouth. The needle poker's breath smelled as if he vomited up shit and garbage, swallowed it, and vomited it back up again.

"You been drinking?" James glared at the needle poker as he shook his head. Reaching his bag, James pulled out a jacket and tossed it to the needle poker.

"Put it on, it'll hide...those," James said and pointed to the entry points on the needle poker's arms.

Then he pulled out a pack of big red and gave the needle

poker a stick of gum.

"And this, will get rid of your ass breath," James said as he waved the stick of gum in his hand. After the needle poker took the gum from James, he unwrapped the aluminum foil around the gum and slipped it into his mouth. The cinnamon aroma from the gum did turn down the stench from his mouth, somewhat. As the needle poker slid the jacket over his body, James winced at the sores that rubbed against his jacket.

He can keep it.

When James turned around, he saw the sheriff getting out his car. The engine and the seizure-inducing lights of the sheriff's car remained on as an officer walked heel to toe to his truck.

"You play along and you get out of this alive. Got it?"

The needle poker nodded his head and wiped his hands on the seat of the truck. James felt the presence of someone appear on his left and kept his eyes straight ahead until the officer spoke.

"You know how fast you were goin'?" The officer shined his light directly into James' face and swept the light over the needle poker's face briefly.

"No, sir, Officer, I must've got caught up listenin' to the radio." The needle poker wiped the sweat on the palms of his free hand onto his jeans and turned to the officer.

He had dark skin, a neatly trimmed mustache, and the cleanest sheriff's uniform James had ever seen. The sheriff's hand, with hiatal leather gloves, remained on the hilt of pistol as he used his flashlight to examine the inside and outside of James' truck.

"Why it take you so long to stop? I ain't hard to miss." The sheriff came closer to the door.

"Sorry, sir. I'm tired, I guess." The needle poker said and as he swallowed, he released a loud glop.

The officer raised his eyebrow and sniffed the air. "Yea been drinkin' tonight, son?" He shined the light on James' face.

"No, but my friend here has. I'm taking him home tonight," the needle poker said, calmer than before, and pointed to James.

"I see that," the sheriff said and sniffed the air once more as he leaned in. The sheriff swung his light away from James and moved it to the back of the truck.

While the officer looked into the bed of James' truck, James' hand reached into his bag and he gripped the handle of his shotgun.

"Let me see your license," the sheriff said without looking at them.

The needle poker reached in his back pocket, pulled out his license and handed it over to the sheriff.

After the sheriff looked at the license, his eyes fixed on the sparkle from the dog tags that hung around the rearview mirror. James began to slide the gun from his bag.

"You were in 'Nam?" The needle poker looked at the dog tags that hung around the rearview mirror, and then turned back to the sheriff.

"Yes, sir." The needle poker rushed his words. James' hold on the weapon loosened.

"My brother served."

"Yeah, when he get out?" the needle poker asked as he smacked on his gum. James heartbeat decreased, and his breathing slowed.

"He served." The officer drew in and continued. "He ain't returned. War's hell and I was in school. Plus, segregation ended. People thought 'cause it ended everything was hunky dory, but it was a bad time for my family. Even harder for them to accept me as deputy sheriff."

"Sorry to hear that," the needle poker said and sat back in his seat.

James shoved the gun under the bag and placed his hands in his lap.

"What you driving so fast for? You running from the devil, or somethin'?" The officer smiled, revealing a gold tooth.

"Ha. No, just trying to get him home."

"Well, I ain't gonna write you a ticket this time, only a warning." The sheriff began to write on his pad, "but slow down 'cause the next officer that pulls you over ain't gonna be so nice," The sheriff pointed his flashlight at James, "and...put the bottle down, son."

James gave him a weak smile and a slight nod of the head. The sheriff handed the needle poker a warning slip. Before returning to his car, the officer tipped his hat and slapped the side of James' truck.

James bowed his wet forehead against his hands and swallowed his anxiety and relief.

Through the corner of his eye, he watched the sheriff's car with the sickening lights speed off into the blackness of the highway.

Turning his head to his other problem of the night, James saw as the needle poker reach down under his seat. Before James could force the needle poker out of his truck, the bastard grabbed James' just in case gun.

"You gotta be kidding me," James said as he laughed and rubbed his lips.

"Don't you move. I saw you back there, I saw you kill those cops. You never planned on letting me go," the man said, and the gun rattled in his hands. The needle poker put the gun in his left hand and started the truck. They headed for the highway. He drove slower than James drove and did a better job at keeping the truck on the road.

"So, you gonna shoot me? I don't think so," James said and went near the man with one hand. As he drove the man's head into the steering wheel like a nail, the needle poker lost control of the truck, and it bounced all over the median, almost into the slope that led to the bottom of a creek.

"Back up," the man said after gaining control of the wheel. The needle poker pulled back the hammer to the pistol; his eye swollen from the damage James caused. James turned to the man, blinking and shaking his head, as they past sign after sign.

"I can't believe this shit," James said. He continued glancing at the man as they drove down the highway, watching the shaking hand that gripped the gun. He sneered when he realized the size of the man. He had the textbook appearance of a druggy, the ones seen in the movies. Skinny, with cracked fingernails from malnutrition, matted hair, yellow-brown teeth, and a smell that overpowered James' odor. The mullet he wore did little to disguise his lifestyle, nor did his choice in music, or the sleeveless shirt, which revealed the entry points that he preferred to inject himself. Although James had noticed how bad the needle poker smelled before the cop pulled them over, he hadn't noticed the extent of his appearance until now.

"Get out," the needle poker said with a trembled voice.

James laughed as the needle poker decreased his speed. He entertained the idea of this man killing him. He took the bait and played along with the intruder.

"You got a name?" James asked the man and observed the infected needle marks between the man's fingers.

Some of the sores on the man's neck and fingers broke open, and liquid globed from the wounds.

"None of your damn business." The needle poker looked back to the road.

"Look shithead, I'm gonna let you in on a little secret. Five seconds ago, I could've snapped your neck. It's true I was stupid by slamming your head into the steering wheel and not getting the gun back first, but I guess that was God's way of giving you more time to live."

After swerving from the skeleton next to him, James turned his gaze back to the road.

"I'm the one with the gun, I'm the one in control," the man said. As he shouted, spit projected from his mouth, the foamy kind, and spilled onto James and his seat. The gun in the intruder's hand remained level with the handle to the passenger's door.

If I get out of this shit with the asshole, I gotta clean this herpes carrying drug head's crap from my truck.

"I used to kill for a living. I was a hit man. Someone owes you money, you came to me. You needed to kill a guy high in power. I was the one to slit his throat. What makes you think I am about to listen to a heroin addict who doesn't even know how to point a gun? What's your fucking name?" James asked and turned his head back to the man. Their sped continued to decrease.

"Shut up!" The man pulled the barrel of the gun to James' head and pulled the trigger.

The recoil shoved the man's head into the driver side door.

"Oh shit," James said and drew his head back as two bullets zipped from the barrel and whizzed past his nose, shattering the glass on the window. If he had reacted two seconds later, the bullets would have crashed into his skull and left fragments of his brain on the window. The red needle on the speedometer dipped below thirty miles an hour.

While James shielded his face from the fragments that dazzled in the night, the driver's door opened, and the man began to leap from his seat. Although James was able to grab the arm of the needle poker's jacket, the needle poker managed to shimmy out of it before he tumbled out of the truck.

After hopping over to the driver's side, James got control of the wheel before the car ran into a ditch. Good thing the needle poker slowed them to twenty miles an hour.

Stopping the truck, James placed it in park. He sat, looking at the rearview as the man limped away, and removed the pieces of glass that lodged in his skin.

"This son-of-a-slut," James said and looked around for the pistol, but it wasn't in the truck. Reaching under his seat, he picked up a box that read .22 cal and bounced them in his hand. He looked at the clock in his truck.

"I got time. This won't take long. Haven't had a little fun in a while," he said.

After leaving his truck, he ran in the direction the man scampered. Because no one shoots at James and gets away with it. Maybe he'd kill him, or maybe he'd scare him enough to cause the needle poker to piss his pants.

Hobbling into the forest, holding his arm that dangled bent in the wrong places, the man still held onto the gun and pointed it at James.

Not even picking up speed to chase the guy, James strode toward him and called out, "There's nowhere to go, my friend."

The man continued to run, and after he tripped, James

jogged to the coward, and stood over his body. Pulling the pistol up from the grass and shaking it toward James' body, he pulled the trigger.

Click.

The man looked at the gun, and then pulled the trigger once more.

Click.

"Only had two bullets in it. I emptied the other seven in a voodoo bitch who gipped me in Myrtle Beach." James lifted the guy up by his hair and slid his body over the rocks and sandspurs that littered the ground.

"Ahh." The man hit James' arms and tugged at his fingers.

"Shut up, it'll be over soon punk," James said and tossed the man's body near a tree.

"Turn around."

The man scooted from James and reached for a stick that lay next to him.

"I said turn around." James raised his voice and kicked the stick away. After retrieving the pistol that fell from the needle poker's hands, he reloaded it.

Crying with his back facing James, the man pleaded for his life.

"Shut up. I asked you your name; you didn't answer me." James placed his hand into the man's back pocket for his wallet. The wallet, a cheap one ripped on all sides, didn't contain much money.

"You shot at me. You fucking tried to kill me. You think I'm letting you off?" James went through the wallet and paused to the sight of a military ID.

"Jenkins, Kent, Staff Sergeant?" James looked back at the shaking man, waiting for James to place the barrel of the gun to his head.

The license revealed the year the man was born, 1947. The same year as James. "Were you in 'Nam?"

"Uhm, yes, I deployed with the eighty second to Shah Valley once, and the second time I was on the border of Laos," the man swallowed loud enough for James to hear him.

"What was your MOS?" James took the wallet and put the ID back. With the needle poker's arms raised, James gawked at the saw work that lined his back and the many scars on the back of his neck. Those were not from heroin needles, they were from shrapnel.

"Uhm, I was an engineer, I don't wanna die...I'm so sorry."

Although being a drug addict seemed a better fate than dealing with The Gentleman, for someone who served his or her country, this was the last thing James wanted to happen to him. This could've been him. Addicted to drugs, unable to better himself, unable to get on with his life, or take care of his family. Selling his daughter's Christmas presents the day after Christmas to get money for blow. Robbing from his wife and her family. This was the other side of the coin and the 'this or that' options of horrible fates. James the druggy or James, The Gentleman's punching bag? He couldn't figure out which was worse.

After James tossed the wallet on the grass, he headed back to his truck and left the man there, giving him an unusual second chance.

Sitting in his truck, he unsheathed his knife and felt the notches in the wood. "Just two." As James grabbed his smaller knife to add to the tally, he shook his head and put the knife down. At one time, this knife was bare. "I can't believe I'm at thirty-six. Thirty-six?" James stuck the keys into the ignition and returned to his original quest of getting rid of The Gentleman.

***

Forty minutes passed before he dozed off again—not even the sounds of Black Sabbath's fast-paced guitar riffs could keep his eyelids from lowering.

"Let me put it on the radio that'll keep me going." He yawned and popped out a cassette tape.

The radio blared *Carry on Wayward Son,* and James sang loud enough for his voice to carry outside of the truck. He rhythmically drummed on the steering wheel. "One mile to

Macon."

He looked at the time. "Twelve forty a.m. I can make it there if I go ninety the entire way," he said and rubbed the sweat from his face.

"He said I could never leave Florida. But I left that bag of dicks behind. Yes!" Relief filled him inside, and he rejoiced by chugging rum from his stash. He bobbed his head to the rhythm with more energy.

But as the air mixed with the smell of lilac, he dropped the bottle of rum and ended his premature celebration. It splashed onto his seats.

"Oh, my God!" He coughed, and his truck wavered all over the road. His tires screeched and left burn marks on the highway.

Blood drizzled from his nose, but no matter how much he mopped it up with his hands, more soaked his shirt. When James looked up, he saw an older man sitting in a chair meant for a king, in the middle of the road, waving to him.

"No! I have time, I have time!" The steering wheel slipped from his bloody hands. The events happened too fast for him to react. Before he knew it, the pickup swerved into a ditch, and then the side of his truck smashed into a large tree.

CHAPTER 5
1974 AND THE GENTLEMAN

Captain Greene barely escaped his Huey, which crashed a couple meters from his present location. It was dawn, and his parachute remained caught in the trees. Every movement rustled the branches and leaves and gave away his position to the enemy. From the height he hung, he could see two ant-like figures humping through the mountains, chopping down brush and vegetation, moving toward him.

"Two-Two-Three, I say again Two-Two-Three, my plane crashed. Let me know if someone is out there. Over." He radioed in his position twenty times and never received a response.

"I've got to get the hell out of here before those fucks get to me." He pulled out his knife and sawed at the entangled parachute to free himself.

"Come on." The strings snapped one by one, and he rubbed his knife against the five-fifty cord faster and faster. As he sawed at the strings, his pistol fell from his holster, and he grabbed it before it landed below him. The chamber opened, and all but one round tumbled into the dense jungle.

"What..."

Turning his head in the direction of the enemy, he watched as the two ants became roaches, and then beetles. The final string snapped, and he descended fourteen feet, his arms flapping in a failed attempt to fly. The hard fall resulted in a broken leg and more cracked ribs. Managing through the austere pain, he lifted himself from the ground and gathered most of the parachute from the tree. Besides the broken limbs, he left little evidence behind.

"Where are they?" He got on his knees as best he could and searched for the rounds from his pistol. But they didn't turn up, and he decided to move away from his crash site.

"Track me now, you pieces of shit." He collected anything that appeared to belong to his chute and limped along the lush trail.

The sun sat on the horizon, and his sense of time wandered into the dense jungle. Struggling to keep a good pace, he often rested and used a large stick to support his weight as he hobbled along.

"My chest burns something fierce. What time is it…ten?" He shook his fist at the broken face of his watch and squinted at the enemy behind him.

The men were now the size of mice, and his current speed allowed them to reach him in less than twenty minutes.

After he took inventory, he released a disappointed moan. He had a pistol with one bullet, two grenades, and the rope from his shoot.

"I don't have time to set these up." He pulled out his pistol and took the safety off. With his cut thumb, he pulled the hammer back; the metal-to-metal sound caused the birds to scatter from the trees. Tears rolled down his face, cleaning three days of dirt from his cheeks as the drops skated down to his chin.

"Well, well…" Were the only words that escaped his dehydrated mouth.

Looking back, he saw the advancing enemy, smashed the pistol into his temple, and steadied his hand with his opposite one.

He applied pressure to the trigger.

His chest rose, sweat fell. He coughed, and blood fell from his mouth.

His legs buckled, and he fell to the ground hacking. His nostrils flared when he saw only one set of dog tags fall out of his shirt.

"It's missing. They have it. Those pieces of shit have it." There was no way in hell he'd leave the earth knowing they had his best friend's tags. He gained his composure and reassessed his equipment.

He hobbled along, dragging his injured leg behind him and coughing up flesh from his lungs. But he still ran; he ran through the acute pain he felt each time his injured leg struck the ground.

Once he felt safer, he stopped and set up his first set of traps.

Most of the trail he used disappeared into the jungle. "This will do," he said.

With tired hands, he worked diligently to strip the parachute string before tightening the finished product around a large tree, low to the ground. The other end he strung around the grenade's pin, creating a trip wire.

The filth on his body provided camouflage, and he stood behind a large tree, tracking the enemy's movement. The tree's pine surface punctured his hand, and the sap of its sticky syrup stuck to it. He developed rashes on his arm. But didn't scratch. He didn't wipe the sweat from his eyes. He didn't rub his burning chest. He remained moving with the wind and using all his energy to stop his coughs and match his heartbeat to the rhythm of the men's footsteps.

"Come on, come on," he whispered.

"*Nhn thay ahn ay,*" (did you see him) one of the men asked. Both wore non-military cloths.

"*Khong,*" (No) another man replied. One of the men carried an anti-aircraft weapon and the other had something else in his hand that flickered in the fading sunlight.

Eight feet, four feet, one foot…

They stepped around his traps.

Desperate, James jumped from behind the tree with his knife in hand. "Come back you assholes." His voice, raspy, was too low to hear.

The men turned to the sound of branches snapping in the

jungle.

James lifted a rock the size of a grapefruit and hurled it ninety miles per hour at one of the men. It hit him in the throat. The man fell, spraying rounds into the sky and using his free hand to rub the newly formed bruises and to help himself breathe.

The man with the anti-aircraft weapon headed for James. His foot snagged the trip wire. The click from the pin separating from the grenade caused James to hobble back to the large tree. As he sat ducking, he jumped as the body parts from the enemy scattered around him.

"Okay, one down," he said.

Then he charged, full of adrenaline, at the remaining man. He snatched his knife from his sheath and staggered. Once the man lifted himself off the ground, still gasping for air, and pushed himself upward, James limped faster to him.

James released his battle cry and fell on top of the man. Fighting for a chance to kill one another, they rolled over the ground. The pain from James' leg became dull.

James smashed the enemy's face into a pile of gravel, while sitting on his knees. Then he gripped the man's chin and slid the blade across his opponent's throat, severing his jugular. As James' silhouette towered over him, blood gurgled through the hole in the enemy's neck. His body jerked then sat still. James was the last man he'd ever see, and he wouldn't have it any other way. This was the first man he'd killed with his bare hands. And it wouldn't be the last.

"I'm safe for now," James said when the man's eyes shut.

As the hotness in his face lessened, the pain in his leg returned, and he almost lost his balance.

"Forgot about this," he said and massaged his leg that tingled and pulsated with each step he took. He limped to the dead bodies and checked the men's person; he found some food, batteries for a radio, weapons, and ammo. He also found Jeff's dog tags hanging from a tree branch and cleaned the gore from them before placing them around his neck.

He stripped the clothes from a body and put them on; they

smelled of rotting cabbage.

"This would last me two days tops. Now time to find a village."

***

His search for solitude proved to be most difficult, and it had been three days since he'd eaten. The sunsets brought creatures of the night. Eyes wandered between the shadows and shapes moved between large bushes. James slept in holes with well-placed traps to keep the phantoms at bay. His leg had gotten worse, and it began to smell, a foul smell that he pulled his face away from after sniffing it. The map he used had to have been outdated because no matter what route he took, he found himself lost amongst the jungle. He wasn't bad at reading maps either; he was one of the best. He blamed his failure in part on his injuries and lack of food and rest.

On the fourth day, his movements became more erratic, and he wandered into the jungle away from trails, tripping over vines and his own feet as he went. All his water and food had run out.

"I'm, so, tired." He fell to the ground, spread his hands, and dug his fingers into the jungle's soil.

A shadow developed before his eyes. A man's silhouette cast over James' face. He tilted his head enough to catch a glimpse of a figure before the muscles in his neck stiffened.

"Who are you?" James closed his eyes.

"I smell flowers."

He didn't fight; he said a prayer only he and God could hear and lay there conserving energy for breathing.

The unknown thing touched James' hand, and the world around James melted into the background. The new serial scenery appeared. The misty haze smelled of dying flowers, maybe lilac, and an older man stood with his hands crossed.

"Dad?" James asked.

But as the man's image came into focus, a villain stood before James. The same face that smiled at him from the fog during his first deployment.

"Daddy's no longer here," the man said and clasped his hands.

"What? Where am I?" James spun around and twirled in the mist.

"My world," the unknown man answered and blew smoke from a pipe. The smell of lilac increased with each exhale.

"Are you…God?" James knew the answer to that question before he finished saying God.

"No, I wouldn't quite say that." The man smirked.

"What's that mean? I don't know how I got here. I…" James touched his chest, knee, and his face. His injuries had healed in the passing minutes, and the rashes on his hands subdued.

"Who the hell are you?" James demanded and closed in on the unknown man's position.

"Umm, not sure this decade. Beelzebub, dark knight, evil dweller, fire demon, Yeehaw, Loki." The man answered with a different accent for each title and stroked his black-inked beard. He worked his way toward James and held out his hands with grace. A smile spread across his face, and his age displayed in the creases of his wrinkles. "You can call me The Gentleman."

James didn't return the offer.

"This doesn't make sense. How do I get out of here?" James asked, walking in the opposite direction into more and more fog. "Where am I?" He raised his voice.

"Why, you are in my home!" The Gentleman twirled around, showing James around his inhabitants. "Pull up a seat. You look rather tired."

"I don't see a—"

A chair materialized near James before he could complete his sentence. Both men sat, and James never lost sight of the man.

"Your eyes…" The Gentleman smoked from his pipe. He bit down on the end of the wooden pipe, and his teeth crushed the hard oak. After tossing away the broken pieces, with the snap of his fingers, he fashioned a new one.

"My what?"

"Nothing." A grin surfaced on The Gentleman's face. "I could imagine this is a lot to take in, but let's not be coy, 'cause I need you to grow a pair." The Gentleman put the new pipe in his mouth and puffed the lavender smoke.

"Am I dead?" James asked as he wiped his face with his hands.

"I wouldn't say dead. I'd say almost."

"What the fuck does that mean? You holding me hostage? You a Vietcong cocksucker?"

The Gentleman's expression changed. A dark presence appeared in the air. "That's cute. You demanding answers from someone who holds your very *life* in his hands."

The two stood and walked to one another. With all James had gone through, he wasn't ready to give it all away to this strange man. His muscles tensed as he took a fighting stance. "You think I'm afraid of you because you made the lights go down? Because you put this stinky ass fog around? I am a fucking war Veteran with more confirmed kills than Attila the Hun, motherfucker."

The dark fog dissipated when The Gentleman laughed—a laugh that echoed throughout the area. He mocked James with a slow clap. "Bravo, bravo, now sit back and listen. Put those pretty blue eyes over here."

James' body fell into the chair involuntarily, and The Gentleman treaded to his own seat.

"What have you done?" James lifted himself from the chair but fell back into his seat.

"I think you are misunderstanding who has the dick and who has the pussy here. See…" The Gentleman veered his body forward and was instantly in James' face. "Whether you live a sorry excuse for a life or you die is up to me." The Gentleman blew his obnoxious smoke in James's face. "You have a choice, but it comes with a price, my *pojke*."

Before speaking, James exhaled the word *life* in the smoky fog. "Let me go, now," he said.

After standing and walking back to his original location, The Gentleman turned his hand into a fist. When he opened it, the image of James' daughter appeared. She held onto a bear and swung from side to side, doing the nervous dance all kids do when they travel to strange places.

"Daddy?" she called and ran to James with her arms up, her bear dangling in one hand.

James eyes widened, and he stopped fighting against the force exerted on him. "Jenni, what…what…"

Just as her body reached James, it dissolved into smoke. Fighting back tears, he gazed around the smoky area, searching for his little girl.

"Do you wanna see her again?" The Gentleman asked.

With his head titled, James raised his eyes to The Gentleman.

"Good, I have your attention now."

"What do I have to do?" James asked and leaned back in his chair. His legs shook something fierce.

"You'll find out in due time. For now, I'll only explain the conditions." The Gentleman sat back in his seat, holding his pipe.

For a time, silence packed the room thicker than the smoke from the man's pipe.

James maintained a staring contest with The Gentleman and beamed into The Gentleman's deep green eyes. They molested his soul and played with its essence, tasted his fear and saw James as he was, what he'd lost, and where he was going. James felt all of this, just as he could feel the heat surface from the man's body, and he felt The Gentleman's yearning as images of death scrolled across his mind.

To his relief, the thought of his daughter festered and battered away the hatred from the stranger. "You can't have my kid…or my wife." James broke the silence.

"Oh, so you have limits?" The Gentleman half-smiled. "Very well, is everything else on the table?" The man sat up, moved toward James, and continued smiling that horrible smile of his. "Please make sure you don't hold back."

"What happens if I don't hold my end of the bargain?" James rubbed his eyes. His hands were now free, which meant, the restraints were gone. Nevertheless, James stayed in his seat.

"Well, it would mean I own you."

"What do I have to do to live?" James eyes remained on his feet.

"Whatever I choose. I could have you just wash my car. Unfortunately, I only get one demand from you, but I do get a good deal out of it. It's a win-win for me." The Gentleman exhaled smoke that wrapped around James, and a contract unfolded in front of him, as did a feathered quill.

James grabbed both items and scanned the document. His forehead wrinkled as he attempted to read the arrows, random shapes, and lines, which represented words. "What the hell is this crap?"

"That is the language of the craziest civilization. You call them the Mesopotamians, Babylonians, Samaritans."

James blinked, and when he opened his eyes, The Gentleman appeared next to him.

"Here, let me translate, if you don't mind." The Gentleman took the contract from James's hands.

"Ah, let us see here yes, I will honor my contract with said Gentleman." He pointed to himself. "And if not, he will have sole ownership of me, some legal conditions, yadah yadah, no curses mumbo jumbo..." He paused, "ah yes, your name here, James Greene."

The Gentleman read on. "On this day, today, of course. Let any who witness agree the deal was fair and just."

"I don't see any witnesses," James said.

"Oh, but there are." With a snap of his fingers, three unknown men appeared; all wearing long flowing robes, and curly white wigs. Their gray skin showed through their powered faces and they rested their lanky fingers, long and boney, over the edge of the wooden gallery. None spoke.

"Do you gentlemen agree that this here contract is legitimate and just?" he asked them.

The contract whisked in front of them. They looked at one another and shot each other raised brows, frowns, and nods.

"Well, we don't have all day," The Gentleman, urged.

The three men nodded at both James and The Gentleman.

"Well then, *pojke*, judgment has been given."

Three signatures surfaced at the bottom of the contract, and the men dissipated into the fog.

"Now, your turn." The Gentleman handed the contract back to James.

"Jenni," James whispered. He inhaled a gallon of air, and his sweaty hands latched onto the floating pen. As James signed his name, James saw in the corner of his eye The Gentleman's mouth watered.

"Well looks like that's set." The Gentleman took the contract from the air.

"When will I see you again, how will I know...?"

"You'll know it's me. Trust your senses. I'll be waiting...." The Gentleman blew out smoke; the word *games* expanded and faded in it while he dematerialized.

"Wait." James reached out to the image and jumped from his seat. His hand waved away the thick fog, but it multiplied.

The smog hid his feet and his hands as he stumbled about the place, searching for a way out. The air thickened, and James fainted from the lack of oxygen.

Chapter 6
Hitching

At dawn, James woke behind the wheel of his pickup with the pain of a thousand hammers breaking into his skull.

"What the fuck?" He wiped blood from his forehead and nose and scratched the blood that crusted on his chin. The door to the glove compartment fell open, and the cotton papers that fell from it caught his eye. They were blank pages; no words ran across the threads.

While rubbing his temple, he picked them up from the floor and looked them over before stuffing them into his bag. "I remember these," he said. "Dad told me his crazy dad gave 'em to him. Blank papers he couldn't throw away."

His gaze wandered from the papers to the hood of his truck, where steam billowed from the hood. Then, he turned his head to the side only to see his truck smashed into a tree.

"No, no, no!" he said, pumped the gas, and turned the ignition. After several failed attempts to stop the engine from knocking, he opened the door and dangled his feet on the ledge.

"Ahhh!" He clenched his side and screamed as if his soul ripped from his body. Tears trickled down his face as he did all he could to push himself out of the car. He braced his hands on the sides of the vehicle and launched himself out of the truck.

When he finally exited the truck, he felt his pain fade.

"What the heck was that about?" He asked as he looked at bright orange sunrise over the horizon.

He approached the hood then jumped away from the steam

that shot from the truck's engine.

The truck had been a gift from his father, one he cherished deeply. When the steam died down, he lifted the hood. It was hot, and he shook off the pain from the burns on his arm. He used his shirt to grip the metal and lift the hood and became mesmerized by the way the engine knocked and sizzled; even though he'd turned the truck off. The engine had overheated, and the impact broke the engine mounts and damaged the hoses. There was a leak in the radiator hose and the steam hissed as it escaped from the opening. He cuffed his mouth to the smell of burning rubber and positioned his head under the hood. Placing his tools in an empty area, James pulled out his rag and attempted to open the cap to the radiator.

Maybe the smells from the fumes made him delirious but James became less rigid and thought of his father as he worked the cap off the radiator.

"Here I am, ole man, remember?" He chuckled as he wiped water from his face and continued working the cap from the radiator. When the cap finally gave way, steam hissed out of the opening.

"I remember the first time I crashed this thing. I crashed it into a tree and stumbled home. The next day, I thought you were going to let me have it. But then, then you took me outside and said, 'Son, you break it, you fix it.'" James' eyes welled up.

"Then, when I came back the first time from 'Nam, you dropped the keys in my hand," he said and poured water from a jug from the car into the opening of the radiator. Steam rose higher into the sky, and James backed away before it could melt the skin from his face. The engine began to sputter and the wildness of the engine's knocking decreased.

While he ogled at the dead truck, gray smog filled the air, the engine knocked, popped, and died. James rushed to the cab and turned the key.

Sputter, sputter.

But the engine still wouldn't start.

Now the thing he cherished with all his heart lay before him totaled.

"Well, I guess you hit the end of the road, girl, huh?" Once the steam died down again, he slammed the hood.

"Goodbye, girl." Reluctantly, he gathered all his belongings, hit the side of the truck, and headed for the road.

He walked to edge of the road, and then stopped.

"Oh, I forgot to get my rum." To his dismay, the truck was no longer there. All that remained was that damn fog and the scent of the man he resented.

"What the?" He raced to the truck's original position and waved his arms. "Where'd it go?" His heartbeat magnified, and he backed away from the space the truck had occupied.

***

"I know I shouldn't do this, but I need to get there quick." He continued walking backward along the road with his arm extended and his thumb out.

After sunset, bright lights flickered against the mist, and a pickup truck zoomed past him, knocking patches of fog into his face.

"Damn it!" James yelled and kicked the rocks on the side of the road. The truck came to a streaking halt, smoke drifting from the tires, and the pickup reversed direction.

"This should be easy." Reassuring himself, James felt the smooth stock of the shotgun he'd taken through his duffle bag.

When the doors to the blue truck flung open, the man in the driver's seat encouraged James to enter.

"Need a lift?" He was a large man with a jolly smile—he reminded James of a young Santa Claus.

James nodded and hopped in. His eyes watered at the aroma of musk and coffee. Seven dip cans lay on the floor, and two sat in the cup holder. The liquid inside them slushed, bobbed, and spilled onto James' boots each time the man hit a pothole.

Young Santa stroked his salt and pepper beard and adjusted his cap several times during their trip. But the two men rode in silence for the better part of the evening before the man interrupted it.

"This fog's bad." Young Santa used an oily shirt to wipe

the condensation from the windshield and the rearview mirror.

"Yeah it is." James readjusted his bag he'd slung across his chest and wrapped his hands on the handle of the gun.

"The name's Hershel, Hershel Law, by the way."

James raised one brow and kept his eyes on the windshield.

"I know you thinkin' that can't be my name. But it is."

"Jeff. The name's Jeff." James turned his gaze back to the never-ending road.

"So where you headed?"

"Athens, or as close as you can get me." James picked his foot from the floor before the dripping dip soaked his boot. He glared at Hershel from the reflection in the windshield and turned his head away when Hershel's gray eyes stared back at him.

"Well, you in luck, my friend, 'cause I'm headed for North Carolina, and I'll be passing Athens on the way." Hershel spit in his can and kept rubbing his chin.

"So where you from?" Hershel turned to James and James stayed silent.

"I'm from here but moved to Ohio when my dad passed in World War II and my mom took her life."

James stared at Hershel as he continued.

"He was from eastern Europe. My dad. Moved to the U.S., met my momma, and then joined up," Hershel explained.

My wife, she came over from Germany after the war."

"Sorry for talkin' about her. She passed not too long ago," Hershel said, and his voice wavered.

"You seen them new scary movies that came out lately? New Halloween, Friday the thirteenth?" Hershel looked at James' hands, and then whipped his head back to the road.

"Haven't had time for that," James said, short and to the point.

"It's crazy how things work out." Hershel swallowed hard enough for James to hear.

"It's gonna be a while before we get to Athens. Got any stories?" Hershel asked.

"None at all." James wished the guy would shut his mouth

to be honest. Maybe he would shoot him after all.

James looked around the truck and noticed the book in the dashboard, *Communist Manifesto*, and looked back at Hershel's thumb and index finger and saw a faded sickle and hammer tattoo. He moved away and searched the ground for an idea of how to proceed.

"I can tell a story that those Hollywood folks wish they came up with. It's not my story; my wife told me it before she passed." Hershel spoke while spitting in a can.

Shifting his eyes from the clock on the radio and Hershel's reflection, James squinted when he saw Hershel's hand go for his pocket. James pulled his hand from out of his bag and didn't stop until Hershel held a tiny black object up into the light.

"Just getting this."

That was too fast. I'll let this guy tell me his story, and then, then I'm gonna pull my gun out and ram it into his face.

After holding up the canister, Hershel dropped a truckload of dip into a bottle in his cup holder and used his legs to steer as he knocked his Copenhagen pack against his index finger three hard times.

"Sorry, gotta get it all packed," he said and James raised his eyebrows, "Oh yeah...,"

James body became less tense, but his hand remained on the gun's handle.

Hershel opened the top, and a burst of minty tobacco melded with the smell of rotten spit. He slugged it in the corner of his mouth and bit down. "I'm ready," he said and began his story. "So after the war, people either were saved by the Americans or placed in displacement camps, or they wandered around to find what they lost..." Hershel slid spit from his mouth.

James continued watching Hershel's reflection in the window.

"My wife's family—her name is Rita by the way—traveled around for months before they found a place to hole up. She told me about the conditions they lived in. Pots everywhere to stop the rain from soaking up the boards. They had two rooms for seven people, and she had to wear men's clothing that they scavenged from the American displacement camps. She told me…she told me that she would…" Hershel laughed and looked at James whose face did not change.

"She told me," Hershel said with a serious tone, "that she'd sneak out to the border with her friends when everyone was asleep. Real early in the morning. She said once that someone died during one of their games, and from that day on, the kids didn't mess with the bartering game they played. All over meat—would you believe that?"

"When they found it, it was a stinky cabin somewhere in Poland, miles from their homes in Germany," Hershel said.

James watched as Hershel's eyes darted from him to the road, appearing to search for a spot where he could exit the highway.

"After she saw some Nazis checking out her location, her dad scouted the area and found small kid bones scattered all over the camp. They left, of course, and some of the families around them went with them. They walked the snow for miles, and the same band of Nazis cut them off. They fought for what felt like hours, and when it was over, they lost, I wanna say, ten people from the group. Ten. But they killed the men who threatened to take her, all the other women, and the young boys. The young boys." Hershel's eyes stretched but his face contracted as the shine from a rifle peeked out from under James' bag.

After Hershel turned his head towards the road again, James could see the giant bulge that formed on the side of Hershel's mouth as he bit down hard on the dip.

"They started off with fifteen." Hershel's hands tightened on the steering wheel, and he continued to move uncomfortably in his seat. His foot smashed down on the gas pedal.

James looked the red needle as their speed increased and began to pass the sixty mile an hour marker.

"They left." Hershel's voice broke. "Excuse me. They left the area, and they got into it with some of the people from their group. Rita's dad, uhm, I think it was Liam? Well, he had to fight off the naysayers and convinced the group to stay together, but they left anyway. Said they had help. Well, after the ones that didn't want to be in the group vanished, my wife told me," Hershel said.

James caught Hershel looking at his hands through his peripheral and sent him a glare that forced his head back to the road.

"It felt like a weight was lifted, they felt they could laugh again," Hershel continued and spit into his canister before continuing the story.

"They found a base not too long after, and they found the bodies of the ones that left near a mine field. Lucky for them, they did leave because that could've been them. Rita told me one morning she saw her father talking to a man, he was dark, even in the morning, and he was dark, not because of his skin but his presence, his clothes. Pure darkness. Anyway, she said the man—she couldn't hear well from where she stood—but the man looked as if he was tellin' her dad to get a box from inside the place they were about to travel to. And that if her dad did, he would save them. Then the man just left like that." Hershel snapped his fingers.

"He left like he had never been there." As Hershel moved his mouth to speak, the radio shot high frequency pitches that sounded like the death of a thousand whales.

"What the hell?" James removed his hand from the handle of his gun. He reached for the knob and attempted to turn the station, but no matter where he put the dial, the sounds of torture and pain scratched through the speakers.

"Turn it off! Turn that shit off!" James punched the radio with the sides of his hand. Lifting his boot, he pounded the speaker on his side of the car and dented the drum of the device. The blaring continued.

"I don't know what' is going on," Hershel screamed over the sounds and maintained his control over the truck as he sped down the highway.

A static noise spat and crackled. Then the noise died and a deep voice said, "Soon."

"Did you hear that?" Hershel asked as his shaky hands steered.

"No," James lied and pulled his bag closer to his hands to hide the way they shook.

"So, well, so well," Hershel said and wiped the dip from his pants that spilled during their panic. "So they went into the base. This was her first time in a Nazi death camp. She'd never seen it before because her family got her out just in time to live with a Germany family. She told me the look on her mom and dad's face when they walked in, she saw the torture they went through in their expressions, and it tore her heart to pieces.

"They searched the entire thing. I mean they searched well before they settled in that day. Rita found this…this medical facility near the back that had specimens, real circus freak show jars. Fetuses, monkey heads, the works.

"She said that the first day she went into the facility, she saw this bolted door in the back. Very mysterious, real piss your pants scary. And she didn't go in, but she said she heard scratches and moans from the room. She took a journal out from this Nazi doctor before her friend got her out of there. When they went back to the camp, she said her father found these two girls, missing teeth, wearing ripped clothes dirtier than a mechanic's rag, and with two different color eyes. I think she said one brown and one blue. Anna and Maria. I think that was their names," Hershel said.

James sat back in his seat and his heartbeat returned to the new normal. He pulled his gun from the bag and focused on his goal from before, getting Hershel out of the truck without killing him. *The big fucker could be a hit man, he could be anything, I gotta do this when he finishes. When he's done buying time, I'll take it out and put it to his head. If he tries some shit, I'm pulling the trigger.*

James didn't hear some of the details of the story as he sat pondering his plan to take the truck and leave Hershel out in the cold. After Hershel finished his boring story, James would pull out his gun, tell Hershel to get out, and he'd drive off, heading for the house in Athens.

They zoomed past a small bar near an apartment complex off the highway. The perfect spot for a sports bar, it was similar to the location in Gainesville that he and Jeff had imagined where they'd build their sports bar. James could see the roof of the place. And not too far from the door, the parking lot where the college teens hung out and finished their drinking.

The letters J and J blazed red.

A cup rattled in the truck as Hershel released more dip into his canister. James took his eyes off the terrain and left his fantasy behind him.

"Well, she figured it out—she rubbed snow to show the words. The girls used this box to hypnotize the whole camp. By the time they figured it out, it was too late, and they had a magic word they used as they played that thing. *Time for a party.* When they said that, hell broke loose in the camp. One of the men killed a boy named Julian. Slit his throat. And Rita told me, whatever that thing did, it made them do bad things. Those girls sat on a perch watching. This monster from the room, he had this paper in his pocket, he was an experiment I think she told me that." Hershel looked at the roof of the truck. "Yeah, she did. He was a monster that looked like a mutated linebacker from the Bears. He had a paper that had a phrase that broke the spell they cast. After they broke loose, the twins set the place on fire. They found a way out, and when they got to the exit, there stood the twins, waiting for them by a hole in the gate. And they had the box in their hands, and a torch in the other. When they got real close to the group, the giant man, what was his name?" Hershel snapped his fingers. "Oh, I think it was Herman. Well, he came out, grabbed the girls, and sent them into the fire. The box fell on the ground, and they ran out of the hole in the gate. My wife said she saw her dad go back for the box."

He's almost done. James tapped his hand on the butt of the gun.

"Well, she said that night, she saw her dad go out with that box when he thought they all were asleep. When he came back, he smelled like a cigar. The next morning, the Americans came and saved them. My money's on the man with the darkness that followed him helped them. My wife agrees. Her dad made a deal with the devil..."

James remained silent, and his hand remained on his gun.

You bought enough time.

"But what is a man to do to protect his family?" Hershel coughed and discarded his dip into a canister.

"I see I didn't scare you." Hershel put his gaze back on the road.

"What's the matter with you anyway? You keep looking out the window, and you're sweating as if you stole something. Sniffing as if you got a runny nose. I see your hands on that gun. What you really running from?" Hershel pressed.

James didn't answer and removed his shotgun from his bag and mashed it to Hershel's cheek.

CHAPTER 7
END OF THE ROAD

"Pull over and get out of the truck," James said and drove the barrel deeper into Hershel's cheek.

"Go ahead and shoot me. I'm already dead."

James released some of the pressure from the barrel on Hershel's face and tilted his head to the side.

"I guess we all have our demons. Just like Rita's father, we all make a deal with a devil to protect those we love. I didn't buy your story for a second," Hershel said with the cold metal pressed on the side of his mouth.

"What do you know? He sent you? Uh?" James crinkled his forehead.

"Just as I thought." Hershel exhaled. "You and me, James. You and me made a deal with a bad man."

James' eyes widened, and he lowered the gun from Hershel's face.

"I made a mistake not too long ago, besides this." Hershel rolled up his sleeve and showed James the tattoo of a heart.

"I loved a girl real bad, and well, I met a man. He said, 'You want her; you can have her for a price.' So I gave in. Funny, I didn't care what the price was."

"Why you telling me this?"

"I guess it's rightfully time I told someone," Hershel rambled on. "At first, life was wonderful, and then he kept coming around, dropping in when he shouldn't have. I found out she had cancer, and that gave him more of a reason to come by."

Hershel swallowed and rubbed the crust from the corners of his mouth.

With every word about Hershel's past, James lowered his weapon and eased himself into his seat.

"When she had cancer, I thought that was it. Then he came by, and I made another deal. Now he's after me 'cause I didn't pay my debt. He killed her..." Hershel's voice cracked.

"What's his name?" James looked at the clock on the radio.

"The Gentleman."

James let out an, "Oh God," and shuffled his hair between his fingers. "What do you owe him?"

Hershel moved his, I-haven't-slept-in-weeks eyes from the road and looked at James. "He took my smarts away. Now, I'm no smarter than I was when I was thirteen. Use to be a physic...phys...yeah—a science person. Then the second time, well, I owed him my life."

Reaching into his bag, James removed the letters he'd received in the hotel and turned them over to Hershel. Line after line Hershel read, and glared at the road after every other word.

"Who sent this to you?" Hershel asked.

"Not sure. Trying to find out. I know the man you're talkin' about," James said.

For a while, Hershel looked at James with a white face, and then moved his gaze back on the road. "I guess he put us here for a reason. I could smell his stamp on you once you got in my truck," Hershel said.

"What do we do now?" James asked.

"He knows where I'm at. No reason to run now."

"I don't know who sent me that, but whoever it is, is trying to help me. I had nowhere to go. That son-of-a-slut wouldn't stop with the games; we played games all the time." James looked at Hershel.

"What did he do?" Hershel asked.

"He would challenge me to answer his trivia questions, or shoot innocent people on the street, or worse." James paused. "He used my daughter to get me to play along." James looked out at the road that skated by faster than they drove.

"I hate to admit some of the stuff he had me do early on, I enjoyed. Getting people who owed someone money, doing hits. But he kept increasing the task. If we played a game and I won, I got something out of it. If I lost, or if it was a draw, he'd have me be his do-boy."

"He would randomly show his face," Hershel said.

"I'm frightened. The only thing that used to scare me was losing my family. I lost that, and now I'm scared of him." James' voice shook as he spoke, and he rotated to face Hershel, holding up his hand with the missing digit. He'd never had someone that he could share his horrors of The Gentleman before this.

"His smell, I hate his smell," Hershel said

James nodded. "I thought I smelled him earlier, but I must've been paranoid."

Hershel brushed his hair back and stared into the road and bug-splattered windshield. "Maybe, whoever helpin' you could help me, too."

"Yeah, maybe they can. I had him beat for a while, got some help from this hoodoo lady in South Carolina. She gave me this shoot stuff that I put in the bullets. Then she tried to swindle me, and I showed her what happens to those who cross me." James held the bag up in the light of the truck.

"What's it made of?"

"Some type of demon weed," James said and put the pouch back in his bag.

When James pulled out a shiny object with a metallic barrel that shimmered and reflected the moonlight, Hershel jerked the wheel, and the tires bobbed on the off road. "I thought we were past that?"

"I just wanted to show you."

After James handed the gun to Hershel, Hershel whistled as he rotated it. "It's nice, but it ain't gone to kill no demon." He handed it back to James.

"Not with regular bullets." James emptied the chamber, showed the iron shells, and dropped one of the heavy bullets into Hershel's palm.

Sniffing with his quarter-sized nostrils, Hershel sniffed hard enough to remove the chrome off the surface of the bullet. "What's that?"

"A lot of shit that'll kill anything that ain't alive, but you gotta aim for the neck or head, otherwise it won't work. At least that's the theory." James reloaded his revolver. "What was your time limit?" He slid the shotgun in his bag.

"Yesterday, five a.m., and for some reason, I'm still alive. You?" Hershel asked.

"He gave me 'til one thirty yesterday to show up, but I think I beat him, or he can't find me, or he's fucking with me."

"Enough about this asshole. You gotta girl back where you from...Jeff?" Hershel said.

"Not anymore. I was married, but well, she left. I pushed her away." James pulled the ring from his pocket and dropped it out of the window. "Been a long time coming, I guess." James paused. "I lied. My name isn't Jeff, its James."

"James, you get called Jimmy a lot?" Hershel laughed.

"I punch people in the throat who call me Jimmy, sounds like a private part. Jimmy. Only my dad and Jeff called me that," James said and touched the dog tags on his neck.

"Who's Jeff then? Your brother?"

"No my best friend. We grew up together and went to college the same time, joined up at the same time."

James reached for his wallet and pulled out the picture of him and Jeff wearing their green Army uniform, James with a cigar in his mouth, and Jeff with smile wide enough to fit a stadium. After holding the picture to the light, Hershel stretched his eyes to the sight of picture, and handed it back to James.

"Sorry about that," Hershel said and James took back his photo and put it in his wallet

"Surprised he was black, Commi?" James snatched the book from the dashboard. "You a commi?" James titled his head toward Hershel.

"Was. Now I don't know what I am." Hershel took in a breath and touched the tattoo on his hand with his thumb. "My granddad was a Soviet, and my dad won't have any of it. After he died and my mother went crazy, I went to live with my granddad in Ohio. He brought me into the business."

"How long?" James asked.

"My entire life. I hid it from my wife—communists don't like the Jews, and I hid it. I told her this tattoo was a mistake. Was supposed to be her initials, R.L. I think it is pretty interesting that you're judging me, after you told me you were a hit man."

"I was a hit man for him. I didn't start doing it because I enjoyed it. But a commi? We went to war and lost blood over that. That's some serious shit. After what they did, after all this shit in 'Nam, in Korea, in Russia. And you being here, you chose that?" James questioned and faced his body to Hershel, waiting for his next words, holding his smaller knife out and twirling it around his fingers.

"We got off on a bad start, I'm not that person any more, James. I'm trying to find out who I am. Just like you."

"Yeah, I guess you're right. We're both stuck together," James said and placed the knife in his bag. He didn't want to see the life of Hershel flash before his eyes after he slit his throat. Thanks to The Gentleman, each man he killed, he saw who they were.

"When was the last time you saw him appear?" Hershel asked as he steered the truck around a decaying raccoon carcass in the road.

"Over a year, until yesterday. Still don't know how that son-of-a-slut..." James stopped when the smell of lilac filled the truck.

Black figures slipped into the holes in the air-conditioning vents. They circled Hershel as he swatted them. The truck swerved and weaved on the broken road and jumped onto the median. Sparks of yellow and amber speckled as the side of the truck scraped the railing.

"Oh no," James said.

Blood fell from Hershel's nose, then his ears. He wiped it away vigorously, but it didn't stop falling, and it spilled onto his clothes. Soon he coughed blood all over the truck.

"Get 'em off me, help!" Hershel said, and his blood splattered on the windshield. When the median turned into vegetation, his truck bounced and hopped on the uneven terrain.

"Shit!" James emptied his soot, and it formed a powdered cloud over Hershel's head that trickled down his body, missing the ghouls. As James pulled at Hershel, the dark objects tugged harder.

Hershel lost control of the wheel and yelled as the black ghosts flew in and out of his body. He gagged, they sautéed his skin, and purple-violet spots spread across his arms and face.

Even as James took over steering the truck, he was unable to put his feet on the brake. To heighten the danger, Hershel's body went into rigor mortis, which caused his foot locked in place on the gas. The size of the tree dead ahead appeared like a skyscraper to James. He had seconds to react. After strapping on his seat belt, he placed his arms across his face, bracing for the crash.

They collided, and Hershel's head hit the horn. James' head hit the dashboard, and three dip canisters toppled. Brown spit blobbed on his pants. As he lifted his head, he touched the sticky ooze.

"Ah, shit in a box," he said and wiped it on the truck's seat. The horn blared, and the high-pitched buzz rattled the glass and shattered James' eardrums. Taking his hands from over his ears, he peeled Hershel's sunken head from the steering wheel.

"Damn," James said and let the lifeless body fall over the wheel. Outside, the tires' rotation knocked up dust that spiraled into the air.

"Holly fuck, what the hell? Fuck you! Fuck you!"

The Gentleman had stranded him once again.

Because Hershel's body fell over the steering wheel, it prevented James from turning off the engine. With his feet pressed against the hump in the middle of the truck, James pulled and yanked at Hershel's body, but was unable to move him two inches.

"Okay, Okay, I'll do it on his side." He left the truck and rounded to the driver's side. The dust from the tires burned his eyes and forced him to cover his face. He slung the door open and smashed his foot into Hershel's leg. It snapped, and white rigid bone ripped through the skin.

After stuffing Hershel back into the truck, James turned off the engine and shoved Hershel's massive frame out of the way of the steering wheel, which revealed the brown mushy stain on Hershel's pants, and he placed his nose inside of his shirt.

James turned the key backward, then forward.

"Come on, Come on."

It only sputtered.

Nothing happened no matter how many times he turned the key and pumped the gas. The front of the truck folded like an aluminum can, and James was unable to lift the hood and make enough fixes to get him to Athens.

When he finally gave up and packed his things, the sun rose through the heavy mist. He took all he could from Hershel's stash, and looked at Hershel's ghostly body one last time before traveling to his next misadventure. It was hard to find things in the truck not covered in the brown spit from the canisters.

"Poor guy." As James motioned to leave, Hershel's body drifted up from the seat.

"The dead meet the dead on their way to death," Hershel said in a demonic tone and grabbed James' necklace.

James pulled away, and the necklace snapped. He scooted away, scraping his butt on the gravel. "No. You were dead!" He picked himself off the ground, and Hershel's body fell into its original position.

***

After twenty minutes of wandering in the muck, he saw a sign on the road that read, 'Five Miles to Athens.'

As he advanced, a mist clouded his vision. The musk of hell and lilac made it harder to breathe, and the sun that lay above the horizon barely hit James' skin. Mysterious shapes wove through the holes in the fog, and he called to them. "Who's there?"

Some laughed, some cackled, others whispered, and some

groaned.

"Got damn blisters," he said and massaged his foot near a tall tree. He looked in his bag at what he had. Cans of tuna, oysters, water, and an apple. Medical supplies, a flashlight, his pictures, the papers from the truck, and his gun.

"I'm so, so tired of this." He put his head against the tree.

"Get up get up. You stay here, and he gets you."

***

James reached Athens after two hours of walking.

He spotted a middle-aged woman wearing old, tattered, 1900's clothing facing away from him, and he called out to her. "What road is this?"

She didn't answer.

"Excuse me, miss," he asked.

Again, she made no response.

"Excuse me, miss," he called once again.

She turned to him; her eyes covered with dried tears and mascara, and held onto a baby in a blanket. "Look what they did to him…look!" The infant's head dangled from ligaments as the mad woman jostled the dead body in James' face.

Surprised and unsure how to react, he veered in the opposite direction and dry-heaved beside a bush. When he lifted his head, he twirled in a circle and scratched his head at the scene before him. "Where the hell am I?"

Near an open window not far from the woman with the baby, a man chopped off his own penis in a butcher's window. It tumbled into the violet grass. A woman in a window down the street sewed her mouth shut as maggots slithered in her empty eye sockets.

James trampled forward into the great unknown. When he saw several women sitting on a post, moving in harmony and mimicking one another's movements, he dropped his bag. They had gray skin and wore swimming caps on their heads.

Children missing limbs and hair ran circles around him, and when one of the little gremlins took a chunk of flesh from his arm, he returned the favor with a knuckle sandwich. The child hissed as he stumbled away from James.

In the distance, the ghosts of soldiers in gray and blue coats jumped out of trenches and battled to the death. The sound of muskets and the first Colts ever welded, cracked against the fog.

As he ran out of the warzone, James walked into a shifty-eyed man with a sly smile. "Pst," the man said and leaned more on the wooden fence that lined the road. James turned and walked to him, gripping his knife.

"You don't look like the others, what is this place?"

"Athens," the man said and cracked his neck.

"Hey, you wouldn't happen to know where Everest Road is, would you?"

"Yeah sure, kid. Watcha got for me?" the man hustled.

"I'm not paying you for directions, asshole." James walked away, and the shifter grabbed his arm.

"You lucky, kid." The man slipped his hand inside James' pocket to retrieve his wallet.

"I'll give you five seconds to give me back my wallet." James curled his fingers into a fist.

"What wallet?" the man asked.

James whisked his wallet from the gambler's hands and pulled the man up by his collar.

"I tell you what, I feel lucky. Just turn down Justice Road, it's a shortcut. It's a big house on the right. Can't miss it," The man said as he held his hands in the air.

"But Justice?" James dropped the man to the ground and shuffled his feet into the direction he pointed.

"Look, kid, roads change over the years. Trust me, pal," he said and patted James' arm.

James pulled away and pushed the man further off the road.

"Trust me," the man repeated as he straightened his coat and pointed to the road.

Turning around, James squinted his eyes to read the sign that said 'Justice Rd.' "This doesn't seem right," he said and turned back to the stranger, but he was no longer there.

***

***

Following the strange man's instructions, James walked down a foggy street named Justice Road, along a trail to a house that looked similar to the one in his picture.

"Not quite it, but damn near close," he said and ran to the steps.

On the second knock, the door unlocked and opened. James jumped as the door crept open.

"I really shouldn't," James said and looked behind him before entering the house.

"Never mind."

Upon entering the home, he batted the swarms of spider webs from his face and spit out the dust that climbed into his mouth. When he pressed his feet lightly on the floorboards, they cracked under his feet and bent in the middle, barely holding his weight.

He walked around the house and kicked the old plates that lay chipped and mangled on the ground. His curiosity led him into the home's hallway. "Hello? Is anyone here?" His voice filled the empty place.

"I got your letter."

He opened the first room to his left. The purple green tint from the window hit a rocking chair that sat in the corner. He scooted into the room, and walked to the desk. James picked up a girl's hairbrush and barrettes with strings of strawberry blonde hair woven in the forks of the clip. A book with the word 'Sarah' written in red crayon lay next to them. Someone had decorated the book with construction paper cut outs of flowers and pictures from turn of the century fashion magazines. Then, he opened the book and read the first page.

JANUARY 15,

TODAY DADDY CAME HOME AND TOLD ME TO COME INTO HIS STUDY. HE WANTED ME TO WEAR HIS FAVORITE DRESS AND SING THE SONG I LEARNED

FROM SCHOOL.

"This is so weird." He put the items down on the desk and looked at himself in the mirror atop the dresser. He knew when to stop invading someone's private entry. Whatever he discovered would remain with him for life.

In the reflection, the fog swirled outside the window. He studied himself and saw the same man from the hotel. Frightened from life, frightened from moving on. A man not sure of what he wanted in life and not quite ready to end it all.

"There's nothing here." His face turned stone cold, and he walked into the living room and went to the pictures on the table. In the black and white photograph was an older man with his hair parted down the middle, standing with his family.

"Not a happy family." He placed the picture on the ancient desk.

"I don't think I should linger in this place anymore. That fucker lied to me, or someone is messin' with me." He walked to the front door.

Then the clank of chains hit the door.

James backed into the table, and the picture fell to the ground. His hands smashed onto a thick piece of glass as he attempted to catch his fall. "God," he said and placed pressure on the wound.

A heavy bang smashed the front door to bits. A man stepped into the home wearing a tight, black cotton suit and his hair parted down the middle. He walked in with a mission on his face.

"Sarah, Daddy's home. Put on the dress I like," he said.

James pushed himself onto the wall, slid his back against it toward the door.

A shriek spilled from the board under his foot.

James winced.

The man rotated his head one hundred and eighty degrees without moving his body. "Well, you came." He smiled and showcased his asphalt-colored teeth. "He told me to have fun with you."

When James pursued the door, his bag fell from his shoulder, and his baseball rolled into hell's kitchen. The man glided over floorboards to James. After the man blocked the exit, he lifted James' body from the ground by his shirt with one arm. Tilting his head to one side, the frightening Quaker opened his mouth and pulled James closer to his horrifying mouth.

James kicked his feet and put his bloody hand into the man's glass eye. It sizzled, and the same kind of liquid that seeps from a bad battery poured down his face. He dropped James to the floor.

As the man went to James for a second attack, the shadow of an owl appeared behind them. It flew through the man's legs and swooped over his head. James stumbled out of the home and didn't look back. He ran to a hill, climbed to the top, and rummaged through his bag for his gun. He took one last look at the crazy Amish man that stood at the door's entrance.

"This can't be happening." James lifted his head and scanned the sky.

The owl from the house flew over his body. It sailed in the sky, circling like a hawk over its prey. Then it swooped down. James moved to avoid it. He aimed his shotgun, burst two bullets from the chamber, and reloaded. They all missed, and the owl began to circle the tree.

Although James ran from spot to spot, the owl followed. James cut to a fork in the road, and it stopped him. The owl pushed him to the opposite road and chased him down a hill, and ran James into a road sign, 'Everest.'

"Ouch." After falling to the ground from the impact, he rubbed his head. Once he looked up to the sign, he sprung from the ground.

"This is it," he said and walked down the slope to the plantation home.

The white two-story house showed its age. The shingles of the roof fell to the ground and hundreds were missing. The door held on to the hedges with luck, and James counted seven large holes in the porch. Spanish moss painted the banister and wove through the edges of the roof. Time chipped and tarnished the

Romanesque pillars holding up the front porch.

Near the right of the house sat a large tree, and blood red peaches hung from its limbs. The roots embedded into the soil, twisted, turned around the property, and stretched out around the only green grass. The mammoth roots stopped at the purple grass that surrounded the entire house like the lakes kings built around castles.

After James ran to the tree and leaned his back against it, the owl perched in the branches and stopped his torment.

"Stay there, crazy ass bird," James said as he looked up the massive structure. He touched the surface—it felt rough and warm on his hands, and he rested his ear against the bark.

"Is that a heartbeat?" James asked. The branches of the tree hung low, some touched the ground. He plucked one of the peaches from the limbs, and the tree swayed.

"Amazing," he whispered and put the peach on the ground. The railing on the porch attracted his attention. The porch was the perfect distance from him, about sixty feet, and the roots to the tree looked like a pitcher's mound.

He sifted through his bag. He sat it down and shuffled through it. He spilled it on the ground.

"My ball! Shit," he said. The flaring of his body caused the peach that sat at the base of the tree to roll onto his foot. He reached for it before it rolled down the hill to the house.

After bouncing it in his hand, he positioned it behind his back and leaned forward. He used a stump of root as a pitcher's mound, wound up, and released. The flesh of the peach absorbed into the grooves of the banister. He took another one from the branches and hit the same spot.

Then another.

He fired off eight peaches and wiped the sweat from his brow. After looking at the missing digit on his left hand, he retired from throwing peaches at the railing of the porch. Spanish moss floated from the branches as he took five more peaches from the tree and put them in his bag.

"The only thing to help my nerves," he said and walked to the house. Holding the picture in his hand up to it, besides the obvious signs of decay, the photo matched the house that lay before him.

As he stepped on the last steps to the porch, his foot broke through. "God dammit." He proceeded to the door, limping on his injured leg.

"What am I doing? I should just leave." When he turned for the step, the stench of lilac forced his feet away from the ledge.

There, on the banister to his left, The Gentleman sat destroying an apple with his bone-crushing teeth. James clenched his bag until his knuckles became white and held on even tighter.

"I was wondering what took you so long," The Gentleman said, rid himself of the apple, and after he elevated off the ground, The Gentleman floated to James. "Nice to see you, too."

James backed away. "This was your plan the whole time. Get me here."

"Maybe." The Gentleman shrugged and brushed the fragments of apple from his brillo pad palms. "Is this image better." A magnum of incandescent smoke puffed as he transformed, wearing a wig, a black corset, and fishnet stockings with high heels. "Oh, Jimmy." The Gentleman waved.

"Wh-I—" James stumbled on the balls of his feet away from the mess before him.

"I can mask my smell, big *pojke*. Something I learned." He pouted.

James' joints locked, and while his brain said *Go*, his body remained stiff with fear.

"Come on. We haven't seen each other in over a year, and all you have to say is, 'What?' I am disappointed." The Gentleman shook his head. "I just need one thing from you, James. No games, just this one thing." He prowled toward him. When he raked his fingers over the rail of the banister, his skin sizzled, and his original figure returned.

"What was that?" he asked and studied James' face.

"I don't know," James said and squeezed the strap on his bag until his hand became numb.

"What did you do?" he said in a maniacal voice.

"Nothing, I just got here, I swear. Please."

The fog became as dark as The Gentleman's suit, and The Gentleman's eyes shimmered lavender.

Once The Gentleman looked at the tree and at the juice on James' hands, he gained his composure. The fog recoiled to its pale lavender-green color.

"No more target practice." The Gentleman straightened his suit and tie. "I bet you felt you had me with those voodoo tricks, but I found you." He walked to James. "What's the fun in all that? You used to enjoy our adventures. In Vegas, you lost all that money to me in Blackjack. It didn't turn out so bad. How many did you kill for me?"

"I didn't wanna do that. I didn't want to…" James inched to the edge of the porch.

"Remember Rosa, Cuba? Yum. Remember the Chinese woman you fucked and stole the fortune from her rich husband?" The Gentleman pulled a leather-bound journal from inside his breast pocket and thumbed through it. "You get my letters?" The Gentleman smiled.

"You sent them? Why are you doing to me? Just kill me." James readied himself for the stairs and placed his foot on the ledge.

The Gentleman's eyes traveled to James' feet. "Kill you?" The corners of The Gentleman's mouth shook as if he was holding back a tantalizing secret. "How you like this place, James?" The Gentleman asked without lifting his head and aggressively parted the pages of the journal.

"What is this place?" James asked.

"This is my world. Nowhere to run, nowhere to hide. I am all around you. I am fucking God here. I determine when you fuck, breathe, burp, and sleep. This is my collection of souls, but you are welcome to stay."

James watched as The Gentleman placed all his attention on the book he held and fevered through. When he turned to the steps to run, he halted. Demons of all shapes and sizes waited for him. Their teeth chomped as they circled around the property. The invisible barrier The Gentleman created stopped them from ripping off James' head and tearing into his chest. The man from the other house stood in the crowd. With his arms folded, he glared at James with his good eye.

"I wouldn't do that if I were you," The Gentleman said, leaning on the porch rail. "I have a lot of friends who would love to get their hands on your blood, and I'll keep them away. But first you have to do something for me."

As he skated from the monsters to the door, James slipped his hand into his bag and gripped his shotgun.

Once at the end of the journal, The Gentleman sneered at the missing pages, slammed it shut, and stuffed it back where it came from. "I just need a teeny tiny favor that involves you going in there."

"Why haven't you had someone find the shit you're lookin' for?" James asked and continued the heavy breathing from his mouth. With The Gentleman, there was no tit for tat.

"You don't think I haven't? I know where it's at. I can taste it, I can smell it, but I can't touch it." The Gentleman became visibly angry.

James flinched.

After licking his lips, The Gentleman neared James, and the stench of lilac twirled and grazed James' cheek. The Gentleman disappeared among the smog.

"Where is he?" James searched around the porch for the face of the demon.

As the smoke spun into a wormhole, a face formed in the middle, and The Gentleman smiled through it. "Boo."

James hurled his body into the walls of the house.

"Oh, that was easy." The Gentleman laughed.

Shaking his rifle from his bag, James cocked it fully and shot two iron-plated bullets from the chamber. The Gentleman lifted his hand, and the bullets spiraled in midair. As he put his arm down, the spinning bullets dropped, melting the porch on their descent. He snapped his fingers, and the gun's gray color turned into a blacksmith's cast iron.

James let go of it, and smoke rose from his hand. He examined his hand—the pain drove him to his knees.

"I am done being *kind and understanding*, and now, I won't make this easy for you. That *skit* only kills ghosts anyway." The Gentleman paced the porch and struck a match for his onyx pipe. "I was going to give you a get out of jail card, if you would've just walked in and got something for me." He cracked his knuckles.

James cried.

The Gentleman rolled his eyes and waved his hand near the scars. They erased from James' hand. "Better?"

James didn't respond. He gathered himself from the floor and placed his back against the termite-ridden wall.

"Do you know your great-great-grandfather was a black?"

"What?" James leveled his eyes to The Gentleman's boots and moved further apart from him.

"Answer me!" The Gentleman smashed his heel into James' stomach

James rolled around as if he were on fire. "Oh, God," he said and spit blood.

"I can't hear you. Did you know?"

"My dad said his...side of the family...came here from Ireland...in the early eighteen hundreds." James wheezed.

"Yeah, part of it, the other part was a slave. Talk about family secrets," The Gentleman said and puffed from his pipe. "And this was the property. The same property where they hanged him." He pointed to the tree. It moved with the fog, and the branches scratched the ground. On top of one of the thick branches, the owl sat fluttering its wings.

"That's right, stay back," The Gentleman said to it as it glided over the roof. He inhaled again and ran to the edge of the porch.

"You see that bastard, and he was nothing more than a *slave* before he learned the powers of Voodoo. Theodore Bailey." He drove his foot into the side of the porch. "Before he died, he kept something from me, and he cursed this place so I can't touch the door it sits in, and no one else can get in that room."

While nursing his wounds, James watched as The Gentleman paraded on the porch, reasoning with why he couldn't enter the room.

"I can enter this anytime," The Gentleman banged on the door, "but not the door to the room where he hid it."

James crawled up from the porch floor and propped himself against the house.

"I really was going to have you open the door and that was it, but since you had to go and piss me off, to show you how generous I am, how bout we play a game, like the good ole days?" The Gentleman grinned and stood next to James.

James shook his head.

"Come on, it'll be fun." He nudged James' shoulder.

"What's the point in playing? You're going to kill me anyway, and you forced me here."

"Now, now let's not blame me. *You* refused to play the game, but I do keep your soul. Rules are rules, James. Rules are rules."

"What do you want from me? You have everything. You want me to go into the house? I'll do it. You happy? I give up, I give up! No more games..."

"*Skit.* Are you listening? You blew that chance, *Pojke.*"

James remained silent.

The Gentleman clasped his hands together and pointed his letter-opener nails into James' chest. "This is the very last game. You find what I'm looking for, and you keep your little soul. But if you don't, I keep you and what's in that house." The Gentleman held out his hand.

"I can't do this again. I can't. I'm sorry about the bullets, I'm sorry," James sobbed and ate the snot that dripped into his mouth. Turning around for the steps, he backed away from the madness of the ghouls that surrounded the property. He had no choice but to face the demon.

The Gentleman put his hand down and took three steps closer. He picked James up by the neck and pushed him to the wall. The back of his heels kicked the house as The Gentleman's grip tightened.

He spoke in James' ear. "I can make this a lot harder than you think," he said and banged James' head against the house, then drew him closer. "Like the good ole days, solider," he said and released his hold around James' neck.

Breaking boards and more of his ribs in the process, James thudded onto the ground. As he rubbed his neck and placed his back against the wall, The Gentleman kneeled in front of him.

"This can all be over. Play this last game, walk into that house, find the papers I want in the room, and you have your life back. I mean it, I don't want to have to force...well..." The Gentleman rolled his eyes. "*You* wouldn't want me to force my hand, because if I do, I keep everything and torture you until I get tired. And I don't tire easily."

When The Gentleman maneuvered out of James' personal space, James stood. He dusted the fragments of the porch from his pants, picked up his bag, and stuffed in his cooled shotgun.

The Gentleman kept his left hand out to James, waiting for a response to his peace offering. After he shook the reptilian hand extended to him, The Gentleman clenched James' hand and pulled James toward him. "Your one and only clue: It all adds up, so find the right door." He caressed the missing digit on James' left hand, his throwing arm. "Sorry about that."

James snatched his hand back and stuffed it into his pocket, hiding his shame.

After The Gentleman looked upon him, he snatched his dog tags.

"No!" James reached for them.

"For safe keeping. You and Jeff were *really* close. Your family likes that type, I see." He rotated the silver-plated tags in his hand and tossed them into the mosh pit of ghosts that bawled around the house. They had front row seats to the show.

"Now that we have a deal, why don't we take a looksee inside?" The Gentleman escorted James to the door.

James advanced to it, shaking after each step. He'd lost his ball in the house, and now, his only link to sanity. The Gentleman tossed it to the ghosts. He could no longer use dog tags to conjure good memories and keep himself levelheaded. Depending on himself alone to overcome what lay before him gave him little hope he'd get back Jeff's dog tags or win the game against The Gentleman, for that matter.

The picture of me and my old man. I still have that. He unhurried his hand to the door handle. After looking at the interest and desperation on The Gentleman's face by way of the reflection in the bronze knob, he closed his eyes, shut out the image, and turned the handle.

The door eased open, and he inhaled the dust from the dying house.

The Gentleman shadowed James' body, and James felt the heat of his breath burn the hairs on his neck. The green laser eyes probed James' skull, and his demon teeth clenched together to devise his sinister grin.

James didn't need to see it, he felt it. He felt that smile. He felt it in his bones and to his core.

"Welcome home, James." The Gentleman sneered.

James stepped into the house to play his last game, his last battle royale.

ACT II:
THE LAST GAME

CHAPTER 8
THE OWL SWOOPS IN

As James followed The Gentleman to the open area, ostensibly the courier, The Gentleman examined the room and paid no mind to the front door that lay open, swaying back and forth.

James used the light from outside to find his way around. From the entrance, he gazed at a staircase that spiraled upward into the heavens and watched as The Gentleman shuffled his feet near a large fireplace on the opposite side.

"Do you mind?" the demon asked.

Not waiting for an answer, he lit the fireplace with a touch of his finger. The flames flared then dimmed. The Gentleman placed his pipe in the fire, and the end ignited with a lavender spark. The light from the fireplace revealed the enormous living room and the spacious ceiling where a chandelier hung. It also revealed the historic landscape of the house and the amount of artistry that went into each piece of wood.

As The Gentleman walked around the staircase, his feet fell against the boards like canons. Peering at the chandelier that chimed from the wind's touch, he gazed up the flights of steps. "I hate this unbearable place."

He took another deep draw from his pipe. "No running, James, I can find you. You can choose from any of the rooms in the house."

"Which room?" James' voice shook.

"You'll find out—I can't give it all away. Three rooms,

three clues. Then you get to guess the number to the magic door." The Gentleman inhaled then exhaled from his pipe before speaking. "Or maybe there aren't any clues. Any questions?"

James shook his head. "I just want this done with. You can have whatever it is, I don't care, I just…I just…" James' speech ended when he heard the swish of the wind bark from outside. With it came a thousand feathers from a bird that almost didn't fit through the door.

Turning toward it, The Gentleman spit plasma from his lips and zipped to where it sailed. "No, you don't."

The feathers that floated from the bird formed a cyclone around James and cajoled him to spin three hundred and sixty degrees. As the cyclone's speed increased, James spun faster, and The Gentleman's face flashed in front of him. Then the gritty face blurred into streaks of greens and blacks. The darkness that swirled around James turned into bright lights, and he lost his footing.

CHAPTER 9
A PARTY FOR A GENTLEMAN

"What the..."

James wandered around a house that appeared alive and full of people. The house, with the rotted wood and ghostly appearance, now displayed a party in the 1850's. Inside, people pranced to the soothing rhythms of classical music that streamed from the musicians.

"What the hell are these?" he asked. His filthy pants and holy shirt no longer clothed him, and now he wore loose cotton pants and a fancy white shirt with an itchy navy petticoat.

After touching his untangled hair, he looked in a mirror. "What the hell is going on? I look twenty-two again."

As he walked around, two Southern debutants pushed him aside and twirled between the crowds of people.

"Watch it, ladies," James said but neither woman acknowledged his presence. Titling his head, he attempted to take a gander at the girls, but layers upon layers of lace and cotton hid all from the neck down.

James stopped exploring the party when he saw a man standing in the doorway with his arms folded and holding papers in his field-working hands.

"Dad?" James questioned. "Wait...the guy's too dark...but still..." He squinted and marveled at the slave's resemblance to his father.

When the slave stood up straight, he moved his mouth to form the words, "Don't follow me," and he ran out of the house.

"The eyes, the dimples, the...no way," James said and

followed.

Once again, a woman ran past him, but this time, he almost fell on his ass. As he watched her float away, he studied her. Her hair, chocolate brown like his, danced in the sunlight. Her eyes, the color of a calm May sky like his, twinkled, and her tanned skin and rosy cheeks would put down the toughest of men. With her dress raised past her ankles, she raced through the dancers, servers, and entertainers, and leapt out into the world. James moved his head to the people whispering and chuckling at a scrappy man wearing a red overcoat and long sideburn chops on his face. Most referred to the man as Mister Greene.

"New money." A small woman laughed as she eyed Mister Greene and walked around James.

"He doesn't even know how to keep his Negros under control. Look at them," a taller man behind James said, and James turned into the direction of the voice.

"Just prancing and doing, their jigs. I heard he wasn't even baptized. Poor white trash does well in Mexico, and then they assume they can meld in with the upper class..." The posh man raised his eyebrow to an old hag standing near him by the large staircase.

"What a bunch of turds," James said but continued listening to the aggravating conversation.

"I heard his daughter was dipping into the slave quarters, that child is a child of shame," the old hag said, and James' hand shook as he checked his watch.

"Well, if you ask me, Mister Greene, the owner of that slave Theo—" The posh man drew his head to a man in a red coat that approached them. "Mister Greene, fine party." He leaned in to give Mister Greene a sign of respect.

"Well, well, if it isn't Michael Haven and Daniel Commodore. Aren't you two a pair of Siamese twins?"

"Good to see you, too. This property sure is a step up from your other living arrangements, don't you think?" Mister Haven said.

Mister Commodore chuckled, and the air he blew from his

hairy nostrils quivered his white whiskers.

Haven wiped his finger along dust that collected on a fabulous table pushed against the wall of the staircase. "Must be hard to keep up, with the forty or so slaves you inherited. Well, not from me, I have sixty, and they are broken in. This would never happen." Mister Haven rubbed the dust between his fingers and displayed it to Mister Greene. "From what I could tell, yours don't act as though they are slaves."

James remained silent and became interested in the exchanges from the men, relaxing on the wall and attempting to pretend to understand some of the jargon they used.

"Yes. I would mention, in your dialect..." Mister Commodore laughed. "You gotta get some help gettin' them under control. You were a slaver? Use those skills, or get one of your old acquaintances to assist with making proper slaves of them."

After closing his eyes and cleaning his teeth, Mister Greene smiled and tilted his head towards the men.

"We don't blame you, you are new money and your daughter—" Mister Haven started, but Mister Greene cut his words in half.

"Well, thanks for the advice, but I may have to warn you." Mister Greene looked over his shoulder, and then came in closer. He lowered his voice, and the two men came closer to Mister Greene, "I heard they was callin' y'all Aunt Fancy and Miss Nancy," Mister Greene said and shook head. "Such hard terms for two married men, wouldn't you say? Especially you, Mister Commodore. I know you are looking to run for senator of the great state of Georgia against that scallywag Tomb in '54." Mister Greene seemed to relish the red-faced men that stood before him, visibly chagrined.

"But what do I know, hell, they could've been referrin' to President Buchanan and Senator King."

Forcing smiles on their faces, they narrowed their eyes as they excused themselves from Mister Greene's company.

"Aunt Fancy?" James asked and closed in on Mister Greene, who looked at the time on his silver pocket watch as the men departed.

"Wait, he may know where the hell I'm at," James said and put his hand out to Mister Greene's shoulder. "Hey you, where am I?" James asked and missed his shoulder.

Greene gravitated away from James. As he walked past a slender man with a neatly trimmed mustache, the mysterious man summoned him and spoke with a heavy Castellanos' accent. He carried himself with the air of a Conquistador. Even for the pristine party, the man appeared overdressed.

Rearing to his new associate, Mister Greene lowered his eyes and held out his hand. "Yes. Yes, I am."

"I am here for your slave, Theodore," the slender man said.

"He ain't given you any trouble, is he?"

"No, no, nothing like that."

Retiring from waving his arms and shouting, James followed the men and listened to their conversation.

"Got him from a friend of mine that fought in the Mexican war…when Old Hickory was President during the good ole days, if you don't mind me saying," Mister Green said.

"Not at all."

"Damn kid does what he wants. Thinks just because he paints good that he gets special treatment. I have to kick in his teeth every once in a while." Mister Greene bowed to a young woman who danced into him on the dance floor.

"I need to talk to him about something," the conquistador said and returned courteous gestures to the men in the party that waved and nodded their heads to him.

"What the hell do you want? He's not for sale." Mister Greene breathed heavily through his nose, and the air fluffed his mustache.

"No, none of the sort."

Greene placed his hand on the mysterious man's shoulder. "Well then, you after his paintings? I take all profits. You gotta go through me first. Let's have some chin music," Mister Greene said and guided Roberto to a group of men who sat in the corner of the spacious living room.

"Those some fine threads, boy, where you get them?"

Mister Greene asked.

"Spain," the man said.

"Spain..." Mister Greene reached for a drink atop a tray one of the slaves held to him. "We ain't at war no more, so all is fair," he said, and Roberto presented him with a shallow bow. As if he were a shadow, James continued treading behind the men.

Mister Greene drank the contents from the glass, placed it on the tray, and continued escorting Roberto to a circle of well-to-do men. The conversation diminished as Mister Greene made introductions. As he stood behind Mister Greene, James eyed each man Mister Greene presented to the stranger.

"This here is John Bynum. Owns the hemp farm 'bout a coupe miles down," Mister Green said.

The man tipped his hat. Roberto shook his hand.

"Here's Collin Edwards. Gavin Turtle, George Forge, and this here Yankee is Martin Herr."

"Martin Herr?" As the two men shook hands, the man gave Martin a sinister smile.

Standing outside the circle, James bucked when he glimpsed Martin Herr's green eyes and used Mister Greene's body as a shield.

"Pleasure to meet you too," Martin said and let go of the man's hand.

"This Spaniard here...what's your name, boy?" Mister Greene asked him.

"Roberto, Roberto Solórzano," he said and looked around at the men.

"Well, Senor Solórzano here wants to buy them paintings from Theo," Mister Greene said. "Ain't that something, Martin? Because you wanted to talk to him too. How about that? I have two customers. His replicas are the talk of the town. I tell you, boys, he can replicate any painting,' and you can sell it as the real thing."

As Mister Greene rambled on about the authentic look and feel of Theodore's paintings, Martin never diverted his eyes from Roberto, and James never took his eyes off Martin.

"Well now, you two look tenser than a 'coon on a Sunday,"
Mister Greene said and swung his head at both Roberto and
Martin.

"So, when can we meet Theodore?" Martin asked Mister
Greene and sipped on his whiskey.

"After we negotiate a price."

"Any price is good for me, but I must ask to see him alone."
Martin pulled from his breast pocket ten dozen Southern Bank
of Georgia notes with the number ten on each corner.

"Very well then. And you Senor Spain, what's your price?"

"The same." Roberto reached in his pocket and pulled out
Spanish Bullions—the silver coins glimmered in the summer's
sun light.

The men's eyes widened as they admired Roberto's
treasures.

As they conversed, an older woman rubbed Mister Greene's
arm. "Where's Elizabeth?"

Mister Greene shrugged his shoulders. "We are at a party,
Gloria. Don't approach me when I'm discussing business," he
said.

"She ran off again and left Flora with the baby." Gloria
lowered her voice when she saw the way the men reacted when
she said Elizabeth's name.

"That's what she is there for. Flora is there to nurse him,"
Mister Greene said.

"But," Gloria whispered in Mister Greene's ear.

James came close enough to hear the words, "I think she
went to the slave quarters again, or so I heard."

Mister Greene pulled away from her and gave her a serious
glare. "I'll find her."

She fled up the stairs.

"All right, boys, let's go before any other incidents arise."

James followed the men who scuttled behind Mister Greene
to the lawn, a lush and green lawn, which covered the entire
property. A carriage waited for them outside the home, and near
the carriage, was a larger than life oak tree that towered over the
front property.

"Gary?"

"Yes, Massa," a dark brown teenager responded.

"Take us to the plantation," Mister Greene said and ushered Roberto and Martin into the cab.

James slipped in the cab before them.

"Not you," Martin said to Mister Greene as he placed his foot onto the stepping post of the cab.

"What?" Mister Greene asked. "You pulling' a fast one on me?"

"No, I'm not. I said I wanted to see him alone. I meant I wanted to see him alone."

Martin handed the Bank Notes to Mister Greene, and he pocketed the money. The door closed.

"It's all right, Gary, take 'em there," Mister Greene said, with impatience in his voice.

"Heeyah!" Gary said, and James heard the whip slash the flesh of the horse. The horse moved toward the plantation side of the property.

As the wheels bobbed over the bumpy terrain, James smashed his head on the roof. Sitting next to Martin, he ensured he was as close to the wall as the compartment allowed.

"Where are you from?" Martin asked Roberto.

James kept his head forward and placed his hands on his lap.

"I'm from Florida," Roberto leaned into Martin and grinned, twirling his pocket watch in his hand.

"*Donde tu eres?*" Roberto asked Martin and positioned his back against the velvet cushion of the seat. "I'm going to be blunt with you. I don't buy that Spaniard crap one bit."

"What do you mean by that?" Roberto sneered and shifted his leg over the other.

"What house are you from?" Martin clenched the sides of his teeth.

James moved closer to the wall as the seat under Martin's hands burned and peeled away from the heat his body expelled.

"Well, I would ask the same of you, Von Aka Herr." Those words caused Roberto's eyes to change from deep brown to red.

"This is my turf, this is mine," Martin said while ramming his finger into his thigh.

"Says who? You are weak, you are all washed up. A humilis. A low ranking one of us. Those negotiations from the fifteenth century are not vows." Roberto spit on Martin's chest. As the dribble rolled down his coat, Martin wiped it up and brought the thick substance to his tongue. He refocused his gaze on the ring on Roberto's finger and adjusted his own.

"It is time for new demons here to put things right. You let that pig run amuck—how many has he taken out?" Roberto said and admired the way his ring sparkled in the southern light. He spoke to Martin like a speck on the wall, like a turd in a toilet bowl, and Martin's disgust with this appeared in the spider veins that pulsed on the sides of his temple.

"Are you saying my house doesn't have this under control?"

"El Castellanos Casa de Robars will take care of him and banish you from this area, too, push you Norse out."

"The...the Robars...huh..." Martin laughed and looked out of the window. "The fuckin' Robars."

His calm demeanor became rage and rampage, and he flung himself at Roberto like a cobra strike. He grabbed Roberto by the collar and hit his head against the cab multiple times. While Roberto scratched at his face and kicked his chest, Martin stood up until the top of his bowler hat hit the roof and he held onto Roberto's neck. He squeezed and squeezed, and ignored Roberto's hands stabbing into his jacket.

Martin endured the pain, punctured Roberto's neck with his fingers, and bled him the way the medieval doctors bled their patients.

Blood ran down the sidewall.

Unable to stop the struggle, James watched Roberto's body become still.

James pushed his body as far up the wall of the cab as possible and shouted each time the men came close to him. No one reacted to his screams.

Martin straightened his clothes and looked out the window.

After ransacking Roberto's pockets for the Spanish coins, he spat on the demon's finger to free the ring. When it didn't budge, he tugged the finger away from the hand and slid the ring off the bottom where the ligaments dangled and blood unmoored from the hole

"Stupid Robars—this man against me. Have I lost it that much?" Martin slid the ring onto his pinky, next to the sparkling lavender one that glistened on his finger.

"Just in case," he said and snapped Roberto's neck as easily as he drew in air to breathe. Pulling up the defunct body, he opened the cab's door and tossed him out. The body rolled and tumbled over the uneven ground seven times before it stopped.

"Everything all right in there?" Gary asked.

"Keep driving," Martin instructed as he shut the cab's door.

"Yes, Suh," Gary said and clicked his tongue.

James went for air, placed his head outside of the cab, saw rows of tiny shacks with ripped cloth used as curtains, come into view. The horses slowed their pace and click-clacked to the slave's quarters.

When the horses' march stopped, Gary opened the cab's door. "Where's the other man, Suh?" he asked as he helped Martin from the cab.

"Seems he fell out not too far from here. Better go get help. I'll be here when you get back."

Gary began to move his lips but stopped and reverted to nodding his head. "Yes, Suh."

"For your trouble," Martin said and dropped one of the Spanish coins into Gary's palm.

Gary dazzled at the coin and dipped it into his pocket. Running to the cab, he jumped to his perch and married his hands to the reins for the horses.

"No slave will accuse a white man of murder, but just in case," Martin said as he progressed to the shack.

Before the cab took off, James climbed out.

Keeping a reasonable pace, Martin reached the shacks before James and ran down the line of homes.

"Fuck, where'd he go?" James asked when Martin skirted

to the right.

He skidded through the maze of homes searching for Martin until he heard screams coming from a shack. His walk turned into a jog, and his jog into a sprint, and he rushed inside the attic-sized house.

"Give it to me now!" Martin held onto a woman while he reached out his hand to Theodore.

James backed into a dark corner of the tiny home.

"Theo…" the woman cried as Martin held his Viking knife to her throat.

"Demon, this ain't your time, and this ain't your place. Let Lizzy go!" Theodore flared his nostrils, sweat dripped from his face.

"Dad…? Wait this isn't my dad," James said to Theodore and stepped further away from the corner he used as sanctuary. "What's going on?"

Theodore kept his attention on Martin.

"Here I am with a knife in my hand with your pretty little wench, and you mouthing off to me? You've got some nerve." Martin turned Elizabeth's face to his and pulled her hair. He placed his lips to her mouth, sucked the color from her top lip, and then inserted his tongue inside. Angling his eyes to enjoy Theodore's reaction, he tossed up her dress and rammed his fingers inside her.

"The-oo," she cried.

Even though Theodore's body jolted like a jackhammer, his hand held onto the velvet sack he gripped.

After Martin retired from violating Elizabeth, he pushed his finger into his mouth and tasted her juices. "Wonder what Daddy would say if he found out that his grandson was the son n—"

Theodore threw a powdered mixture into Martin's face, and his eyes spackled and oozed lavender tar from the tear ducks. His death lock around Elizabeth's neck loosened. She ran to Theodore, and Theodore ran to grab her.

"Come here, wench," Martin said with his hand on his eye and snatched her back by her brown locks.

After pulling her by the hair, he slit her throat with his knife. With her eyes still open, she dropped to the ground, covered in a bed made of hay that covered the floor. Martin flung the knife near her and spread the blood from his hands onto his shirt and his face.

"Let's see how this turns out now." Martin exited the shack, covered in blood.

"No...no...no." Theodore knelt over her. He cradled her head in his lap, rocked back and forth, and pulled her eyelids down.

"Get up! Get him, get him now!" James screamed to Theodore.

"How could he?" James asked and charged from the shack after Martin. In the distance, James saw Martin snatch the plantation home's door open and jet inside.

At the sight of Mister Greene and a gang of twelve men hightailing it his way, holding torches, a thick rope, and enough rifles to supply a small platoon, James retreated to the crummy shack.

Theodore still held Elizabeth's body when James returned. Once the sounds of a village drifted closer and rattled the indisposed shack, Theodore pulled out a clear bottle, rubbed a grainy substance over his forearms, and downed what remained in the clear flask. James shielded his face from the flash that omitted from Theodore. After it faded, he marveled at Theodore, who rocked his body and stared at a foreign inscription inked on the roof of the shack.

"Bind the soul to the soul of nature, sheet by sheet. The blank slate connects to the mind, and the blood can read. Let the soul fly, let it fly in the eyes of the dark." His eyes rolled into the back of his head, and his shadow cast the wings of an angle.

"Wow," James murmured.

The shadowy feathers separated from the wings and sailed out the window.

"Get out here now, boy, or we're going to drag you out."

The men eddied around the shack. They shook it, and parts of the foundation fell apart. One of the men burst the door open and exposed Theodore chanting with Elizabeth's blood body in his arms.

Mister Greene fell to his knees and put his hands over his mouth. "Lizzy, no, not Lizzy. I trusted you, you black heathen." Mister Greene pushed off the ground and darted toward Theodore.

He pummeled him, kicked, scratched, and punched his face, and when he saw Theodore didn't respond to his beating, he went to his daughter's body and lifted her head from the blood-covered ground

Acting in Mister Greene's place, his posse dragged Theodore out of the cabin by his feet and resumed the beating. When they tired, they tied his feet to rope about a horse's neck.

The man slapped the horse's butt, and it hustled toward the home. Theodore's body bounced four feet then crashed to the rocky trail. James could see pieces of his skull crack and watched as liquid dragged on the rocks leading to the large tree.

James watched, horrified. "My God…"

When Gary pushed the coach to the shack, Mister Greene climbed in holding his daughter's lifeless body. His wrecking crew followed the horse to the main house and halted it from rejoining its kindred. Theodore never screamed.

"Moan, Goddamn it, moan and beg for your life like my Lizzy!" Mister Greene screamed from the carriage while holding his daughter's body. "Hang 'im, hang 'im!" Mister Greene yelled.

While James watched this unfold through his tears, Martin watched and smiled.

When James was halfway between the house and the plantation, the men forced Theodore's head through a noose and tightened it on his throat.

One of the men kicked his feet from under him, and he hung in midair, his eyes still rolled into the back of his head. They pulled and pulled and hoisted his body to the top until his head hit the limb of the tree.

For five minutes, he swung from the rope, chanting in an unknown language, and then his body stopped. James peered as the feathers from the shack circled over the body and molded into an owl.

The men cheered and lightning crashed down on the home. Theodore's face paled, and his body deflated. The branch that held him up by his neck drank his blood, and the blood spread into the fibers of the tree and down into the roots.

As Martin slipped away from the crowd, James headed back for the slave quarters. "No, you don't," he said. James ran even when his chest burned.

After his marathon sprint to the shack, he bent over to catch his breath and fell into a wooden stool beside the door. He brought his head up, when Martin rushed inside. Fragments of what remained of the frame, crumbled to the floor.

"Where'd you put it? If I was a voodoo shaman, where would I put it?" Martin ravaged the walls, kicked up the dirt, and tossed the bed of hemp and hay into the air.

James stood in the corner, kicking and punching at Martin. He ran to him to deliver his angst but teleported through the monster, taking traces of his evil with him. He coughed and rubbed the nastiness from his tongue.

Martin went to his knees, panting, and dug in the soft dirt.

"Ahhh!" he screamed and beat the ground where the makeshift bed had sat. His eyes changed from green to lavender, and the bones on his face became more jagged. His nails grew, and his skin darkened.

When Martin saw the unturned earth on his fist, he slowed his slew of rage and dug up the spot. His transformation reversed. James held onto what was left of the wall and exhaled hard through his mouth. "What the *hell*?"

Martin dug until his hands scraped something hard underground. He separated and scooped out the dirt around a chestnut object then pulled it up. He held a book made from leather and removed the dirt that covered its outer shell.

"What's this?" He grinned and opened the book.

James peered over Martin's shoulder and gazed upon the pages. It was a demon's wet dream—spells, potions, and information on herbs and techniques written inside.

"There are several pages missing." Martin slammed the book closed and brought himself to a mirror that hung from a string in the corner of the room. "You handsome demon, you sure look like *skit*." He snapped his fingers. All the dirt fell away, and his suit was as new as the day the tailor created it.

Martin exited the shack, the door no longer on the hinges; he kicked it out of his way. James waited before following and collected his courage. "I've never seen him like that before," James said. "Get up. He can't see you. Just follow him," he told himself. "Someone is trying to show you something."

Obeying his conscience, he pursued Martin. And noticed Martin run to his main target— the house.

James' strides didn't match Martin's, and he fell behind. He bent over periodically to catch his breath before gaining his strength and sprinting.

When he reached the house, he had to weave through crowds of people frozen in time. He snapped his finger in Mister Greene's face, who stood with his mouth open. He didn't even move when a fly landed in his eye.

No one blinked, flinched, or scratched their privates. All but Theodore were stationary, and the blood from the tree continued spreading, traveling toward the entrance of the home.

James lifted his feet over the veins that spread across the porch and leapt over lines of blood. He hedged to the already open door, opened it more, and walked to the staircase.

After colliding with a servant that stood in mid-pour, he poked the young slave that stood holding up the drink tray. Martin stirred the ashes in the fireplace, and then threw the poker like a javelin when he didn't find what he was looking for.

"This is impossible! Where is it?" He turned his head to the ceiling, and his gaze fastened on Native American patterns glowing and rotating in a circle above his head.

"There you are," he said and ran to the banister. Before his foot hit the bloodstain that soaked into the house's foundation, he stepped back.

Martin held out his hands and waved his fingers. Some of

the blood receded but stopped at the door, and he proceeded to the banister. Skipping every third step, he glided down the hall.

James remained standing near the exit, his eyes glued on the stairwell.

Loud screams and the searing of flesh lead to Martin returning from upstairs holding his hands and tumbling down the steps. "What have you done to me?" When he tilted his head up to the swinging body outside, he wiped away tears that rolled down his puffy face and set his sights on the open door.

The bull saw red and charged to the porch. James forced his feet from the path of the monster.

Stopping at the doorframe, Martin leapt over the porch and landed on the lawn; the lush green lawn transformed to purple at his touch.

"Where were we? Oh, yes," he said and leered at Theodore's swinging body.

An owl picking bugs from its feathers barreled a hate-filled glare at Martin.

"How are you able to do that?" he whispered. "Doesn't matter, because you won't be able to leave this place, and your soul is mine." Martin snapped his finger.

Mister Greene took a deep breath and swatted the fly on his face. The men on the ladder next to the tree dropped to the ground, and the uproar of the crowd ensued as if it had never stopped.

James remained in the doorway, gawking. Theodore's body swung, but the life was no longer there. The resemblance of Theodore to his father brought a feeling of altruism, and he pictured his father working on a classic car, restoring it to its new state. He saw his father preparing Thanksgiving with no knowledge of cooking after his mother ran off and joined a band of hippies. He cried to the image of his father's casket that he came home to after the war in 1974.

And the dying face of Theodore resembled his father's dead face in that casket.

At the base of the tree, an invisible hand etched the words:

JAMES YOU CAN KILL 'HIM. YOU GOT IT IN THE BAG.

CHAPTER 10
THE FIRST DOOR

A rush of air closed the door and knocked James inside the house. Yellow feathers and purple light dripped from the sky, and the patterns above him swirled then vanished.

When the feathers fluttered to the ground, The Gentleman broke them down to dust. Blood from the porch crept along the doorframe. While his hands swung with the wildness of a feral child, a ruby ring slipped off his finger and bounced to James.

"No you don't." The Gentleman ran to the door and shut it completely. The remnants of the feathers separated into different directions.

One landed in James hand, and he crammed it into his pocket and retrieved the ring near his leg.

The Gentleman used his finger and torched the door's outlining. A lava color burned on the lines he created, and The Gentleman's breath cooled them into igneous rocks.

Rubbing his head, James looked at his current state and grunted at the sight of his mucky shirt and oil stained pants. He grabbed his bag and stuffed inside the fruit that fell from it.

"Try something like that again, and I take another of your relatives," The Gentleman threatened an invisible force inside the house, his nostrils flaring as his eyes changed to lavender.

"What he show you? What he show you?" The Gentleman subjected James to an interrogation.

James looked at his face and noticed he looked the same as the day he'd ravished Theodore's shack. "Nothing, he showed me this house, is all," he said and walked to the staircase.

The Gentleman's face contoured to his customary grin. "Something's different about you."

James remained silent. His posture improved with renewed confidence, and his head slanted upward. He stood under the stairs and looked at its never-ending steps. His hand touched the rail. Some of the wood came apart, and he crumbed pieces in his hand and blew them away. Spiders crept out of the cracks onto his hand.

"So, this is where I go." James looked back at The Gentleman and wiped the spiders from his arm.

"Sure is, sure is. But first, you sure he didn't show you anything else besides this house, because I would hate to find out otherwise." The Gentleman sneered.

James pressed his lips together, shook his head, and continued up the staircase. Grasping the railing, James took steady steps. The boards came apart under his feet and some departed to the basement. He didn't halt, only climbed.

After climbing the forty steps, he looked down, and The Gentleman was no longer there. When he turned his head to the hall, he saw that grimacing smile and demon eyes shift in the darkness.

"Hello," The Gentleman called.

"So, where to?" James asked and remained where he stood. Seeing the demon in the other world and being able to endure that image provided him with a sense of composure.

"You choose the door, *pojke*. I have no part in this. I have to admit, this is the most fun we've had in a while." The Gentleman nudged James' arm.

James pulled away.

The Gentleman turned to the hall and clapped his hands three times. One by one, numbers and Norse writing swirled onto the doors and burned with a lavender glow. A grandiose grandfather clock materialized on the wall at the end of the hall.

James remained in his position, not distracted from The Gentleman's words. The Gentleman's playful face melted when he saw James' stoic pose. For the first time since James had known him, The Gentleman was at a loss for words.

"Let's up the ante." The Gentleman pointed to the clock. It rang when the big hand struck midnight. "You have until six to find the room."

James scratched his head.

"I know he showed you something." The Gentleman retracted, and his image became the darkness.

James moved forward and viewed the five doors that stood in front of him where the hall intersected. To his left stood the master bedroom.

"First door, first clue." Walking to the master bedroom, he followed the soiled carpet and touched his hand on the eroding baseboard lining the bottom and middle of the wall

His footsteps echoed in the empty space as he approached. Lavender flames burned the number fifteen on the frame. After pressing his fingertips against the icy frame, the door unlocked and wavered open. Bad vibes flooded from the dark room, and he raised one eyebrow and backed away.

"What?"

A gray hand reached out and grabbed his belt buckle. It pulled and tugged, ripping skin from his stomach. He used the rug to ground his feet and sent his heel into the massive arm, severing the bone. But the arm never let go. The formation of a large body with stringy hair parted the darkness, and the eyes, sunken in, sparked in the absence of light.

James snapped its fingers one by one and pried off the cold hands that held him hostage. He fell to the floor, and after getting to his feet, ran from the terrible being. The bunched carpet tripped up his feet and caused him to buckle into the walls of the large hallway. He stopped fleeing when he felt it was safe to catch his breath and proceeded down the main hallway.

"How big is this place?" Wind whistled against his ears, and its coldness raised goose bumps on his body. As he peered down the hall, his eyes enlarged to the site of the hallway stretching to infinity, and he placed his hand on the wall to keep from developing vertigo.

"This is impossible," he said and closed his eyes. After opening them, the stretching of the rooms ceased, and he stopped leaning on the wall.

"What's that, a seventy-eight?" James asked to the second door in the row to his left and covered his ears. Howls and screams vibrated from it and rattled his head. A high-pitched sound buzzed in his ears until he moved away from it.

James began to read the numbers on the neighboring doors.

"Thirteen, fifty eight…minus fifteen?" He touched the cold surfaces and clenched his teeth.

"Six." He pointed, and a red substance flowed from underneath it. He moved and backtracked to the room with the fifty-eight burning on the egress. A mellow woman's voice sang with the harmonious sounds of the sea breeze, beckoning James to come hither.

"I guess you are first," he said and reached for the knob. As his hand neared it, a warm presence materialized to his right; it burned the hairs on his face.

"I wouldn't do that," A tall man spoke while admiring his fingernails in the dense lavender gleam from the window.

"Who the hell are you?" James backed away from the door to face the man and grabbed his knife.

"Roberto Solórzano at your service." Roberto bowed and then lifted his head to James.

"You, you're the guy he…you," James tightened his grip on his knife and walked away.

"I am he." Roberto vanished from in front of James and reappeared to his right.

"How the fuck you do that?" James moved around to Roberto's new position.

"Like this," Roberto said, disappeared, and reappeared in different locations around James.

"Stop it, stop it," James said as he waved his knife in the red smoke that lingered after Roberto faded, missing him by mere seconds.

"But back to business," Roberto said and reappeared in front of James.

"Stay back." James held his knife up and stumbled over his own feet as he receded.

"I'm your guide." Roberto turned his eyes up to the ceiling, "He sent me to help you along the way."

Remaining silent, James caught his breath and moved toward Roberto.

"Once you put that away, we can speak at length." Roberto directed his gaze at James' knife.

After looking at the knife as if it were a foreign weapon sent from the gods, James slipped it back into the knife hilt.

Roberto smiled then turned around, peeking over his shoulder. "Did you, by chance, obtain a ring?"

"A what?" James rubbed his fingers over the ring in his pants. "Maybe. What's it to you?"

"Nothing, only curious, Senor."

"You, you a demon?" James asked and rubbed his shoulder as he trailed behind Roberto.

"Yes, I was a demon."

"What? That doesn't make sense."

"It does. The Gentleman…it doesn't matter. I am your guide."

"What's a guide do?"

"Make sure you don't die," Roberto said and continued down the hall.

"Do you understand the game, James?" Roberto drug his feet over the carpet and kept his hands in front of his body as they sluggishly walked down the hall.

"I got three rooms to choose from. Three rooms to get a clue from, and then I have to pick a room in the house where it's at. Pretty simple."

James scrunched his face as Roberto sniggered in response.

"Am I right?"

"Yes, yes, never mind," Roberto said, raised one finger in the air, but lowered his hand.

When Roberto u-turned down the hall, James stopped walking and grabbed his shoulder. "Wait, why we turning around?"

"I walk to gather my thoughts. Like I said, I don't care what room you choose, I just make sure you don't die." Roberto jerked his shoulder, and James' hand slid off.

James spat on the gothic black coat that hugged Roberto's slim body. "Fuck you." He stomped down the hall. He stopped when he heard a crisp piano jazz piece liven the dank hall. The heavenly sounds cajoled James to place his ear on the door and take in the half notes. His hands felt the door's Norse writings that sat below the number thirteen, and the lavender flame wrapped around his fingers. "Is this a room I should go in?"

Roberto shrugged as he wiped James spit from his arm.

"Some fuckin' guide you are," James said.

"Like I said, I make sure you don't *die*." Roberto raised one corner of his mouth.

"Yeah, yeah…shit in a box. What if, the thing from before is here, too?"

"There's only one way to find out," Roberto said and stepped backward.

James removed his short barrel from his bag, checked the chamber, and turned the cold knob. The door opened with one push.

After the door swung open, he cleared the room, swiping from corner to corner.

In the middle, a boy sat at a piano and played a jazz piece with ease. The mood lightened, and James released his suspense and sat on the bed near the window. The door shut of its own will.

"Hey there," James said.

The boy didn't respond and played through the last a few bars of his song. As he touched the keys that set above the bottom set, a chilling voice darkened the room.

"This is Eric. Are you James?" a dark voice that didn't match the boy's appearance came from the piano.

"Did that, did…" James directed his attention to the piano Eric ran his fingers across. "But how'd you?"

The boy turned to him, revealing his rosy cheeks, pumpkin skin, and curly hair.

"Eric can speak through me. I speak with the sounds of music, James," the piano said.

James remained quiet.

The boy swayed back to his piano and played a trill. His fingers slid over the sleek white keys and smashed the black notes on the top and bottom levels of the piano. On the top of the well-crafted instrument, a pipe jetted steam from the top of the valve and the other pipes closed. One by one, they released steam as Eric hit the keys, plucking the strings of the piano.

"How old are you?" James asked and moved closer to Eric.

"He is older than you."

"When he'd get you?" James shook his head.

"He was nineteen. It's been so long," the piano said, and Eric effortlessly played up and down the piano.

"Would you stop speaking through that thing and talk to me?"

"You eva kill a man?" Eric asked. He turned to James halfway, his voice kind.

James liked it much more than the haunting sounds of the organ. "I've killed many men." He pictured the dying faces of the cops from Valdosta.

"I've only killed one…"

CHAPTER 11
RIDE THE TRAIN

It was 1936 in Elba, Alabama, and the sun rose early in the summer mornings and fell late on the summer nights. The crickets and frogs sang for dominance of the night and mosquitoes stealthily forced their needles into unsuspecting skin. While he hid behind a long leaf pine tree that stretched up one hundred and fifty feet, Eric June let the bugs bite him and focused on the men that circled outside his property.

On the porch of his house, his mother, Mother June, stood. Behind her stood his cousins and siblings: Frank, Ivan, Jenna, and Harold. At the door's entrance, his sister Margareta grasped the hinges and kept her head down.

Mister Brown, moving his sunburned face and raking his long gray beard, the owner of the priority his family farmed, stood with a gang of nine men. One of the men in the party made grotesque gestures at Margareta, causing her to run into the house.

"Where is he?" Mister Brown called to Mrs. June, who lowered her eyes to the crude members of his pack.

"I don't know." She shook her head. "We are good to you, Mister Brown. My Eric would never do such a thing," she said and pushed her kids behind her.

"You betta hope you find 'im first, Junie, before we do," Mister Brown said, and the men left the area.

Eric's heart raced, and his mouth dried. The light of the moon revealed blood all over his hands, and he rubbed as much of it on his pants as possible. He waited until the men no longer were in his line of sight before heading to the back of his house. Near the tall stalks of sugarcane, he dug up a spot and retrieved a box that carried tools, playing cards, and some papers.

He ran and jogged for three hours before reaching the tracks. Once within meters of them, he slowed his pace to a fast walk.

"This is it," he said. Eric took off his bag and banjo. He rubbed his shoulder and wiped his forehead with his handkerchief. His mother created the handkerchief when he had pneumonia the previous year. It had music notes all over the cloth, with stars in between each note. She made it with his favorite colors: yellow and green

"I'm gonna miss you, mamma," he said and held it.

A fist collided with Eric's stomach, and he cowered over in pain.

"Gosh, what the hell, Barry?" Eric said. Barry, a tall, slender, dark-skinned teenager laughed and playfully shoved Eric's arm.

"We almost left you, man. That train coming soon," Barry said.

Three other boys—Donald, Jerry, and Thomas—went to Eric and playfully tugged and hit his arm. Wearing baggy pants held up with string and ribbed cloth, the boys tied different colored bandannas around their arms.

"What held you up?" Barry asked Eric.

"They came to my house. I had to take a lot of back routes and hide out."

"We gon' finally hobo it, man," Donald a tall, pumpkin-colored boy said.

After they showered Eric with greeting and formalities, Barry stole their attention by putting two fingers into his mouth and blowing air through the tight hole.

"If you too scared go home, we are gonna be men. We were seventeen and eighteen until yesterday, now we're men," Barry said, and the others listened.

"We in?" Barry folded his arms and viewed the group.

Unable to fight the hunger pains rumbling in his belly, Eric rubbed his stomach as he nodded his head along with the other boys.

After they found the perfect spot to set up shop in Columbus, Georgia, the boys traveled to town and displayed their talents. The crowds of people who went to see them perform rewarded them with change, enough for them to have a good time for weeks.

As the days went on, Eric enjoyed his time with the newly formed gang that bantered together. Filled with adventure and enough close encounters to tell to generations of grandchildren. Following a poker game that almost cost him his life, in which he won, Eric became more confident in his card-counting skills and used them on the people he encountered during their travels throughout the southeast.

***

Searching for his next sucker in Charlotte, North Carolina, Eric approached a well-dressed man with a deck of cards in his hand. He addressed himself as Eli during the exchange, and tripped Eric up by shuffling the cards multiple times.

After Eric won the man over with a card trick, the man invited Eric to accompany him in a poker game. Eric wanted to show his skills and his ability to play poker with the best of them and accepted Eli's offer.

"Go around back and meet me there. We'll sneak you in as the help," Eli said and left Eric by the garbage that oozed of rich folks' unwanted food and Thanksgiving turkey in the summer.

During the game with Eli, Eric helped him win 5,000 dollars. Of the 5,000, Eli gave Eric ten percent of the cut. More money than he'd ever had. Along with the money, Eli offered Eric a chance to escape his hobo life and meld into the life of gambling. Eric refused the offer, but Eli provided information to meet him the following day at the train station at ten.

***

Fall came, winter froze, and spring sang, and then 1937 welcomed new fortunes for Eric. Jerry's death the previous year inspired him to pursue a new life with Eli. They traveled all along the east coast and even trampled into Canada for a spell. During their travels, Eric read *This Side of Paradise*. It was Jerry's favorite book, and he kept it after Jerry passed.

He sharpened his poker skills and even developed a better understanding of body language of the men that played against Eli. He only played his hand at poker in the colored-side of town when he and Eli separated to take care of personal ventures. During these games, his ability to mark men before the first hand and predict their next move grew stronger.

Eric earned enough money the year prior to buy fancy suits and to afford three meals a day. Still, the breaking up of the gang after Jerry's death sat in his mind when he wasn't chasing girls or working as Eli's *counter*.

Today, Eli promised to take Eric to The Boardwalk in New Jersey. They were going to play a high roller, and they'd get a large sum of dough if they won. Eli told Eric, 'Kid, we'll be able to take off for a year in Paris after this one.'

After getting pie and catching up with an old friend, Eric traveled to the train station to meet Eli.

"All right, kiddo, we got the best of the best tonight, so get on your A-game," Eli said and tapped Eric's cheek. "Fifty big ones kid and you get ten percent." Eric stopped walking and stared at the back of Eli's neck.

"Five thousand dollars?" Eli didn't answer Eric. He smiled and continued walking down the sidewalk.

"We taking the Atlantic City. There's a fine place there, owned by Nucky Johnson."

"Who's that?" Eric asked.

"Son," Eli said and took the cigarette from his lips, "he's the most important person in this entire state and the most powerful man in the North East."

"You know the drill," Eli said to him once they arrived at the hotel, and he patted his shoulder. After changing into his clown outfit, Eric ran to the alley, around the dumpsters to the kitchen door. After he knocked on the door, a man took him down the hall and upstairs to a small room.

"All right, this guy's the real deal—from Ireland, and his father made thousands off us Yanks during prohibition," Eli said to him and met him in the hall before they ventured into the room. "Stay keen, and we using the other tricks for this one." He knocked on the door.

The door inched open, and Frankenstein's kid brother peeked out. "Yes?" the man's voice scratched.

"Ace's high but not on Sunday," Eli said, and the man allowed them to enter.

In the dull room, a recorder played 1920s music. The dust and dirt that sat in the cracks of the vinyl caused the record to pop and crack. Near the back of the room, rich men bargained at black jack tables, craps, and poker. Cigarette girls offered drinks and smokes.

"Mister Eli, you know slavery ended over a hundred years ago?" Garrett Doherty shuffled cards in one hand and drank whiskey in the other. He wore a white, three-piece suit and the finest pair of shoes Eric had ever seen. He dressed his scarf across his neck, down his chest, over his shoulders, and across his lap.

His eyes followed Eric into the room as he finished his whiskey.

"My half-witted friend, ready to lose your fortune?"

"I'm ready to triple it," Eli said and pulled on his coat's flaps.

"Who's this lad?" Garrett asked Eli while looking at Eric.

"Eric here is my assistant, helps me with bags, cleans my car—I pay him well," Eli said and pulled open his coat.

"I see, five thousand dollar buy-in, unless you don't have that?" Garrett raised his eyebrow.

Eli reached inside coat, retrieved several bank notes, and dropped them next to Garrett on the table.

"Two inks, and the watermark—not playing with fakes anymore, I see," Garrett said and handed the money to the tall man that stood next to him.

When the man returned, he gave Eli poker chips.

"Eli, why you tagging this boy around with you?" Garrett asked and his shuffling attracted Eric's attention. The ruby ring on Garrett's finger sparkled. The ring looked ancient, and the inventor chiseled Gaelic around the Ruby's golden crest.

"What we playin'? Seventh Street, straight poker?" Eli asked and counted his poker chips. He had thirty-eight total, which equaled the 5,000 buy-in he gave to Garratt.

After releasing one of the cigars from his humidor, Eli bit off one side of it and struck a match. The flame flickered as he held it up to the tip of the cigar. He puffed the heavy smoke and exhaled victorious smoke rings into the orange light.

"I see you are celebrating already," Garrett said, leaned back with one arm around another chair and one leg resting on his lap.

"Don't mean to be an abercrombie, but I'm all aces at this game," Eli said and blew smoke into Garrett's face.

Garratt waved his hand to move the smoke from his face and raised on side of his mouth to Eli. "That so? Well, then..." Garrett placed the card deck, with solid red back outlined in blue, on the table. "All who are in please join the table. Time to start five-card stud. We'll have Mister Kelley here as the permanent dealer."

Three other men left from the black jack tables or the bar and sat at the velvet table with Garrett and Eli

"Thanks for joining us, Fredric Mullen, Roy Arnold, and Michael Savage. Did I get your names correct?"

"Ay," the man Garrett identified as Fredric Mullen said. He had dark hair and eyes. He wore his glasses down to the bottom of his nose and sat with his feet crossed at the table.

"You have a good memory, Garrett," the man Garrett addressed as Michael Savage said. He had an Afrikaans' accent and wore a leopard skin scarf with his suit and alligator boots, which commanded the table's attention.

Roy Arnold, a business Tycoon from Georgia with his dark-gray, three-piece Brooks Brother's suit and silver-plated pocket watch slung low in his inside pocket, dressed the best out of all the men.

"I ain't here for acquaintance. Bidding will start at twenty-five for the first bids and go up to fifty. The next round will increase to fifty, one hundred, and the round after that," Garrett paused to chuck his whiskey, "Ahh, one hundred to five hundred, big and small."

They all held onto their chips, smoked their cigarettes or cigars, and drank their whiskey or beer.

"Mister Kelley?" Garrett turned to Mister Kelley, who stood behind him with his white-gloved hands crossed in front of him.

"Master Doherty?"

"Get a chair for the lad. Seems Eli forgot his manners," Garrett said, and Mister Kelley obeyed.

"I don't want him sitting behind us, he could give this Yank information on our hands," Roy Arnold protested.

The other men agreed, and Garrett instructed Mister Kelley to get them a bigger table. The larger, oval-shaped, gave each man enough space to ease Arnold's suspicions, and Eric sat at the end next to Eli, directly across from a mirror near the door.

"Is that better?" Garrett asked.

The men nodded. Mister Kelley stood behind the table and shuffled the deck of cards Garrett had shuffled earlier in the night.

"Count the cards before we begin. Let us be assured there are fifty two," Fredric Mullen demanded.

Mister Kelley gave a slight nod of the head and counted the cards one by one.

"Face up. I wanna see them," Michael Savage demanded.

Garrett smirked at the men's request and drank his whiskey. "If you need more to drink, just tap the table, and someone will serve you," he stated.

"Fifty, fifty-one, *fifty-two*." Mister Kelley dragged the words fifty-two into the next hour.

As Eric counted along with Mister Kelley under his breath, Garrett took interest in Eric.

"Now then, shall we play?" Garrett held his hands together

after no one spoke. "Shall we Mister Kelley?"

Mister Kelley shuffled several times and gave the deck to Garrett to cut.

"Huh, let someone else cut it," Roy Arnold stated.

Mister Kelley took the deck from Garrett before he could touch the cards and placed them in front of Roy Arnold. He cut the deck three ways, placed the cards back, and slid the deck to Mister Kelley.

"Oh I forgot to mention, the first, third, and fifth streets will be face down," Garrett said to the men.

"Making it harder on us," Fredric said and pulled his glasses down further.

"All right, kiddo, you my good luck charm, so keep it coming," Eli whispered to Eric.

Eric sat in his chair, eyes fixed on the cards and barely blinking. Garrett watched Eric using a mirror that pointed at him.

All the men placed their ante into the center of the table to start the game. Mister Kelley took off his jacket, rolled up his sleeves, and dealt the first street to each player face down as Garrett wished. He dealt the cards swiftly; they fell close to the hands of each player.

Each man looked at his card, and then put it face down completely or held up one corner of the card with their hands cupping over it. And after Garrett looked at his cards, he pulled his head up to Eric studying the men.

During the final street, Eli raised his bet to five hundred. After peering at Eric from the mirror, Garrett folded. This left Eli and Roy to duke it out to the last street.

"Well there, let's see you cards," Eli said.

Eli won with two of a kind. Roy lost with an Ace high. As Eli pulled his winnings to his chest, he placed his ear on the pill. "What's that? I'm taking them to the bank?" He lifted his head and laughed. "You got that right," he said and played with his chips, letting them fall through his fingers and kissed their surface.

"How's about we take a break and let Mister Eli enjoy his

winnings for now?" Garrett said.

Eli's face straightened, and he fixed his jacket. "Don't like the way you looking at me, Mister Garrett. It'll be over soon." Eli walked to the bar, and Eric scooted from the table and trampled behind him like a lost puppy.

When the third round began, only Fredric, Eli, and Garrett remained. During the last hand, Eli displayed a wide smile. After all the men went, it was Eli's turn to display his hand. He showed them his full house—three queens and two kings—a hard hand to beat and an impossible one to get.

"Well then, I'll cash the winnings," Eli said and slid the chips to his chest. Ashes fell from his cigar and burned the outer shell of the chips.

"Not so fast," Garrett said.

When he reached for Eli's hands, Eli's eyes crossed and his smile turned into sour milk. "I won fair and square."

"Fair and square? That lad over there won." Garrett tossed his scarf from his neck and let it float to the ground.

"I'll play him. He wins. You keep this pot. He loses, you lose," Garrett said and rubbed his eyes.

"I won, end of story," Eli said and tugged the chips to his side of the table.

After Garrett relaxed in his seat, he cleared his throat and cracked his knuckles, then stared at Eli.

"What's mine is mine." Eli puffed his cigar and placed the chips in order of their value. "You know, I had a lot of fun playing with you." Eli blew the thick smoke in Garrett's direction.

"Shut your dirty mouth." Garrett pushed back his coat and pulled out his pistol. He zeroed it to Eli's head.

After Eli stared into the barrel of a .22 pistol, Garrett adjusted his aim to Eli's chest and fired. The blood that came from his body burned, and it smelled of hot copper and cold steel in the room. The cigar in his mouth dropped to his pants and burned a large hole between his legs; third degree burns seared his penis. Even though Garrett dethroned King Eli and blew him off his pulpit, still, Eli's dead hands clutched a fortune he had yet to spend.

"Eli, Eli!" Eric said, eyes wide.

"I gave him an offer, he didn't take it. Just push him to the ground."

Eric looked up at Garrett, and his brown face became a pale blue.

"I said push his body down." Garrett leaned in and sat the pistol on the table.

Eric pushed Eli, and Eli's body slid off the table with the chips and cards stuck to the dried liquid that spilled from the hole in his chest. The smell of burning flesh resonated from it— and the blood that trickled from his wound extinguished the cherry on the cigar melted on his pants.

"Ah!" Eric screamed when he saw Eli's face.

"Mister Kelley," Garrett said.

Mister Kelley bowed to him and left the room. He returned with two men and a body bag.

Eric didn't move, not to scratch his nose not to rub his eyes. Eli was his only family or contact and his guide to the circuit of gambling in the U.S. With him gone, he would need to find another gang and another source of income.

"Mister Kelley, get the small table," Garrett said and brushed residue from the gun off his suit.

Mister Kelley placed the smaller table, big enough for four people to sit around and a wooden box on it. Inside the box were yellow, red, and white chips, with Gaelic writing on each side. Star patterns that ran across their seams caused Eric to see sunspots in the dim room.

"Have a seat, lad," Garrett said to Eric.

Mister Kelley pulled up his chair.

"I'm sure you've never had white folks treat you like this, but believe it or not, in my country, we're treated the same way by the Brits. Scumbags make me sick, so I know how it is fer you. My country is in civil war over freedom." He motioned to a server. "Bring this boy a drink. What do you like to drink?"

"I like, rum," Eric said in a raspy tone.

"Good, good." He tapped the table in front of Eric. "Don't

be frightened of me. I just want to prove I'm the best poker player in the land, and I can't do that with a bastard like yar friend Eli in the way," Garrett said while moving his hands. "You must be thinking how I knew you were more than a good luck charm."

Eric lifted his eyes to him. His heart raced with time, and the beads of sweat on his forehead fell down his face. They splashed on the carpet that held Eli's blood.

"I watched yer eyes and mouth, and you're a card counter, one fer poker..." Garrett said and sounded astonished. "You know, I can read people, and that's how I win. But you, you count cards and calculate the outcome."

"I don't have no money," Eric said to Garrett and put his head to the floor.

"I don't wantcha money. I want what's most precious to you, sumthin' you couldn't live without, and if someone stole it from you, you'd kill a thousand men to get it back."

Eric reached into his pocket and felt the groves of his harmonica. He placed it, now with the name Eric June engraved on its silver cover, in the center.

"That isn't it," Garrett said and sat back in his chair.

Eric grabbed his handkerchief. He closed his hands around it and hesitated before placing it next to the harmonica. After taking in all the air in the room, he committed to placing it in the center.

"That's the one," Garrett said. He took off the ruby ring around his thumb and placed it in the center. "Since you have two items, I guess I should put two as well." He pulled out a small compass from his pants. Painted green and worn around the edges, he held it in his hand.

"My father used this compass to find his way back during the Great War. Some say its bewitched—finds what you looking for." Garrett put it in the center near his ring and Eric's items. "Now then, let's play poker."

***

The two played several rounds; Eric won three of the five games played.

He lost from folding or from a bad hand.

He sweated enough to fill an ocean, and his shirt and face showed that. The demeanor of Garrett and his clandestine existence rewired Eric's concentration, and the blood that his feet slid over hindered his focus. Garrett, amused, displayed poise as he watched Eric suffer under the pressure.

"This is the final round," Garrett said to Eric, and the majority of the people in the room gathered around and placed bets on the winner.

On the last hand dealt to Eric, he received a ten of hearts and festered all his strength to resist the urge to jump out of his seat, because on the board sat: one nine of hearts, an Ace of hearts, and a ten of hearts.

And Garrett's final card, an Ace of clubs.

"Everyone leave!" Garrett looked around the room.

"I said leave!" Garrett expelled whiskey from his shivering lips and didn't settle down until all the people from the room were out the door.

"Not you, Mister Kelley, not you," Garrett said and pulled his arm as he walked away. When the final guest closed the door behind them, the lights brightened on their own. "Well then, what are you betting?" he said to Eric.

Eric rubbed the moisture from his palms onto his pants and lifted his cards while he weighed his options. Garrett's revealed cards showed Ace of clubs, King of clubs and a Queen of clubs. Eric looked at the burn pile then back at the deck. Avoiding eye contact, he peered at Garrett's cards before looking at his own. He repeated the process three times while tapping his hand on the table.

"I'm...I'm all in." Eric slid his chips across to the area where the spotlight orbed in the center of the table.

After smiling at his two cards facedown, Garrett brought his eyes to Eric who sat shaking in his seat.

"Well, boy, welcome to the grownups' table," he said and pushed in all his chips. "Seems we have to see who bluffed the best."

Eric turned over his cards and showed Garrett three of a kind and ace high.

Garrett's eyes filled with hate and defeat. "Well, well," he said and turned over his cards showing Eric two pairs of aces and all high cards.

"I...won? I won," Eric said in disbelief and stood up with his leg shaking like a rickety fence.

"I never lose," Garrett said and slammed his hands on the table, splitting it in two. Some of the chips fell in the middle, and his compass fell open on the ground.

After picking it up, Garrett rotated it in his hands.

Eric didn't move, and he faced the man he'd defeated, the man who'd shot Eli.

I'm gonna die. Eric backed close to the door. He had no intentions of finding out what Garrett really was. Inside, Eric knew, he was something other than human.

Garrett smirked and rolled the compass from hand to hand.

"Well, there's something very special about this compass. Eric?" Garrett called, with the same expression on his face as when he'd killed Eli.

"Yes, sir?" Eric asked.

"This compass finds my treasure," Garrett said and opened it, revealing its face. The dials on the mechanism spun counterclockwise and clockwise and slowed their rotation after settling on the North marker. A faint yellow glow beamed on its face.

"Still works," Garrett said and closed it. "You use this compass to find my treasure, an abandoned train not too far from here. It's in the tenth compartment. You'll be rich for years to come. Follow where the arrow points," he said and played with it in his hand. "Once it's green," Garrett looked down at the compass then up to Eric, "you're there."

"But it won't be easy." Garrett finished the whiskey that Mister Kelley handed him from the bar. "The ring's the key." Garrett stood up from the table, and Mister Kelley slipped his coat on and wrapped the scarf around his neck.

"Maybe we'll meet again, Eric."

When he and Mister Kelley departed, the appearance of the room changed from the inside of Nucky's grandest casino to the basement of a segregated hotel.

Before grabbing the items on the bare floor, Eric sat in the chair until Mister Kelley closed the door entirely, and went for his bag. Once he freed himself from the oversized clothes, he pulled out his suit then stopped, folded it, and placed it back. Then he retrieved his hobo attire. He didn't want to dirty his good suit while he searched for the thing Garrett had given him. Before leaving, he placed *This Side of Paradise*, into his coat's pocket.

***

Eric walked into the alley behind the large hotel and bundled up to fight the cold. He blew out white breath while looking at the pocket watch for the time—five a.m. The sun would soon rise. Evidence of its return peaked on the horizon and teased the clouds.

After opening the compass, he followed the directions of the dial. It moved on its own, not guided by the force of gravity but the force of magic, and the colors changed to a green yellow as he walked down into the rural terrain of New Jersey.

The compass took him up a ridge and down a steep hill; he shook away frost on leaves as he hurried down the hill and crunched the frozen dew on the grass as he sought the path laid out by the compass. Below the hill, a compartment of a train sat tipped on one side. Its door, battered from the elements, held on with rusted nails and hinges. The compass in Eric's hand flickered green as he approached the cart.

"How many of them are there?" he said and touched the cart's cold surface with his hands. He looked left and saw five other cars. To his right, he saw four more.

Following the lines of trees next to him, he took the short cut to cart ten, but the line of trees blocked him from entering. He ran back up the hill and penetrated the shrubs, and again, the large trees near the entrance and the vines and vegetation that grew around felt like cement in the shunted cracks of the train.

"He said the tenth one, and I can't get to it."

Eric went back to the sixth car and pushed the door with his hands.

He kicked it with his feet and ran into it with his shoulder.

It didn't give.

Looking around, he found a pickaxe not too far from the start of the hill and wedged the object in between the door, pushing it against either side

He pushed and pushed until finally the doors separated. Using the object as an anchor, he hopped into the train.

The door shut.

Eric placed the sharp edge of the axe into the crack of the door, but it didn't reopen.

He banged on it and yelled for help, which knocked handfuls of dirt and old wood on his forehead.

"Shit," he said and raked it from his head and face. He lit a match from the matches he kept with him for Eli's celebration.

When movement from the train jerked Eric to one side, the match blew out. Eric stood up, and the sound of gears grinding stopped him from lighting another.

A diesel engine ignited, and the *chaga-chaga, toot-toot,* of a train launched. As the train moved forward and away from the area, ice fell from its body. The heat of the engine vapored the snow on the metal gears, and a levitating stream followed the train as it wrecked the landscape. The train sped down the broken tracks like a bullet. It hovered over the steel and flew over areas where tracks were missing and bulldozed vegetation that stood in its way.

For the sake of seeing around, he lit another match. It wavered in his cold hands. Then the flame sizzled out.

Eric struck another match and it blew out. His nostrils expanded like a bagpipe to the stench of the breeze that killed the flame—the smells of New Jersey's sewers gripped his senses. He struck another match, and the same breeze eliminated another one. Moving to the wall, he shook another match from the box and ran the sulfur head of the stick over the phosphorus strips on the box. It too blew out.

"Okay, okay, let me put my hand around it after I strike it," Eric said and raked another match against the box. This time, the match remained lit. Its flame bounced on the cabin's walls and provided enough light for Eric to see. Looking at the ground, he saw big red shoes pressed against the hay. His eyes progressed to grimy, multicolored silk pants, oversized.

Moving the flame up from the ground, the light from the match exhibited a filthy white shirt with suspenders snug against a rotund body.

Warm liquid seeped from Eric's pants. His match flickered to and fore on the man's face. He dropped his match, and flames broke havoc into the area.

The light that cracked and popped provided a clear canvas of the thing standing before him. The man wearing white make up and red lips spread his mouth apart, and grubs and roaches crawled in-between his clam-colored teeth.

The clown flopped one foot after the other forward and let out an, "I eat children for breakfast laugh" from his wormy mouth. Then, someone to Eric's left pulled his arm.

Eric turned to this person, "Jerry?"

"I'll explain later. Let's book it."

Eric did as Jerry instructed. The clown collided with the wall of the train as Jerry pulled Eric toward the exit. They jumped outside of the sixth car and witnessed the terror outside produced from the train's speed.

"Jerry, Jerry, but you died." Eric hugged him and cried from disbelief and joy.

"I miss you, too," Jerry said, and he tugged Eric along across the unsteady latches connecting the two carts together. The turbulence from the speed of the train propelled them into the door of the seventh cart.

"Prepare yourself," Jerry screamed and heaved the door open. He shut the wild and unruly world away from them and turned his attention to the obstacle ahead. The cart's walls flowed with a gray liquid.

Men with pale skin and faces of death lurked, hawked, and

zombied around one another's space.

After Eric sucked down the vomit that swam in his throat, he reached for the exit.

Jerry took his hand off the handle. "We just have to run, trust me." Jerry slothed through the men, moving with crouching tiger motions.

Eric's eyes watered from the smells of death. As the smells intensified, he coughed out its essence.

"I can't go this slow," Eric said and rushed to the door at the other side of cart.

His fast motion brought on undead hands, clammy and rough, and they latched their wrinkled skin onto Eric's body.

"Get back," he said and dropped the pickaxe.

"Let him go, you son of a bitch." Jerry retrieved the axe from the ground, and with both of his hands around it, he battered the head from the creature's body.

The ghouls chased after them but Eric and Jerry belted for the exit of the cart. Soon the other walkers stopped their tired walking and veered towards Eric and Jerry. They broke the door open and used the pickaxe to sever the lock. When they ran out of the cart, they landed outside to the unpredictable motion of the train that created its own weather system.

As Eric balanced on the edge of the rusted rail, inches from the eighth cart, Jerry held onto him by the shirt.

"I gotcha," Jerry said, using all he had to help Eric onto his feet.

"We gotta jump," Jerry said as the wind from the train's speed pushed in his cheeks and lifted his eyelids. Once on the other side of the eighth cart, Jerry slung the doors open and they flooded into the room.

Once they closed the door, the sounds of the storm decreased. Near the exit, a woman stood with a black veil over her face.

Jerry picked up a board from the ground and held it to the match in Eric's hand. The wood erupted as the fire burned on its tip.

"Don't look her in the eyes, Eric, no matter what," Jerry

said to him.

They ran to the door and darted away from her, but the woman grabbed Jerry's arm and he squared his arm over his eyes. Pushing the flame into her face, she hissed at Eric. She lifted her arm and smacked Eric away. His back banged into the cart, and he slid down it, out of breath.

A long, laced piece of cloth, from the same material as her black dress, hung from her chest. She lifted it over her head, revealing her cleavage and the pale, milky skin of her wrinkled face and her gray eyes.

"No Jerry no!" Eric crouched from his location and hobbled to the woman.

"*Féach isteach i mo shúile agus lig dom go bhfuil do anam...*" She spouted off chants and curses as she pressed her nails into Jerry's skin.

Blood drew under her cracked nails. Eric slapped Jerry's face and pushed his body away from her, but the grip she held repelled his efforts.

He took the pickaxe and placed the prying end in-between Jerry and the flabby gray arms of the banshee. He jabbed it deep and twisted.

She screamed and loosed her grip. Her face and hair became more gruesome, and liquid dripped from her ears. Eric snatched Jerry's shirt to drag him outside into the blistering speed of the runaway train.

Leaning over the railing, Eric took a deep breath then heaved. Shaking off the daze of his possession, Jerry stumbled to Eric.

"This it, Eric, but I...I want you to know that this car, shows you a horrible truth." Jerry put his head down and led Eric to the entrance of the ninth cart.

"Okay," Jerry said and released the air he held in his lungs. He braced himself and slung open the door to the cart. The door slammed without their assistance, and they continued down the middle of the cart.

"This is the quietest one," Eric said and held his foot in mid step to the image of a pumpkin-colored girl standing in the center, her feet bare, and her hands held out. Blood dripped from her veins, and her face filled with tears as she bellowed to the ground in a dress torn with bloodstains. She still held out her arms.

Eric ran to her in a half sprint. "Maggie, Maggie no," he said and held onto her body.

"Eric, she's not real," Jerry said and yanked on his shirt.

"How long you know?" Eric cried and rocked his sister back and forth.

"I couldn't tell you when I first saw you in the first train. It would kill you like it did me, but that ain't her, Eric." Jerry pulled up his friend. "We gotta go. It just wants to keep you here and then kill you. We gotta go," Jerry said, but Eric went back to his sister's body.

"Why'd you leave, Eric, why'd you leave?" Margaret said. When she turned over and sat up, she bent the cracks in her grayed face and the dried blood flaked from her face.

"Why'd you leave!" she said and slumped up from the grimy floor.

"No, I didn't. I killed 'im. I stuck that knife in his stomach like the pig he was. " Eric pleaded like the strings of a blues player's guitar.

"Look at what you did!" she said and the arms formed slits and allowed blood to fountain from her body. Eric touched the blood that dried on contact.

"That ain't you sister, Eric. Maggie would never blame you, and look at her face." Jerry pointed and pulled on Eric's clothes.

When Eric looked up to the image of his dead sister, her sorrowful face became demonic and frightful.

"You're not Maggie, you're not her," Eric said, and his tears receded. His courage returned, and he lifted his body from the cart's floor.

"Why'd you do it?" the ghost disguised as Margaret said in three different voices.

"You ain't her," Eric said with more confidence and backed away to the exit.

After Jerry slung the doors open, they reintroduced

themselves to havoc outside. The water system the train created evolved to a Martian-like atmosphere with high pressure and ice-cold wind.

As they trampled outside, the speed of the train decreased, which reduced some of the shacking. Eric held onto the rail, it was the only thing keeping his feet to the floor. His sister was gone. He left and she died.

"Your mama still needs you, and with that money, you can take care of her," Jerry said and placed his hand on Eric's back.

"It's my fault she died. I left her, I left Momma." Eric's knuckles became yellow as he gripped the rail.

"You gotta be strong, Eric," Jerry said, and turned Eric around to face him.

"You gotta be strong," Jerry said. Eric took in as much air as he could before releasing it and he turned to the final compartment that lay before them.

"You're right, my mother needs me."

"So this is the last door," Eric said.

"Yeah, it is," Jerry said to him, using the wall of the cart to balance himself as it twisted over the invisible tracks.

"Let's go, let's go," Eric said and pulled Jerry's arm, but he refused to budge.

"What's wrong?"

"I can't go with you," Jerry steadied himself and walked to Eric.

"Why not?" Eric asked and the train felt steady compared to the way his heart went into a seizure.

"This where he said I can't go," Jerry said to him. "All these years, you helped ole Jerry, every time. Now, I gots to help you. It feels real good, real good."

"But you have to, you gotta," Eric said and a hellish jolt from the train caused Eric to stumble forward. *This Side of Paradise* fell from his coat and the bumping of the train tossed it to Jerry's feet.

After picking it up, Jerry read the cover, "*This Side of Paradise*, you kept this, this whole time." Jerry looked at him and opened his favorite page.

"We'll meet again." Jerry felt the cover of the book and dispersed with the fog.

"Yeah, yeah I did," Eric said to Jerry's reflection.

The tenth door, the prize, the reason for the torment, rocked four feet away from Eric. As he fumbled Garrett's ring from his pocket, he turned and faced the door. The ruby face beamed to a hole in the door and cart

Eric hopped over the raggedy bars that held the carts together, and when he slipped, he grabbed the railing. The ring bounced from his hands.

"No," he said and grabbed it before it fell into the train's wreckage. He lifted himself into the bay of the tenth cart and jammed the ring in the hole. Nothing happened. Then he noticed that the outer patterns of the compartment matched the Celtic scribbles that traced the ruby of the ring.

"I guess you turn it," he said and turned the ring to the right.

It obeyed his commands, and he walked into the tenth cart alone.

The sun punched through the holes of the cart and provided enough light for Eric to spot bags in a corner and an envelope tucked underneath one of them. He ran to the bags and opened one of them; he picked up gold coins and permitted them to fall through his fingers. The exploration of the other bags revealed more gold and jewels, and he counted over fifty bags total slumped in the corner.

"I could buy so much…" His celebration ended when his brain recreated the realization of his sister's suicide and Jerry's brief reunion.

"I wish Maggie were still here," Eric put his back to the cart and looked up at the ceiling.

"Maggie why?" he asked. "It should've been me, and Jerry got shot because of me and I ran…,"

The train's extreme speed reduced, and the shaking from the wind slowed. The rotation of the gears decreased, and soon, the entire train became motionless—the beast rested.

The smell of lilac snaked inside and a shadow rested on the

bags. Mourning, Eric ignored the man's entrance.

After the man cleared his throat, Eric lifted his head to the man in black that smelled of fear and disgust.

"How'd you get in here," he asked him and popped to his feet.

"Backdoor," the man neared him.

Eric tightened his hands around the pitchfork and raised it above his head.

"The name's The Gentleman and I heard you were really good at games," the man said.

CHAPTER 12
THE SECOND DOOR

A s Eric ended his tale by way of his piano, the room became silent. James slid closer to the edge of the bed and focused on Eric's hands.

"Just tell me, I'm tired of these riddles." James sprung from the bed and launched in Eric's direction. His face became hot, and he had no control over the natural instinct to act before thinking.

"That's the story he told me to tell you. So that's the story I told." Eric spoke instead of the piano. His voice was low, calm with a slight tremble. That tremble appeared because of James, no doubt.

The sound of a gong rung in the room and vibrated the door. It shook the metal gears of the piano and caused the hammers inside the piano to strike each string.

"Two a.m.," said the voice of The Gentleman.

"What? I just got here?" James asked and kicked the wall nearest the door. It turned to fire, and he pulled away before it blazed his oil-stained pants.

"He runs on his own time. His six a.m. could be two hours from now or three minutes." Eric played the keys of the notes on the piano to create the sentence.

"You can help us? I mean you can kill him?" Eric brought his hazel eyes up to James and stood up from his piano. On the seat was his imprint. It looked as though he had sat at that piano for decades and this was the only time he'd been away from it.

Bewildered and angry, James threw his hands into the air and marched around on the broken boards in the room. How would he be able to kill that demon? That demon was something far worse than hell and controlled every fiber in James' body. He caused James to see the family of the men he killed, the things he took away from them, the lives he shattered; he was a real son of a slut. There was no killing him, no outwitting him, only surviving and hoping that he forgot about you once you finished doing his deeds.

"If you tell me the room," James thought he was sly, "I'll kill 'im." James continued walking toward Eric.

"I can't. If I do, we all die." Eric backed away from James. After looking at the ground, Eric looked at James.

"The clues are *all* around you." Eric gazed at the door, and then back to James.

"Great, more riddles. My time's running out. Just tell me!" James ran to Eric and ripped the seams from his shirt. When he saw the ugliness of his face in the reflection of the glossy rosewood of the piano, James loosened his grip around Eric's shirt and walked backward toward the door.

As his hand lingered over the knob, James moved his head to face Eric.

"I'm sorry, for that," James said and raised his eyebrows to prevent the sweat from hitting his eyes. "I'm not that guy, Eric. God, I wish I was, but you are betting on the wrong man."

Eric stayed silent and turned back to his piano.

"Hey, what did he take from you? And don't tell me using that evil ass piano," James asked as he turned the knob of the door.

"My sister killed herself, and I gave him myself for her, myself for her." Eric began to play a benevolent jazz piece to suit James' departure from the room.

James shut the door, and the number and the Norse writing withered away into the dank hall.

"Keepin' count, I see," James said and dusted off his hands. Looking at the face of his watch, he saw the time didn't match the clock at the end of the hall, which floated unanchored to the wall. He tapped the face of his watch, shook his head, and got on with discovering the maze of a house. His watch remained stuck on twelve forty five.

"Hey guide. Hey fuckin' guide, where you at?" James asked and looked into the emptiness that wrapped around each corner as he searched between the dusts that swirled in the light of the nasty fog from outside.

"Thanks for nothing, you son of a slut."

He stepped nonchalantly over broken boards and the mess of the floor that came from the fifth room. While he hugged the walls to guide him down the opaque space, he felt a cold arm grip his side.

He jumped away in fright, panting as he stood up from the ground.

"What the hell," James said and beamed at the claws and faces imprinting on the wooden latex fabric.

They moaned to him, groaned to him. The ghost wanted him, and they wanted him ground up into a meaty stew and served with a side of scared shitless. Panic seeped in his stomach and slushed around with the rum.

Bouncing down the hall was an old ball. James' game winning ball. It had to be. It had brown spots and pieces of white fabric torn from the red stitching that spiraled around it. As it rolled down the hall, lights brightened in the hallway, and James chased it as if it was a rabbit and he a greyhound.

"It can't be…," James said out of breath and ran around the left corner. The color on his face returned when someone picked the ball up from the ground and bounced it in their hands, smelled the leather, and threw it up into the air.

"Jen, Jenni," James said to the ten-year-old girl that stood in front of him, wearing a flowery dress and her hair in pig tails. She was the same age as the last time he'd seen her, the previous year, and she wore the exact outfit she'd picked out for her and Daddy's day out. His precious little pumpkin.

"Hey, Daddy," she said, and her smile revealed her missing front teeth.

"You look the same, the same as the last time I saw you,"

James said and walked toward his daughter. "How'd you get in here?"

"He let me in." She swung from one side to the next with the ball in her hand. Grasped in her tiny fingers, the ball looked like the size of a grapefruit. Then, she tossed the ball up into the air, jumping to assist with the height it traveled.

James followed the ball with his eyes as it sailed and smashed into the ceiling. It remained lodged in the ceiling briefly, before gravity brought it down. It fell into her hands.

James jerked back. He daughter, his lovely pumpkin Jenni, was now a developed teenager. She wore the same floral-print dress. The end of the dress set high above her thigh. He'd never allow her to leave his house in this fashion. Oh, the boys he'd kill if they touched her and the clothes he'd burn after she bought the too tight shirts and the too high shorts and skirts.

"You always loved this ball more than me. I know you wanted a boy," she said with a splash of sass in her voice. "That's why Mom said you named me Jenni—because you couldn't name me, James."

"Jenni?" James squinted at his teenage daughter.

"God, Dad, you are so weird, totally," she said and rolled her eyes after looking at the ball in her hand. She flung the ball down the hall, past James, and his gaze followed the ball's descent.

Upon turning his gaze back to his daughter, her boobs enlarged, her hair became crinkled, and she pushed it to one side. Her face looked as though someone shotgun blasted makeup on her face with bright blue, white, and red colors, and her skirt was six inches too high. Higher than her floral dress. This was college-aged Jenni.

"Dad, I'm in love with a total hunk," she said as she smacked the gum in her mouth.

"What?" James tried to find reason in how his daughter morphed through phases of maturity before him.

"I said I'm in love." She began to twirl the gum on her index finger.

"With who, pumpkin?" James played along with the

situation.

"With him." She perked up her chest, and in a blink of an eye, The Gentleman stood next to his daughter, grimacing at James.

"No...no. You better not touch her, I swear, I swear to God." The level of angst that James felt caused a blood vessel in his eye to burst, and blood spilled from his tear ducts. His worst fear: The Gentleman and his daughter.

After removing the rusted blood from his cheek, he looked up and witnessed The Gentleman placing his reptilian hands over his daughter's petite frame, forcing his lips on hers. She didn't push him away. She welcomed his crude advancement and bit the top of his lip.

"Jenni, no. Get your hands off her," James said and lunged in their direction. The seam at the middle of his jeans ripped as he trucked down the hall to snap the neck of the man that had tortured him since 1974.

Turning to James, The Gentleman waved, and James' daughter, still holding onto The Gentleman's dark coat, turned and smiled. No matter how fast James ran, his motions slowed the same way as in his nightmares.

"Daddy, it's okay. He said he'd take care of me, like you never could. Always too busy playing solider or beating Mommy when she couldn't make you happy. That's why she shacked up with those hunks and spent all your money. It made her happy. You were the worst dad of the year, a real jerkoff."

James didn't stop and increased his speed to the awful couple, but once he was close enough to smell the banal scent from The Gentleman's skin, the lights dimmed, and they left. James slammed into the door, which knocked him to the ground.

Regaining his composure, James jumped from the floor and looked around the hallway, more unfamiliar than before. He walked away from the door where the fraction 1/5 burned on the wood.

"Dreadful sight, isn't it?" Roberto appeared at an intersection.

Rubbing his head, James moved past him and down the

other side of the hallway. "Why show up now?" he said without facing Roberto.

"Like I said, I am a guide, not your fortune teller."

"Guide yourself off the roof of this shitty ass house." James placed his back on the wall, but lifted from it as quickly as he rested when he remembered the hands that had reached for him after he left the first room.

A red smoke formed Roberto's image near James. His aroma, warm and crisp, resembled the smell after the sun dried the rain. It smelled of fresh soil and lemons and warmed James' nose with each inhale. It smelled the way summer did, but without the happiness or the summer love.

"Maybe, there is something, we can come to terms with," Roberto said

James noticed the way his mouth salivated and how his eyes lowered to his pockets. His eyes focused on the imprint of a ring.

James reached for it and pulled out the silver-colored piece; the ruby middle blazed a faint red before becoming dull. James smiled as he studied Roberto, who appeared like a dog at the hand of an owner with a ball in his hand.

"You want this?" James waved the ring near Roberto and his head followed. And James pulled it back before the dragon hands lunged to snatch it.

"Bargaining chip," James said and pocketed the jewel.

Roberto gave him an irritated smile, and the deep grayness of his eyes returned.

"So, Mister Guide, what's the next room?"

Roberto's head snapped in the direction of the hall, and he held his hand up, proffering James to take the lead.

"How you become a demon anyway? Does someone come to your doorstep one day and say, 'Hey, you wanna be a fucked up son-of-a-slut'?" James walked side by side with Roberto down the hall.

"Not quite. You are recruited, and then you become an apprentice, either while you are alive or before you die. A demon has to take interest in you," Roberto said and moved his stare away from James' pocket when James' caught him staring.

James moved the ring to the opposite one. "I see. So who found you?"

"A Latin god that commanded the forces of the vanguards during the fall of the Benzamine Empire. He was not kind, and he was stern. When the Romans pissed him off, he destroyed them in almost an instant and sent them back to the times before the gods. He commanded with a flick of his pinky." Roberto lifted his pinky and flicked it.

"Wow," James said.

"Yes, Felix Donde la Casa Gaius."

"When'd he recruit you?"

"It was, 10—" He paused, his expression thoughtful. "1016? I cannot remember the year exactly, but the events that year are as vivid to me as the sun in the sky. My brother, my favorite older brother, second of the six children that my mother begot, stained my name and took everything from me. He even went as far as convincing my wife, if she lay with him, he'd help restore our lost fortune. When she found out it was a lie, she took her life." Roberto drew in a sharp breath. "I got revenge."

"You kill 'im?" James asked and glanced at the clock that appeared in front of him no matter where he was in the house.

"No, but I did something far worse. I created a situation in which he assumed the men he owed money would be at his house wearing animal masks, and I removed all his funds so that he could not flee. I convinced his wife to play a prank on her husband and wear a mask to scare him, get him back for not being home when she needed him. To sum things up nicely, when she came home, wearing the macabre mask, he stabbed her five times." Roberto smiled.

"I watched across the field as the events played out, and a deep feeling of ecstasy surfaced. That feeling has stayed with me since that day. He appeared to me, in the same field that I stood watching my brother as he realized he had murdered his wife and I didn't even turn to him, my longing for revenge took away any outside distractions."

"He said, softly, 'I am ready to move on, you will take my place'." Stopping in the middle of the hall, Roberto placed his hands in his pants pockets and rocked on the ball of his feet. "Now I'm here."

"Why you?" James asked and stopped a few feet ahead of Roberto.

"He told me it was me or my brother, but where my brother lacked in patience and creativity, I made up for it. And that day proved it."

James nodded and stood waiting for Roberto to provide him with information to the next room.

"You know, The Gentleman…Theodore took a lot of his power. Therefore, he cannot focus on multiple souls at once. It takes him some time to react. He's probably doing his trials again." Roberto continued scanning the ceiling, and James looked there, too, attempting to discover what Roberto found intriguing about the moldy structure above them.

"How'd he become a demon?" James asked and relaxed more around Roberto.

"He was a demon in his real life. As a teenage boy, he would go to villages in his home in Iceland and steal a maiden, take her virginity, and return her to mock her future husband. He would run with the wolves in the ice tundra's of Newfoundland, and the Natives there, he created the worst games. How long can you serve without food?" Roberto turned to James.

James used rum for sustenance until his brain told him to refuel, and then he'd suck down hotdogs at gas stations, go fishing near lakes and rivers, or get some fast food, if it was close. Food didn't taste the way it once did, therefore it didn't matter what he put in his mouth. And he had no idea of when he'd last eaten a home-cooked meal.

"And games that involved the demon wolves in the area. Some of those early settlements by Leif Erickson. I remember Gaius telling me about the time The Gentleman was shushed in a tavern in Vineland. He destroyed the village and watched as they burned and listen to them cry. He created games, sick games. Tar and feather people on a hot day and inject a village with syphilis to make a foul out of a village that conformed to Christianity."

"How you know all this about him?"

"We demons do our homework. Take a look at the photo of your great grandfather," Roberto said and James reached in his pocket and turned the photo over.

HERE'S TO THE BEST YEARS OF OUR LIVES.

"What…this wasn't what it said before? It had the address on it," James said and hurled the photo into the hall.

"He loves games, James. Who writes their address on their photo anyway? He used your desperation to get you here."

James sulked, leaned against the wall, and closed his eyes. He shut out the pain in his stomach that ached since he walked up the steps and looked into the emptiness of the hall.

"And he made you feel. Not normal feelings you get when you've done something wrong. Deep yearning and remorse." Roberto walked to James and placed his hand on his shoulder. "Van Herr, oh Van Herr." Roberto looked down to James. "He hates that name."

James began to shake. The thought of The Gentleman appearing when he was vexed made him jittery. He moved away from Roberto and braced himself for the roof to cave in on them.

"Don't bring him around," James said and retracted from Roberto.

"Listen, you are the scum of the earth, the lowest form of Demon, a vile, a small vile, not even a house leader of a Providence. Kicked out because you couldn't control your temper and fled to America on the pretense that you were some country leader from a town no one heard of." Roberto's teeth snapped at the air, and he inhaled, and then moved his eyes to James.

"See, nothing. Wait for it—he hears everything, and eventually he'll come, but it takes him a decade to appear."

"How?" James labored to Roberto away from the wall he

smashed his back into.

"When he owns you, you leave an imprint in his mind, where you are, what you think about, he knows. Think of it as a psychic link. But his is broken and receives delayed messages."

"How was he before all this? I mean, how was he before he lost some of his powers?"

Roberto's zealot face transformed to a serious one. "He was able to overpower me, and I owned all of Western Europe and South and Central America. He could crush a man's face by thinking about it. Now he has to have contact. He could make people do things with an idea. Now he has to orchestrate it physically. He was able to rape a woman with his eyes alone. Now he must do the act himself. The only reason he is able to do it now is because this is his world. But even still, he is limited."

James gulped at the words.

"Now, I am here," Roberto shouted to the walls with his sinewy voice.

"Where do I go?" James beckoned Roberto to remain on topic and to leave the dreadful subject of The Gentleman alone.

"Look for…" Roberto's words pacified and he gurgled red spit. He placed his hands on his throat, attempting to relieve the pressure that bent his throat inward.

"Shit!" James said and turned around. He ran down the hall and rounded the corner. The latent screams of Roberto and the cracking of bones shot a shrill of nervousness up James' spine.

"I gotta do this alone," James said and prepared himself for the rest of his journey.

As he strolled down the middle of the black brick road, he found the second door, door number thirty-one. Flinching at first, his hand slid on the wooden skin, and his fingers traced the Norse letters that carved on the door in a siren light. His face relaxed, and his body became less rigid. He shook out his limbs in an attempt to remove the anxiety that seeped through his pores.

"Okay," he said and took one last glimpse at the ghouls in the hall. "This feels right." He pushed it open.

Inside, a man drifted in the corner near the window, peering at what used to be the house's backyard. Viewing the back of the man, James saw a mural from an F. Scott Fitzgerald novel; a back that belonged to a time not too distant from his grandfather's generation. A perfect replica of the roaring twenties.

After James closed the door, he progressed toward him. "Hi, I'm James," he said with his hands reaching to the stranger.

The man glared at James and loose wet hairs hung over his eyes filled with tears. His flushed face dripped with sadness and his untrimmed mustache didn't conceal the despair in his halfhearted smile. Then, the man looked back to the window. And James slowly lowered his arm.

Nevertheless, James came closer. Without turning around, the man held up his vibrating hand, stopping James. His hands fashioned cuts, and burns.

"I need your help," he asked the stranger who refused to turn to him.

The bulb that swung above his head, a Thomas Edition, hung in the center of the room over a bed with covers neatly folded into each corner. James looked around and saw a journal sitting on the edge of a desk.

Closing the curtains, the mad man lifted a glass from the desk where the journal was, emptied the contents of liquor into his split, and bruised lips. When he snapped his fingers, an already sparked cigarette materialized.

James watched the blaze and studied the man's mannerisms: hopeless, restless, and lost.

"You smoke?" the man asked him.

"No, no…," James said and lifted an eyebrow.

"I hear these are bad for you," the man said and gave the cigarette a look over before putting his unsteady hand to his dehydrated lips for another hit. The ashes on the tip, three inches long, fell on his shirt and produced more holes on the moth-ridden fabric.

"That's what they say now," James said attempting to progress the conversation. With his feet moving forward and his eyes on the complex man, he resisted raising his voice.

Heel to toe, he placed his feet, and using the least amount of pressure as possible, he anchored his weight on his opposite side.

"The name's Frank Hansberger. I was born and raised in New England, moved to Louisiana after I got married," he said and inhaled from the cigarette until it became all ash. When Frank's hands began to shake, he veered his attention away from James once again.

For thirty minutes, James endured the oddities of Frank, and at times, the room filled with unpredictable silence. James became impatient with Frank's reluctance to engage him with the same urgency he had. Three times too few, Frank spoke to James in unstructured sentences that would even confuse a schizophrenic.

"Frank, I don't know what's wrong with you or why you are a recluse, but buddy, I need something from you and bad." James' proximity to Frank allowed him to feel the heat emanating from Frank's crazy.

"Stop!" Frank threw up his arms in panic, and the perspiration on his face fell down his neck and besmirched his shirt. The moisture speckled James. He smeared it from his face.

"Stop," Frank, said calm and less rigid. He grasped the curtain and cowered in the corner away from James, who resisted lurching to him. James merely witnessed the Mad Hatter having a nervous breakdown.

As Frank transitioned to a man of confidence, he adjusted his shirt and coat and walked around James. "You know, I remember when my father got this suit for me. Wanted me to go into the finance business and compete against those Wall Street fellows," he said and brushed off the invisible dust from the coat. "You'll find what you need in there." He pointed to the journal on the table.

James' gaze drifted back and forth, and his forehead scrunched. Trying to understand the man's motives caused him to have a headache, and he rubbed his temples to ease the tension.

"What?" James asked and his voice sounded exhausted from their erratic exchange.

Frank sneered at him. He reached for the journal, ripped out two pages, and tossed them into the air. He did this all while staring at James with a delirious expression. The Mad Hatter reemerged, and Frank receded.

"What's wrong with you?" James asked.

Frank turned back to the window and smothered his nose into the cloth of the curtain. "The question is will you be able to get rid of him?"

"If you help me, I will." Eric had asked the same question. The truth was, James didn't want to be a hero and only wanted out of the game. He was ready to hand over whatever the demon wanted from the room.

He walked to the table and took a break from Frank's display of the inside of an insane asylum.

Turning his head over his shoulder, Frank blew smoke from another cigarette he created. "Occam's razor," he said and his focus returned to the window.

"Occam what?"

"No, Occam's razor. Means the explanation requiring the fewest assumptions is most likely to be correct. Just look at what's in front of you, what's always been there, and you'll find your answer," Frank said, and his breath condensed onto the rustic glass.

"You're in front of me? Are you this Occam's bullshit? Tell me the room crazy ass." James began to walk into the direction of Frank but stopped when Frank burst into laughter. After ringing James' ears with his high-pitched chuckles, Frank placed the dusty curtain into his mouth and began to chew on it and make awkward and childish sounds.

"I don't need this bullshit!" James launched at him, grabbed his arm, and placed his knife under Frank's chin. "You are going to tell me what I want to know, one way or the other." He pressed the blade against Frank's skin.

"Huh." Frank retired the last of his cigarette, and his image burned in the molecules of the air. His escape forced pieces of the ripped paper to float and wander down to the ground near James' boots.

"No come back! Don't do this!" James flared his hands in the space where Frank had stood.

"Shit in a box!" He pushed the table into the wall, and the journal fell open to the ground. After picking it up, he separated the pages and observed the words written on the top and bottom, on the sides, and in spirals in the center of the page.

"What the hell is a ragamuffin'?"

"A muckraker?"

As James flopped onto the bed holding the journal, one of the lockjaw producing springs sliced the side of his leg. Rubbing the cut, he moved away from the bed and headed to the window. "Man this bed is worse than that hotel."

The curtains quivered. James moved them to reveal the outside. "Let's see what this looney bastard was lookin' at." However, beyond the dirt-covered window was the green and purple mist of The Gentleman; it moved and shaped itself like the clouds in the sky, with shapes of horns, nightmares, and demon's eyes. James shut the curtains and retreated to the desk. He scooted the chair out, flopped into it, and placed the journal on the mahogany top.

Studying the hemp paper with the beige, water-stained surface, he ran his hand down the center of the binding. The words, written in cursive with indigo ink, came from a man with great penmanship. When James closed the book, he lingered at the initials scripted on the edge of it. *Journal of F.D.H.* Fancy

Leaning back in the chair, he flipped the journal to the first entry and read the confessions of Frank Hansberger.

Chapter 13
OH, ADELA!

December 02, 1922

The depression is over, and my friends are getting along as they once did. Now that President Harding is doing well, parties have begun again among the rich. I know this because my "Friends" mail me invites that find their way to my trash.

None of these things interest me as much as they used to. At one brief moment in the terse existence we call life, I salivated for a chance to be in the company of others, yelled at the radio during political debates, and pushed away crowds to catch a good fight. I even purchased the weekly paper to monitor the stocks. Now, those papers are mountains stacked on my porch, enough to build a bridge that sails across the Gulf of Mexico from Louisiana to Florida. I used to be so intrigued with politics, mechanics, and finance. A gift from my father. It's all balderdash to me now. Background noise.

Doc says I should write in a journal to ease the pain of her... "Let go," is what he tells me from behind his bushy whiskers. Nevertheless, how do you let go of such beauty? Moreover, how do you fill an emptiness that can challenge the depths of any abyss and that deepens inside me every day? How can you stuff away her beauty into a closet and never peek at it ever again? My Adela, I could never let go. It doesn't make it any better for me since I still have her body.

I still see her face when I open or close my eyes. She speaks out to me in the whispers of the wind and in the sounds of the morning. I see her when I first wake, in my dreams, at work, and in the streets. Her face—I can still feel her soft skin that became milky white in the winter and the color of yellow sands in the summer. Her smile, with her cordate shaped lips, and the apricot smell of her. Oh, Adela. With hair browner than cinnamon and saturated in God's essence. Eyes of serendipity. They froze me. Shakespeare wrote what is in a name? So much, so much.

The monotonous activities during the months she took ill linger in my brain. I can hear her coughing as the fevers took. I feel the warm water on my hands from those days that I saturated her forehead to bring down the fever, and I can still smell the nectar of the strawberries I fed her in the squalor room I live in now.

The doctors pumped her with funny medicine too often, and I didn't like it. One of the colored men, Billy Lee, gave me herbs from his grandmother that helped her sleep. If it were not for him and the medicine he provided, she would have suffered more than she did.

In addition, I didn't care if it was old slave magic he used. It helped. Before her, the people I lost in life were my distant grandparents whom I rarely visited. Subsequently, their passing didn't affect me. However, when I lost my Labrador Chocolate to old age and heart warms, his did.

The last day she was on this earth stays in my mind and never leaves. She said to me, "Frank, it smells like sunshine."

"Yes, dear, it does," I said as I entertained the hallucinations she experienced, but I felt this one was different.

Her eyes closed, her chest fell, and her hand that I held until my fingers became numb let go of mine and went limp. It took me two days to leave the bedside, even after they removed her body. Her body now sits in my embalming room. It has been a while since I have gone there. I would sit and stare at her face for hours, days. I preserved her body...

***

James slung the journal across the table and lifted from the seat.

"This is so fuckin' boring," he said and left for the door. He jiggled the knob, yanked the door open, and blundered out of the room. Then he reappeared inside. The same dank walls, the scratched up table, the itchy wool curtains that wavered in the windless room, and the same Thomas Edition that swung from before, even that damned journal sat on the desk. He lifted the journal up to see if the initials were there. They were.

"No, no, no," James said and walked back to the door. He ran out and ran back inside. The same room.

Back and in and back out.

Out.

In.

Out.

In.

He did this strange dance for three minutes before he stopped trying to escape.

"You got this, James. Read this boring journal, and then get out of here." He steadied himself and headed for the table. He flopped down in the uneven chair, and it creaked with his weight. He slid the leather-bound book to the edge of the table and picked up close to where he stopped. As he lifted the corners of the papers, they flapped against his hand. His hand began to shake, and he attempted to push down the paper that resisted his force.

"Shit." He lifted his hand and allowed the papers to move on their own. It stopped on another entry.

December 08, 1922

> *I washed my face and went to the stash of greenbacks, where I kept my half a dollar coins. In addition, I snatched lavish dresses from Adela's closet and ripped the one she wore off her frozen body and stuffed it inside the bag with the other items.*
>
> *"I'll see you soon," I said to her and fled from the house, but not before kissing her lifeless face.*
>
> *The witch's castle was the tenth house on 10th street. I went to it and walked up the plantation steps. There the witch will bring my Adela back. Back to me once again.*

"Wait—Ten," James said and reread the previous passage.

"All these doors are ten. Eric's story he had to go to a ten and this story has a ten, too." James lifted from the desk. The legs of the chair drug across the splintery floor and scraped up shavings of wood.

"Now to find ten," James said but after he opened the door, a parade of zombies slumped toward him, blocking the entire hallway. He shut out their clammy faces and arms before they could scratch off flesh from his face and arms.

"What the fuck?"

As the moans and scraping at the door withered away, he tried his luck once more and swung the door open, pulling back in case something reached for him. While the door opened, a tunnel of wind pounded his face and body, and the floor in the hall became a large hole that emitted a faint blue light. Pushing himself over the edge of the doorframe, James looked down into an abyss with depths as deep as the pain and hurt inside him. He searched for the bottom.

"How?" Backing away from the massive sinkhole in the hall, he used his body weight to close the door. He brought his tired eyes to the journal that sat open on the table. As he treaded back to it, he lowered himself into the chair that felt like it might crumple under him.

"Okay, Frank, you win. I'll read this boring ass journal," James said, and the journal flipped to the next entry.

"Thanks for speeding this up Frank. I can't get mad at you for that. I have to admit it's creepy though." James strengthened the paper and glared at the first paragraph.

December 26, 1922

I woke outside to the chirping of birds. It was still Christmas day. The rich neighbor's children played with their new gadgets and gizmos and trolled along merrily.

I sat thinking about all the time she'd taken from me because of her needy habits and her insistent nagging that we look the part. I also took the week prior off from work because of the fatigue and headaches. These nuisances prevented me from playing sports, going hunting, and being a part of Gene's group again. They forced me to spend time with Adela, and I feel she wanted it that way. I regret to say, I wish I had never gone to the witch to bring Adela back to life. This was not the woman I loved. This was not the woman who made the rain fall like sunshine.

I thought about what we had done on that Christmas Eve; we'd killed John. We killed him and left his body in the alley, like road trash for the garbage men to dispose of.

My venture to the house proved troublesome.

My feet forgot how to work, and my ears forgot which way I should stand. I launched at the door and collapsed in the living room, and when I saw Adela resting on the couch, I took this journal and fled. I didn't take the machine so she would remain asleep.

She'd done a swell job being Natalie. No one recognized her as Adela. Her blue eyes helped. And the burgundy wigs she wore added to the disguise. She did such a good job as Natalie that I could not stand her. I wanted to get away from her and reverse the spell from the witch. I wasn't ready to bury her, however.

During my walk along the ridge of the road, I saw a man sitting on a wooden fence near my neighbor's home.

"Hi there," he said to me.

I waved to be polite and lifted my brows to the smell of flowers the breeze blew my way, maybe lilac. "Hi," I said to this strange man and remained on course.

"She's eating your soul, but I can give it back to you," he said and hopped off the wooden seat.

My feet became stuck to the ground. "What are you talking about? You, sir, need help. Good day and Merry Christmas." I turned back to the road wearing yesterday's garments.

"How's the upchuck? Black? Nasty like the chew?"

"I—I don't want to deal with magic anymore. I don't want anything you can offer," I yelled to him as I walked backward and further away from the truths he spouted from his hairy lips. Perspiration poured from my body and my face became hot.

"Well, when you are ready, I'll be waiting," he said and left. Left without another word, and in

the blink of an eye. I assumed this man was part of my newfound and sick imagination and brushed it off as such.

Forging forward for five miles, I went to Billy's house and failed giving my salutations to all the other families in the neighborhood during Christmas. All of my concentration was required to fight the aching pain and fatigue.

They yelled to me, "Merry Christmas, Mister Frank."

I gave some smiles or simple waves. I only had one thing in mind, how Billy's grandmother could help.

After walking into the house, I saw his grandmother slaving over banana pudding and humming. I staggered to her, fell at her feet, and groveled like a man on his last string. Her tears as she looked into my face didn't better my situation or settle my mind.

"You soul rotten, you dead. I been praying for you, but she took you. You should've taken what I gave Billy. You should've taken it." She sat in the chair.

Billy pulled my body from the ground and sat me on the couch in the living room. My head bowed heavily, and I heaved the broken promises of the witch about Adela.

After lifting my head, I saw Billy assist his grandmother from the kitchen next to me. Her hair was loose. The gray and black strands mixed with white lay on my arm as she rubbed my head.

"What do you mean, ma'am, that my soul is rotten?" I said and tightened my chest to suspend my shakes.

"She means you dying, and there ain't nothing she can do," Billy said and walked to the screened door with his head down and hands

behind his back.

His grandmother picked up a box from the side of the couch and set it in my lap. "This will break the bond, but that witch ate so much of your soul. You ain't got nothing left," she said to me, face full of tears.

I took the box from her and my hands shook. This was the same box Billy brought to me weeks ago that was supposed to wash away my angst for Adela, the same damn box he shoved in my face.

"Is there anything, anything at all?" I asked in desperation. "There has to be something, there's always something. I-I can't die." I rubbed my mouth. I didn't wish for death's arrival any longer and wanted to live. Live away from her, this imposter of Adela in her body. I pulled the hourglass from my pocket, two-thirds at the base.

"This you time," she said.

I stuffed it back into my pocket and looked out the window. She told me something I'd guessed about the hourglass for quite some time.

"You go tah the witch that done that, that be dah only way, but....but she died weeks ago," she said and laid her tears on my hand as she kissed it. "I prepared it for you in the box, please drink it. It'll make you feel better and take away her control."

I opened it and inside sat a mason jar with swamp water. After popping the top, I placed my nose at the entrance.

Pungent. The stench drove my head away from it, and after three failed approaches to bring the bottle to my face, I finally slammed it to my lips, chipping a tooth in the process, and took several large gulps until the glass was empty. My eyes burned and my head wanted to unscrew from its base.

I coughed and coughed up ash.

I coughed up a pound of it, and Billy's grandmother rubbed my back.

After I stopped, Billy cleaned it and placed it in a large container. His grandmother lit the container and the flames glowed blue and yellow from the flames. Real voices yelped and I grabbed my stomach as it twisted like a wrung out shirt. When she spit on the flame, it fluffed into nothing and took my pain along with it.

Trying to stand, I almost collapsed, and Billy helped me sit on the couch.

"Are you sure she died?" I asked her.

She nodded.

Billy handed me a paper with the obituary.

I saw the old woman's face and date of her death December 10, 1922. I crumpled it in my hand, yelled at the wall. I threw it across the room and crumbled.

"I am so sorry," she said to me.

I hugged her tight. She had tried to help me before, and I didn't acknowledge the warnings. Now with clairvoyance, I see how selfish I was, how stubborn I became, during the time I sought to bring Adela back.

"You have tah kill her. That is the only way to get rid of her soul. You gotta let go, 'cause that ain't you love. The one in her, she ate you. Baby, I am sorry," she said to me sincerely and lovingly. No wonder Billy treasured her.

I kissed her forehead, shook Billy's hand, and headed home. This woman, this witch, had taken my Adela's body and usurped it, violated and cajoled me to commit murder. I wanted her expelled and away from where she came.

As I entered the dark room, her petite frame stood, Adela's frame stood.

"Adela, darling." I crept inside. I played the scene of how it would unfold in my head repeatedly on my way home. I would grab her and say, *"Leave!"* with the voice of a god, and she would crumble to the ground and depart.

But that's not how it happened, I'm afraid.

When I slung the door open and pounded my feet inside, she kept her back facing me, and I touched her shoulder.

She turned around and gripped my arm. *"Now you knows,"* she said octaves lower than the voice she used as Natalie.

I took my arm back and backed into my chair. I didn't use the voice of Zeus or perform an exorcism with my words. Defeat settled in.

"Old woman, leave her body," I said with my hand on my chin, and my gaze darted from corner to corner.

She laughed and examined the dress and body she'd taken hostage. *"I don't think so."*

I flung from my seat.

"Ugh, Ugh, Ugh, you touch me or do anything out of line and I mutilate and defile her body until you don't know what is left, and I tell them coppers about the murders. The ones I had to clean up after you slept outdoors, you know, John, that hobo." She struck a match and sucked on the cigarette she held. *"Robert told those cops he thought he saw your machine that night."*

I stood opening and closing my fist as if I was inflating a blood pressure device, ready to launch and take her away from Adela's body.

But how? I had no knowledge of magic, no knowledge of what I had invited inside her. All I had was patience and the hope that Billy's grandmother found something to help.

And I released my hand.

"Koulye a, ou chita gen imajine ti gason ak fè menm bagay mwen di," *she said, and those eyes flashed blue, they burned a hole in the darkness of the room. Of those words, I only made out* 'Fancy, do as I say' *and that was all I needed to understand.*

We sat in the dark for an hour, and she lit another of her cigarettes from the end of those fancy handles the gals use, and the light of the moon cast over her eyes the way they did in the talkies, when the girls readied themselves for their big monologue.

And I sat thinking of the ugliness that bronzed from this beauty. It sours the stomach.

"You knows, excuse me," she cleared her throat, "You know, I like talking like this, and I like this life," she said and blew the smoke in my face. "And I don't want to lose it, so play nice."

She sat in my lap. She kissed me with those lukewarm lips, and I felt no love, no emotion. Only rage and the taste of cigarettes bit my tongue.

Like an obedient mule pulling the haul behind me as the farmer whipped my back, I nodded.

She lifted herself from me. After staring out the door, she walked out of the house; and God knows to where.

When she left, I released the pressure that I'd held in during the exchange and rotated the hourglass between my fingers.

"This is all the time I have left?" I said as more sand fell. The falling of the grains triggered pain, and I grabbed my stomach. The pain of it all put me on the ground, and my existence became black—at least the vomiting stopped.

***

January 01, 1923

Lights went on, then off, on, and then off. This happened over the course of five minutes, until I sat up and looked at her.

"Time to go outs, we's gotta party," she said to me and pulled me off the ground.

I didn't want to go, but what other choice did I have? Sleep in the embalming room again and lock myself away for days?

There was no dichotomy from her. She found me. I even tried to go to Billy's place. She stopped me before I could leave, and she reverted from sleeping as much. The times I thought I was sneaking out of the house before when she passed out, she had been watching me.

"What are we doing to-tonight, Adela," I hated calling her that. Forced to use those words, forming those syllables, my insides turned into liquid from the flames that spilled in my belly. I hated calling her by MY wife's name. I preferred calling her Natalie like everyone else did. Adela, you say, more like demon whore. Save Billy and Gene, I don't know a man who hasn't slept with her.

However, if I refused, she slapped, wailed, kicked, made fools of us both in public, and worse, cut and damaged Adela's body.

My, how time changed within a week. The effort it took to stand up from my squalor I created in my temporary slumber, broke the skin on my face, and shot pains in the back of my spine. Enduring it, I heaved out the door and met with the sunshine, a long overdue appointment we had.

Shattering my stiffness in my bones and ligaments, I slid to the door to our, my *house and slumped on the couch nearest the mirror.*

"That's a good boy. I like when you call me Adela." She smirked and walked to a bag on the ground. After opening it, she tossed me a full suit. How much money do I have left?

"Clean up, you look like hell. You look like death's at you. Or maybe it is?" She laughed and placed her earrings in her ears. "When you pass, I'll tell 'em...I'll tell 'em, 'He wanted me to have everything officer, everything.' They'll look at this paper you signed, and I'll have your estate, your house, and everything your daddy passed to you."

"I don't remember signing that...yesterday?" I said as I lurched up from a sweat stain I created on the grandiose fabric we imported from France, and I looked at the old woman in the mirror. I saw the nastiness for what she was.

"Ugh, Ugh, Ugh," she clicked and grabbed another one of my hunting knives from my closet. My Closet. *She cut deep into the skin and drew blood.*

"I'll get ready," I said and shunned my eyes from her emotionless displays and disrespect for Adela.

"That's a good boy. We shouldn't be late for the New Year's Eve Party. I hear it'll be a bang!"

After taking the clothes, I ran upstairs.

I looked at my face in the mirror; looked at who I'd become.

This, this old man of thirty-five, with bags underneath his eyes, large enough to fit the garbage the witch shops for.

His pale skin from lack of sun, sunken cheeks, and my teeth from lack of hygiene. My teeth became gravestones that cracked and appeared chiseled on my molars; happened faster than I expected. Thank goodness, it was only my molars for now, so no one was the wiser.

I wet my face. It was a daring task now and took all of my energy to complete.

My hands shook as I shaved all but my mustache. I cleaned my nails—bitten off, frail, and yellow—and scrubbed the dead skin from my body. After brushing back my hair, I noticed clumps of hair in my brush. Clumps and clumps of hair. My semi-black hair. Soft and subtle, hair that women had admired came out, and the curious man in me, reached for my head and pulled more from their roots.

Then, panic and short breaths overtook me.

I didn't resist the need to plunge to the floor and draw in, and cry. I let it happen. Oh, that woman had to have heard me, listening from where she pranced in the common room, because as I whimpered into the gray slacks that covered my knees, she knocked on the door.

"Hurry up!" she yelled.

Ignoring her calls, I pressed my head into my knees harder, almost losing air.

When the bathroom became cold, the smell of apricots entered, a smile spread across my face.

"Adela?" I asked, and there she stood with those sea green eyes and beautiful presence. It glued me to the floor.

"Let go...," she whispered.

"Honey," I said and sprung from the ground and inched to her lovely presence.

As the witch resumed her beating of the door, Adela's image washed away.

"No...no...come back." I reached out my arm.

The witch continued banging on the door.

I looked at the door, white without life, and sat there and thought, I could sit here, ignore her, and smell the essence of apricots Adela left behind until I am forced to leave this warm bathroom.

No, no, I had to do as she said, or she would do far worse to Adela's canvas. I mustered up the nerve to stand and wiped the fog from the mirror.

"Let go," I said those words again.

Brushing my hair to one side, I did a great job covering the spots where I was missing hair. After taking all the hair from the floor and putting it in the wastebasket, I placed the rest of my clothes on and opened the door.

Still standing there with her arms folded, she looked at me, not moving, dreamy, and not as pleasant—that is an understatement.

"I told you to hurry up!"

When I didn't respond, her gaze narrowed. "What were you doing in there?" *She looked over my shoulder as she inhaled the aroma from the bathroom.*

"Losing my hair. My hair is falling out." I said

She touched my face. Her hands smelled of gas. After peeling them off, I raced down the stairs.

Walking into my *living room, I put on my tie in the mirror. As I looped it and created a noose around my neck, she crept her slimy hands over my shoulders and ran them across my chest. I clenched my jaw and looked away from her. She had turned a benevolent flower into a weed.*

"Let me tie that for you, dear," *she said and took my tie away from me. Tying it tight, she scooted the knot to my throat—causing me to gag slightly.* "There now, let's go," *she said and patted my back.*

After loosening it from around my throat, I walked behind her out the door, and my hands involuntarily shadowed the back of her neck. Then she whisked around, and I slapped my hands to my sides and lifted the corners of my mouth, assuring her that all was well with the world.

As we neared my friend Gene's private club, where the celebration would start soon, I had half a mind to kill us both and run the car into a ditch, but she watched my every move, and any movement of swerving off the gravel road, she pulled at my arm and kissed my neck. Demon woman.

We pulled up and went into the ballroom where the party commenced. While showing the witch off as her pseudonym, Natalie, I attempted to rid myself of her throughout the night.

"Gene, Gene," I said. I was glad to see him. "How are you?"

He nodded and downed the rum from his glass. "By the way, I love your friend Billy. He delivers as he promises each night, fine man. Oh, congratulations, I have to announce this." He left me and ran to the stage, and as I put my hand to my head, I could only imagine what announcement he had in store for me.

"Excuse me, everyone."

Chatter decreased, and everyone gave his or her attention to Gene.

"I have to congratulate my friend, Frank, on his new engagement with Natalie. Everyone let's have it," Gene said and instigated the clapping.

As I waved to the smiling faces, I plastered a withering smile on my face, and the demon woman grabbed my arm.

"Isn't it wonderful?" she lied to me.

To keep up appearances, I kissed her and

touched her face. The crowd whistled and cheered me on.

"I despise you," I said as the crowd's glass-shattering volume hid my words, but she saw my lips.

"Okay, everyone, drink! Drink until you can't anymore, and then drink some more, but remember it is illegal to be sober in here." Gene spread laughter around the joint as he waved a cup of bootleg alcohol, that the authorities would never discover—the witch arranged for that.

"Seems I have to freshen up," she said to me as she bounced her hair in her hands. In her language that meant, "I'm going to blow a guy in the back alley, then I'll drink and drink, smoke and smoke, and when I come back from doing all those vile things, I'll lay a fat one on your lips."

"Okay," I said through my teeth.

I peered at the clock during the party so many times I forgot all the dull and uninteresting conversations around me. I watched the arm tic and the short arm trying to catch it, but it never seemed to move fast enough. I timed the second on the clock and synchronized my inner rhythm with it, and I even timed my drinking to it.

While I played the game with time, I watched as my time passed me. When the sands from the hourglass fell, I counted the seconds in-between the next.

Coming to where I stood in the dark corner of the room, Gene left his podium to speak to me, and I thanked him silently for it.

"Frank, it is so good to see you again." He shook my hand and his face turned from happy to distorted.

"What's the matter?" I asked as his hand pulled away.

"I am afraid they found John's body. They're calling it a lover's quarrel—he had a male partner down in the colored side of town," he said and gave a depressing grin.

"Too bad. He was a good guy," I said and masked my lies behind the glass near my lips.

"I wanted to ask you, Frank, do you trust Natalie?" His face was serious.

"Yes. . . Why do you ask?"

"Well, besides from my wife telling me of her stealing. It has been given to me that she took out insurance on your house, and she comes by my club during off hours, or so my security tells me."

"Wh-who told you that?" I asked and searched my memory for the instance of signing the insurance for my house. I only saw the life insurance.

"Well, a good friend of mine saw her in old man Melvin's office. He is a shady attorney—will create any legal document for the right price—and Melvin told him about their little deal."

"I will speak to her tonight," I said to him.

"Also I smelled—"

Before he could finish, she joined us.

"Natalie!" Gene said, and his eyes widened as she shimmied her shoulders in between us.

Gazing at this witch with a drunken face, I wanted to stab the smile from it, fifty times.

"Frank, I wanna go look at the stars before the count down," she said, and the smell of petroleum became unbearable.

"Okay. Gene, we'll be back."

"Be careful," he said to me.

I gave him a cry for help in my eyes, but I don't think he heard me.

After we pushed through the back door, she burst into laughter. "Oh, Frank," she said and grabbed my tie, "I'm going to miss all these good times."

I remained silent and looked into the sky.

"Roof! The roof—we'll see the fireworks from the river." She screamed and pulled me up the stairs outside the building.

As we skidded up the stairs to the fire exit, my hands touched the cold wet surface of the rails. Spiraling upward, she stumbled over every other step until we finally came to the roof.

I hesitated before placing my foot on the wet concrete.

After we walked along the roof, she headed for a fire truck-red canister that sat near the edge of the building and dumped heavy loads of what smelled like petroleum, the exact aroma on her body, around the building and down certain areas of the roof.

This was the plan, blow Gene's place up, collect the insurance money from me, and open her own joint—I finally came to the realization of it all and couldn't help but laugh at the situation she placed me in, or I had placed myself in.

Kicking off her shoes, she began spinning in circles with her hands spread as I once had during the summer rain in Montana. One minute, she was happy go lucky. The next, she was the old demon woman.

Pacing my steps, I walked to her as I read the time from my pocket watch. It said 11:55. I pulled the hourglass from my pocket and saw five pieces of sand that remained. I slipped it in my pocket when she stopped spinning and brought her attention to me.

"I am afraid this is your last night, so let's make it memorable," she said out of breath, and while she stumbled to me.

We danced to the sounds of the music that blared below us, and I felt nauseated. I peered at the edge and an idea sat in my head.

Let go.

While staring into the trickles of moonlight that shimmered over the water, a gust of wind veered us closer to the edge. Close enough that the people in the street that counted down to the New Year appeared right next to us.

Ten, nine.

My heartbeat matched the nervousness in my gut as I kissed the forehead, with the imposter inside, of my Adela.

Eight, Seven.

I twirled her to the ledge, and then spun her into my chest; I felt the bosoms of my wife press against my petticoat, breasts that I would once have traced with my fingers until she couldn't bear it.

Six, five.

I hugged her body so close.

Four, three.

I looked into the deep blue eyes and swore they turned green for just a moment and Adela's voice said, "Let go," through the witch's mocking grin.

Two.

I danced her to the ledge again.

One.

I dipped her body and kissed her lips. Firecrackers like the sounds of guns popping off and loud bangs and hooting rose from the streets like heat and fluttered from the sky like ash.

"Whoa, I liked that one," she said while I dipped her further.

After I stood, I let her body dangle from my arms. She lost her footing, and her body leaned

*further back. I held onto her hands, the wetness
from the rain required a tighter grip that I didn't
want to produce—I didn't resist it.*

*"What are you doing, pull me up! Pull me up
now!" The blue in her eyes blazed red.*

Let go. *I heard the words from Billy's
grandmother, from Billy, from my inner
conscience, from that quack and now, from Adela
herself.*

Let go.

So I did.

*Relaxing my muscles in my hand seemed
effortless, and her hands with the lavender paint
on them slid away from me. With her eyes
stretched wide enough to see all of Louisiana, she
teeter-tottered, and then her feet swept from under
her. Reaching out for the ledge, she missed it, and
her body rotated, flipped to the ground, and
landed on the cold cement.*

*No one heard the splat from her body falling
at thirty miles an hour to a hard surface. No one
heard the breaking of her spin, and no one heard
the rupture of her stomach. They were all too busy
kissing and jumping, drunk in ecstasy.*

*As I peered down upon the concrete that her
body panted with blood, I didn't see my Adela, but
the witch.*

I let go.

*Backing away from the ledge, I retrieved the
hourglass from my pocket, wishing the death of
her reversed the magic and released me.
Nevertheless, like all things in realty, this didn't
happen. Holding it in my hand against the light of
the New Year, I saw the last blade of sand fall to
the bottom of the hourglass and crooked when my
heart palpitated until my aorta fissured. I bent
over and hugged my stomach.*

This was it. *I thought this was the big sleep. Hacking up flesh as I stumbled, I floundered to the ground. A fish out of water is how I would have appeared to a spectator. I rolled my body around the wet roof, but no matter which angle or which position I assumed, the unbearable pain stayed with me.*

During my Julius Cesar death, a shadow removed the light from the moon, and a man's shoes stood in front of me.

"*Gene, Gene, she fell...*" *I sent those words from my dying lips and as I looked up upon his face, I saw it was not Gene. It was that man, the man from the perch. The man with the flower smell. I coughed out my lungs and rolled from him, ready to roll myself next to the dead corpse near the dumpsters—how Romeo and Juliet of me.*

"*What...W-hat do you want?*" *I said and held my hand on the edge of the roof.*

He sat next to me, ruining the nice suit of his.

When I smelled apricots fall from the rain, I put my back to the ground and looked at the stars. I loved how they aligned to the rotation of the earth. The rain felt like sunshine on my face and I knew, I knew Adela caused that to happen. Adela wanted me to live. She wanted me to move on, to let go and start a new life.

"*I can save you, I can save you,*" *he said to me.*

"*All right, all right...*"

CHAPTER 14
MIRROR, MIRROR

"I guess everyone's got a story."

After James closed the journal, he lifted himself from the desk and approached the door. He opened the door. Hesitating before exiting the Mad Hatter's room, James searched the hallway for holes in the floor, ghouls, or anything else that might surprise him. To his left, he saw the lavender flame, and to his right, the grand clock levitated in the hall. Then he fled into the darkness of the hallway.

The number on the door faded, and the clock on the wall struck three thirty.

"It is now three thirty, James…hurry up," The Gentleman said in a motherly tone.

"Fuckin' time." His feet touched the sticky boards as he walked in the center. "I know the room, I think, it's ten. But I don't get the door numbering. Maybe that's what he meant add up. Let's see which one added to ten." He grazed his hand over the odd numbers he passed on his venture.

"I wonder if he really killed him," he said and trampled along the hallway.

"Hey guide, where are you?" James asked and searched in the darkness for Roberto. "I guess he's actually dead."

As he rounded the corner of the house, he glanced at a mirror placed in between a room with the number fifty-six written on top of it, and another with the number ninety-nine. The reflection of his face caught his peripheral. No matter which mirror he looked in, he was not a replica of what he once was and became a shell of himself.

Touching the mirror, he ran his hands on the muck, and the image in the mirror touched its own face. James shook off what he had seen and squinted at his reflection.

"Did you move?" he asked it.

Nothing happened.

He flexed in the mirror, jumped up and down. He shadowboxed, and the image replicated these movements flawlessly. He lifted his shirt, and the image in the mirror had the same sunken in chest from months of malnutrition—caused from using alcohol in place of food.

"Just my imagination." He progressed down the hall looking for his next room. His own image remained in the same position, peering at him, watching him leave. The wheels turned in his head. The rusted and broken fragments in his head sparked.

When he returned, the image waved and smiled. A lump in his throat forced its way up, and he swallowed hard to push it down. The thing in the mirror moved freely without him.

"This is, this is just a mirror," he said and reached for the glass surface. A pale cold hand and blue veined arm reached out to him. As it tugged on his shirt, he yanked away from it and used his knife to slice the outer skin of the mermaid colored arms. It released its clutches, and James' feet gave way as he tripped over the bunched up carpet.

"No, No!" he exhaled and looked back at the image. The events that proceeded terrorized him. First, the hands pierced the mirror's barrier. The mirror's sold state liquefied and its plasma surface wavered. It reflected a distorted image of the house and the clammy skin pushed through it.

Then the head, a decomposed version of James. Missing loads of hair, teeth, and hallowed gray eyes. The thing moved its zombie head around the edge of the mirror sniffing for James.

Once it spotted him, it smiled.

The cholesterol in James' heart sizzled and pumped through his veins.

As it hung over the edges of the mirror, the gray mud plopped from its lips onto the floor.

Lastly, it placed its foot through the mirror and shimmed out of the hole. After standing from a crutching tiger position, it used its ice sickle fingers to push away its lanky hair.

"There you are." It pointed.

Giving himself a pep talk, James crawled at the boards on the floor.

"No this is not the time to freeze." He pushed off the carpet and picked himself up, and the gum-like blood stuck to his body.

"You are not me...you are not me," he said to it as backed away into the hall, turning around to see the distance between him and the creature.

"Why not, your body is dead, I am that vessel, I am you," the thing spoke. It even had James' voice.

"No...No. I am here I am here," James said to it.

The thing walked closer and closer.

With each step it took, it moved faster and faster.

James lifted his feet, but they fell hard. His shoes felt like they had lead bottoms. When he twisted his body to race down the hall, he ran in slow motion.

The thing reached for him, and its cold hands snatched the skin from his wet shoulder.

"We belong together, you and me, James." Its nails dug into his shoulder and punctured blood vessels.

"No!" James screamed and pulled out one of the fruit. With his palm open, he pelted the thing's eye, and it burned and sizzled.

After freeing himself, James ran. In the hall, a ladder descended from the attic and banged on the floorboard. James slowed his advancement, but after looking at his corpse behind him, trampled up the steps into the unknown room. The doors to the attic snapped shut behind him.

CHAPTER 15
LILAC IN THE ATTIC

As he stood up in the attic looking around at his surroundings, the door of the Attic shut. He turned the door as the light from the hall faded and attempted to prevent it from shutting. It shut, and he kneeled down to pry the door open.

"Come on," he said as the veins on his neck popped out and pulsated. His exhausted hands tugged at the string that released the steps, but nothing permitted the latch to open. The howls from the corpse convinced him to move away from it and further into the attic.

"Never mind." He walked into a statue of dolls that tumbled to the ground. Someone ripped out their eyes and gutted the stomachs of the dolls. He picked one up and looked at the mangled eyes and the disheveled hair.

"This is some weird shit." As he moved to toss the doll into the pile, it animated, and the head spun around to him.

"Are you my mommy?" the thing asked with a voice as if the batteries were dying.

"Screw this." He tossed the doll into the pile, and the stack toppled over. As he walked down the open area of the hall, James stopped when he heard the sounds of little feet running around him. As if, rats were scarring across the floor. He turned around. The dolls lay in the same pile where he'd left them.

After he turned around and went on his way, the feet continued once again. James twisted in the direction of the dolls and the pile remained untouched. He began to walk backwards and monitored the dolls while he left the area.

"Are you my mommy?" they asked in that deep horrible voice and feet wandered around the room but the dolls remained in the pile

He bolted in the direction of a bright light at the end of the hall.

The light flashed, and with the flash, the attic transformed to a dark courtroom from the nineteenth century. He covered his nose to the stench of lilac that molested the air.

"This is so awful," he said.

While James walked further into the room, he looked at the benches aligned evenly along the wall. He bumped into one of the spectators in the seats and brought the attention of a one-eyed man wearing a black cloak. When he smiled, he had snakes for teeth.

"Sorry," James said and stepped away from the serpent being. He attempted to blend in and sat in the benches two rows from a spotlight in the center of the room. In the gallery with the church benches, wicked-looking people from several different times and several different social classes sat. They threw rotten meat, fruit, and soiled clothing at the man who stood in the middle of the spotlight.

The man in the center, with broad shoulders and hair along the nape of his neck as thick as the hair on his arms, held his hat in his hand and put his head up to a face that caused James to press his back into the wooden seat.

"How do you plead?" The Gentleman asked from his seat on the bench, which towered over the onlookers. Even though it came from fifty feet above, The Gentleman's voice sounded as if he were sitting right next to James. Behind The Gentleman, a flag with Norse letters that rotated around the outline of a wolf in the center draped behind him.

After the man looked back at the gallery that taunted him and pelted him with rotten food, he placed his attention on The Gentleman.

"How do you plead?" The Gentleman asked again, raised his gavel, and hammered it onto the woodblock. The power of it rattled the room.

The onlookers laughed and pointed to the man who danced in the center of the room, unsure how to react to anything.

"Kill him," a homely woman shouted, ripped the tooth from her already gummy mouth, and flung the rotted thing at the back of the man's neck. It struck him, but he kept his attention on The Gentleman, perched high above.

"Hershel?" James squinted at the back of the man. He recognized the flaps of skin that folded on the back of his neck and looked like a bumpy landscape in Shah Valley. The same valley where he'd lost Jeff, a valley with an evil wind, but not as evil as the hairs on the arms of the demon striking the wooden block as if it would open up the dam that kept James' sanity from finding him. That demon with his green eyes, emerald eyes, lost in hate and unapologetic actions.

How'd I get wrapped up in this? He readjusted his legs.

"Shit in a box," James said and lifted himself from his seat.

"How do you plead, Hershel?" the demon asked and sneered at James as he walked around the back of the gallery. The Gentleman's cold stare demanded James take his seat.

Once he slumped down into a bench, The Gentleman looked back to Hershel in the middle of the room. "How do you plead?"

"Not...guilty." Hershel placed his head down.

James guessed he was staring at his hands or the hat that he held onto as if it contained a way out from the madness of it all.

"His voice is so clear," James said.

"Clear, clear, clear," a man said. He wore a mask with a bird's beak, flapped, and hopped on the top of the benches, pecking the heads of some of the mob, but he refrained from touching James as he hopped over his head and continued to torment the others. "Clear, clear."

"Not guilty?" The Gentleman leaned back in his seat and shook his head at Hershel.

The crowd digested his actions and followed the *Not guilty* plea with a wave of boos and heckling that offended James.

"Fatty, fatty, touch the baby, fatty, fatty, fatty," a straw man, skinny enough to hide behind a telephone pole, said as he waved a flag that read, '*Bang*.'

As the man increased his chant, more of the ghouls assisted him, and soon, the entire room ranged with the words *Fatty, Fatty touches the baby*.

The Gentleman stood behind his pulpit, brought his hands together, and joined in with the madness.

"Fatty, fatty touched the baby," The Gentleman said and clapped along with the crowd, which encouraged the loudness to continue.

"Fatty, fatty touched the baby," The Gentleman said with calmer and more controlled tone.

"What?" James asked and looked around at the fellow spectators that sounded the cadence.

Hershel remained in the middle, but his head was no longer down, and his massive fingers went to his face. He began to sob. "I didn't mean to. I didn't want to."

"You didn't mean to? Fatty, Fatty touch Lolita. Fatty, Fatty likes them young." The Gentleman clarified the meaning of the irrational chant.

"No way," James said, and his neutral position on Hershel changed to dislike, the same dislike he'd felt before Hershel revealed he had a dealing with The Gentleman.

"Little, little Sara, Hershel. How old was she when you told her, 'Let's play a game'?" The Gentleman used Hershel's voice. He leaned in more, his bench lowered to Hershel's eye level, and he traveled forward, close enough if Hershel reached out he would be able to slap The Gentleman's sinister face.

"I didn't mean to. She reminded me of a girl I fell in love with when I was thirteen, Gena." Hershel sobbed more. He sounded like a pig with asthma.

"Well, I will give you lil' Miss Sara developed for her age, and she wasn't a virgin but still, Hershel. She didn't even say yes," The Gentleman said, and the crowd mimicked the word 'yes' with a snake's lisp.

"James what did he tell you I made a deal with him for?" The Gentleman rested his chin on his hands.

Non-coherent sounds came from James' lips as he pondered the conversation Hershel and he had on the road.

"James doesn't know." The Gentleman's laugh set off the crowd.

"I'll tell you, James," The Gentleman said and looked at Hershel.

Hershel turned to the crowd and searched.

James knew he was looking for him and he moved his head away from the light and further into the shadows.

"You raped a girl not even sixteen while your wife was in the hospital. Then you asked me to make it go away," The Gentleman said and raised himself over Hershel, towering to the ceiling where the constellations of Pisces, Aries, and Mercury swirled and rotated.

James noticed a battle underway on the opposite of Aphrodite, between Hercules and Mars. "Crazy," James said and gawked at the red segment lines that formed the body of the gods.

"And he says, Not Guilty." The Gentleman drew on his pipe and blew smoke that wrapped around Hershel and lifted him from the floor. "What does the jury think?" The Gentleman said.

Eight men wearing white-as-snow wigs and black orbs appeared.

Hershel lowered his gaze to the men in the jury. Their stand floated off the floor and leveled where Hershel suspended.

"I didn't mean to. I didn't mean to touch her. Please," Hershel pleaded.

The Gentleman rolled his eyes. "I didn't mean to touch my daughter's friend, blah, blah, *bullshit*. You wanted her, you wanted lil' Sara. Those teenage breasts, her fair skin, that red hair. You wanted her bad—look at you. Me describing her is exciting you all ready," The Gentleman said and laughed as he hit his block with his gavel to quiet the unsettled crowd.

"How can you judge me? You have done far worse,' Hershel said through his fingers.

"Great comeback. Good one. But I don't give a *skit*, and I

do it without guilt. I don't make excuses for my actions." Lavender spit spilled from The Gentleman's lips to Hershel's shoulder.

The men in the jury continued their silent deliberation, the same as James remembered they'd done in the jungle.

"This is crazy." James rose from his seat, but as he tiptoed around folks sitting on the benches, The Gentleman's stare drove James back to his original position.

"Good *pojke*," The Gentleman said and moved around to Hershel, who continued to plead with men who didn't acknowledge he existed.

"Well, we don't have all day," The Gentleman said as he tapped his fingers on his gavel and yawned.

The peanut gallery yawned with him, except their yawns were obnoxious and overbearing.

James even found himself yawning, too.

Nodding, as they did when James first saw them in the Jungles of Vietnam, they looked at The Gentleman. Then at the left of the jury bench, a lanky man stood. James guessed he was in his seventies but couldn't be certain from where he sat. The lanky man opened his mouth, and out of it, he said a word that caused the hairs on James' body to stand up and leap from their cuticles.

"Guilty." The man sat back down beside his comrades.

His voice sounded the way James imagined God would sound pissed off. It was deep, and it traveled through James' veins and pumped through his heart, an internal voice calling, *Don't say anything, just sit there, and listen to me.*

"Guilty, guilty," the straw man said and pumped his fist in the air to encourage the others to join in.

As did The Gentleman.

Hershel's body floated down to the floor, and The Gentleman lowered his bench to become level with Hershel.

After he left his throne, The Gentleman walked to Hershel, who trembled.

The toothless hag that had pelted Hershel came behind James, placed her mermaid webbed hands over his eyes, and began to speak in her broken language. "Who dat, me, it's me! Beat me, beat me!" She jumped up and down, and her fingers became blinders on James' eyes, allowing him to see glints of the trail underway.

Pulling her fingers off his face, he swung her over the bench and onto the floor. The commotion he caused led to ghouls heckling him as they did Hershel, who stood in the middle, anticipating The Gentleman who faced him.

But the ghouls and foul beings took their attention off James when The Gentleman shouted, "Guilty!"

The place became a chimpanzee playhouse. The barriers that kept the peanut gallery from running to the bench and tearing away at Hershel's flesh dissipated and floated into the constellations above James.

Mars stood over Hercules, and he slashed his throat and began devouring his body. Bit by bit, he ripped away a limb here and there and placed the mangled piece into his mouth.

When James moved his head down from the hypnotic ceiling, he winced at the sight of the ghouls destroying Hershel's body and shoving pieces of it into their mouths. They even spread his blood over their bodies and took pieces of his skin and bones as keepsakes. They mimicked Mars' actions.

The Gentleman had returned to his bench and smiled at the events that took place in front of him, enjoying Hershel's demise. "We'll meet tomorrow, Hershel." The Gentleman smirked.

During the chaotic scene, James maneuvered around the crowd of things and headed for an exit. He touched the walls— cool and like dry skin. He felt for a knob or trick door and knocked on the wall with his ear to it, listening for a hollow echo.

"Stop," The Gentleman said,

The beasts stopped their carnivorous feast on Hershel's body. They looked up at The Gentleman, and then they rounded to James doing his odd knocking and sliding with his body pressed onto the wall.

They all laughed and pointed at James, then the navy blue

walls that felt like skin became scarlet, and James pulled himself from them.

"Where are you going, James? The fun just started," The Gentleman said and grabbed a scroll from his desk and brought it to his face. "Who's next?"

"Renee Benoit. Renee Benoit." The Gentleman answered his own question and scanned for someone to appear.

Out of a door, which appeared on the side closest to the bench, men the size of bouncers emerged, dragging a large woman. She had scars across her face, deep scars, and gray hair tossed on her head. The dirt on her skin made her look darker than she was, and James could see her ivory skin between the grime.

"Mrs. Benoit. I meant Miss." The Gentleman sneered and brought his pulpit down before her. With the wave of his hand, the peanut gallery returned to their benches, and the barrier he created rematerialized and shimmered in the room lit by the stars above them.

Mars returned to his original position, and Hercules grew back his head and arms.

"You do not scare me, ha!" she said with a heavy Creole accent.

"The white queen—is that what they called you?" The Gentleman asked.

James took a different seat, one close to the door the woman came from.

"What is it today, gluttony? Ugh, ugh, ugh." She clicked the sides of her mouth and turned around to the crowd behind her.

They hissed and gleamed at her blue eyes.

James got a better look at her face as she swung around and lifted her dress to the crowd. Laughing, she turned back to The Gentleman who laughed at her.

"Is that supposed to make them angry? Today, today, Renee, you pay for..." The Gentleman ran his hand over the scroll at his desk. "Being ugly," he said and giggled to the point he almost dismounted from his chair.

Renee became less confident. She stopped her taunting of

the crowd behind her, she slumped her shoulders, and she stared at the floor.

"You steal women's beauty because you are an ugly, ugly woman. Poor Frank Hansberger—you drove him to insanity. All for beauty. The ugly queen with enough odious looks to scare the dead."

The crowd burst into laughter.

Renee turned her face to them, somber and sad, then back to The Gentleman. Her former display of pride was gone.

"The walk of shame!" the straw man said, and The Gentleman hit his gavel to quiet the gallery.

"How do you plead?" The Gentleman said.

The audience became silent, waiting for her response.

"Not guilty," she said and lifted her head up to The Gentleman.

The jury filled with the Torres from before. They deliberated, then within minutes, the tall man stood up, and with the voice of Zeus he said, "Guilty."

"Guilty, guilty," the crowd reiterated.

"Miss Benoit, I sentence you to…" He held his gavel up and held the crowd with the suspense. "The walk of shame."

Once the gavel struck the wooden block, Renee fell to her knees. "No, no, no!"

The men who'd brought her out dragged her to the hole in the wall.

"Noooo."

James flinched at the shrillness of her voice. It became an echo as the doors shut. He leapt from his seat and maneuvered to the door before they closed completely.

"Who's next?" The Gentleman surfed the crowd and zeroed on James, who jetted to the only exit he could find.

"James Greene," The Gentleman said, and the doors reopened.

The bouncers grabbed each of his arms. As they drug him to the center of the room, he caught a glimpse of Renee touching the surface of mirrors on either side of her as she crawled on the floor.

Tugging and kicking as they tossed him in the center, James wrestled from the ground and looked up at his worst nightmare gleaming at him from a skyscraper chair.

"James!" The Gentleman said as if he and James were close friends who hadn't seen one another in years.

James remained silent and tried his best to keep the shakes from becoming obvious to The Gentleman and the gruesome spectators heckling behind him.

"James!" a bird voice squawked.

"James Greene, welcome," The Gentleman said and his seat lowered to James' eye level. It drifted closer.

"Why am I here?"

"You came here. Since you came here, I thought we'd have a little fun." The Gentleman crossed his leg over the other.

"I still have one more door, and then I have to pick the one where it's at," James said and took a step back.

"How is this gonna affect the time?" James asked and stared at the crowd throwing rotted pears that slapped the back of his leg and splattered on the ground.

"This better?" The Gentleman snapped his fingers, and the clock on the wall appeared from the hall. It froze, the small and large hands rewound back to four, and then it disappeared.

"Now James, it says here you are a wife beater." The Gentleman raised the corner of his mouth, and wet spittle escaped his lips.

James looked at his shirt, and a white tank top, stained with blood and dry beer, clothed him. "What?" James pulled at the threads and smelled the horrid odor from the pit stains.

"I felt this fit you better." The Gentleman tossed the scroll.

"Why am I here?" James took another step away from The Gentleman, and the bench hovered closer to him.

"You came here. I didn't tell you to come, and since you are here now, I figured why not give you a sneak peek of what's to come."

"Let me go. Let me go, and I can get what you want."

"So you and the knave can talk it up about me?"

Knave, James thought, and before he could attempt to

define the word, The Gentleman intruded on his thoughts.

"Means male slave, like you and all the other male souls I have. And especially in a literal sense for ole Theodore. He'll come here soon."

The Gentleman gallery chanted, "Theodore."

"You are wasting time getting to know him, James. Wasting time."

"You're wasting time." James found his balls that had fallen to the floor.

"What?" The Gentleman sounded vexed by James' response.

"You are wasting time. Every minute you keep me here, is a time where you don't have what's in that room. Just tell me where it's at. These are games women's play. If you are so amazing as a demon, then why play games? Are you a *humilis*?" James straightened his back and glared at The Gentleman.

"Learn a new word, and think you are some hip kid." The Gentleman blew smoke from his pipe and stood behind his lavish podium. "Let us see the slut for a wife you had, James. Mrs. Greene loved to invite the officers into your home while you deployed and ignored the phone call from your dying father, while Major Bens piled her from the back. But don't worry— Jenni's not home. She's at a sleep over." As the smoke left his lips, it swirled to the wall behind The Gentleman and created a hazy projection.

James lifted his head to it and lowered his eyelids at the sight of his ex-wife doggy-style on his favorite bed, on his favorite Egyptian thread covers, while one of his good friends, Major Bens, gave her the screw of her life.

"Stop," James said and turned his head away from the XXX porn of his wife. But he couldn't drown out the moaning that came from her mouth or the grunting from his. The phone rang, and James knew it was his father reaching out to his wife.

"Stop. No."

When The Gentleman lifted his hands, the images of his wife fast-forwarded to James coming home and greeting her at the door. She with a tissue knotted up in her hand and pretending to care what happened to his father or the hardship he faced in Vietnam, sickened him. It had been easier for James' father to dial his number instead of 911 because he had him on speed dial

"I still remember the day I showed this to you, James. She spent all your money while you were deployed and that didn't send you over. But when you saw that your father had been calling her while she was being pile-driven by Major Bens, you lost it." The Gentleman reenacted the motions of Major Bens as the peanut gallery chimed in.

Lifting his head to The Gentleman, he regained his composure and took a deep breath. "What does it matter if I beat my wife? You still can't get in that room, and you don't even know if it's in there."

"I know where it is." The Gentleman clenched his teeth and cracked his canines. His hand came down with the force of thunder, and the loud clash from the impact silenced the peanut gallery. The projector behind him faded.

James turned around and saw some of the spectators cower away from the invisible barrier that separated them and move closer to the wall.

When lavender blood spilled from The Gentleman's tear ducts, James smiled. Knowing he'd irritated The Gentleman for a second was enough for him to die satisfied.

The Gentleman straightened his bowler hat that had canted on one side of his head while he lashed out at James.

"He said you were a humilis, didn't even have a Providence or something like that. And here I am thinking the guy that calls himself The Gentleman must be a real son-of-a-slut, but he is just a bag of dicks. Can't even get into a room that a slave bewitched," James said.

"Enough!" The Gentleman snarled, and the bones on his face became more rigid and jagged.

James knew when to quit, and he stopped egging-on The Gentleman. He stood, allowing his words to swim in The Gentleman's head and eat at his conscience, if he had one. See-through white chains appeared around his ankles and wrists.

James smirked and dissuaded himself from wrestling with the chains.

"James the wife beater!"

James veered his head to see who called out.

It was the straw man once again.

"Yes, James, how do you plead?" The Gentleman's groomed appearance returned, and he raised his chair to the highest height; almost touching the war that broke loose above them.

"Guilty," James said. He played along with The Gentleman's twisted game and swallowed hard when he saw The Gentleman sit with his mouth open, gazing at him.

"Guilty, I agree." The Gentleman raised his gavel and drove it into the wood block. Pieces of the maple-colored wood speckled from it and rained down on him.

"Guilty!" The Gentleman sneered, and the barrier that held the ghouls back evaporated. They lurched toward James.

He began to back into the bench, away from the gallery, and he wrestled the chains that held his hands bound and his feet together. "No, get away from me."

They came to him, creeping with their hands out, their mouths open, and their teeth showing.

"You need me." James looked up at The Gentleman.

He looked away and kept his face to the stars, gazing upon Mars who massacred the lot of the gods that once swarmed in the heavens.

"You need me!" James said again. "You need me." His voice became raspy and filled with uncertainty and confusion.

Before disappearing from his pulpit, The Gentleman returned a short-lived look at James, smiled and vanished.

"No…" James looked at the evil souls that intended to rip off his face and dismember his manhood.

"No." He swung his arms around and knocked a hand full of them back. After shifting his weight and pivoting off his back foot, James avoided the straw man pulling at his shirt and skirted to the only exit he knew. Banging on the door with his hands clasped, he turned around to monitor the distance between him and the crowd. While banging on the walls and searching for the handle, he shuffled his feet to prevent from falling. The chains tightened and restricted his ability to move freely.

"Let me out, you need me…" As he spun to the other side of the area, his hand caught a hook underneath a lamp and ripped his arm, but not deep enough to require stitches.

"Ah. Not again, not here." Fleeing from the wall, James found himself back in the center of the room, and the ghouls circling him. They began to swarm around him like a whirlwind, tightening their radius with every rotation.

"Get away from me," he said and tripped as the chains between his feet shortened to two inches.

"Get back." As he lifted his arms, his blood projected from his wound and hit the face of the straw man. He recoiled from James and held onto his face. The others in the crowd screamed louder and tightened the circle.

"Kill him!" The straw man protested, still holding his face that oozed and gulped a nasty gray slush.

"Kill the wife beater," he said again.

They all chanted. "Kill the knave's son."

The chants became a single phrase. "Wife Beater. Wife Beater." Their claws reached for James' face. They pulled at his clothes, and they shredded his flesh and separated his arm from his socket. He witnessed his ligaments stretch away and heard the bone crunch and snap from the joint.

"God!" he said and tilted his head up at the damage Mars caused the other gods. As Mars celebrated his victory over the other gods, lavender line segments shaped a different figure behind him. It was the outlining of The Gentleman.

His hands appeared around Mars' neck, and then he snapped it and stared at James.

After he faded from the ceiling, the letters *Mine* connected the dots in the red aura. Then white-hot light flashed and erased the destruction of the ghouls around James.

ACT III:
FIN

CHAPTER 16
THE THIRD DOOR

Still screaming, James lay on the floor in the home, holding his face in his hands. There was silence, and the silence caused him to remove his hands from his face and look around him. No gallery, no pulpit, no jury bench. Only the tacky wallpaper his grandmother presumably picked out, the horrible carpet, and the moldy ceiling above him. He rolled onto his side, lifted himself up, and placed his back against the wall to stand.

Feeling his left arm, he glided his hand up and down it, convincing himself it was there and not in the mouths of the straw man and his gang of horribles. He pulled at his old raggedy white shirt that looked as though he had used it as his oil rag while working on his car, but he liked it better than the wife beater he'd worn at his trial in the attic.

"When did I?" James asked and felt the urge to move to the next room.

Around the corner, Roberto stood, leaning on the wall and looking out of the window. But he was dead? It appeared Roberto and The Gentleman worked against him.

"You, you..." James charged to Roberto before he could ask James how he was. "You let me go up there. You didn't even tell me."

"What?"

"We had a deal," James said and neared Roberto.

"We did?" Roberto said and placed his hand on his chin and looked to the moldy ceiling. "How do I know I could trust you?"

Roberto said and moved from the wall and stood in front of James, then disappeared and reappeared closer to the window.

"We had a fuckin' deal. I am so sick of you fuckin' demons with these riddles and games. You have no idea what he did to me." James pushed Roberto into the wall.

Roberto disappeared then reappeared behind James.

"He made a fool of me, making me as your guide. Not even a humilis would ever be in this position," Roberto said and reached out to James. "You don't know what he did to me." Roberto put his arm around James and flexed his muscles, causing him to choke.

"Let go... of me," James said through his narrowed windpipe.

"When you left for the attic and the other room, you know what he did to me? He left me in a room, where a minute feels like three weeks!" Roberto tightened his hold on James' neck.

Attempting to rip the arm from around his throat, James placed his fingers in between his neck and Roberto's forearm.

"In this room, he drops water on your head, and you can't move. You can't move." Roberto drug James down the hall on his heels.

"I was there for three months. He can change time here James. He changed it to three months for me and placed me in his special room," Roberto said, and his arm that wasn't strangling the life out of James, levitated over James' knife.

James felt the life in him fading, and the darkness created a gradient vision as he looked into the light of the lavender flame of the lamps fixed on the sides of the hall.

No. I'm not dying in this evil ass house.

His eyes popped open. He wedged his hand into his pocket and prevented Roberto from putting his inside. Biting down on Roberto's forearm, James used the last of his strength to free himself. He bit down until he drew blood, but it didn't taste metallic, it tasted like summer. He fell once Roberto released him. After gasping for air and rubbing his neck, he kneeled on the ground and reached for his knife. It was gone.

And Roberto held it in his bloody hand. He advanced on

James.

James popped up and took a fighting stance. The blade slashed the air and cut James' elbow. His blood projected from his arm and sprayed Roberto in the face.

The liquid sizzled Roberto's skin and he backed away from James and patted the blood from his face before it could do more damage.

James rammed Roberto into the wall, pressed his forearm into his throat, and smashed his knee into his side. He may not be able to kill the Gentleman, but he damn sure could do damage to his partner.

"I thought we had a deal!" James allowed his body weight to add to the pressure he placed on Roberto's neck.

"Post mortem," Roberto said as James forced his elbow deeper into his throat.

"What?"

Roberto turned into a red smoke then vanished from the area.

"Face death, James. Face death." Roberto's voice carried.

As the smoke cleared, James backed away from the remnants of Roberto. He returned to searching for his next-door and lurked down the hall, touching the surface of the doors.

"Door 108. Door shit in a box." It would have been easier if he had his bargaining chip still, but Roberto couldn't be trusted. James' muscles became sore as he traveled down the never-ending hall. His body was not used to the amount of walking he did since he entered the house. While the outside of the house showed there were over twenty rooms, the inside was a grand labyrinth with over a hundred.

James stopped and slid to the ground.

"This never ends." He wiped the wetness from his head and tilted his head back, resting on the wall.

"One room after the next, one crazy adventure. One shit my pants ghost shows its face..." As he looked up, he saw the number to one door change from sixty-seven to minus fifteen.

"What," he said and popped up from the floor and ventured to the door.

"Negative fifteen?" He closed his eyes then opened them to reassure he saw it correctly.

"We are meant to be together. You can't escape fate," something called behind him in the hall. It pleaded as it cowered on the floor, holding the black syrup that poured from its eyes.

James' shaky hand jiggled the knob. He forgot how to open a door and rammed his shoulder into the frame. He had overlooked the thing that had chased him in the hall before he fled to the attic.

"Come on." He could smell the decaying breath from the creature as its footsteps drew closer. He dared not look back, for what he'd see would surely freeze him where he stood.

The door finally gave, and James fell inside, he kicked the door closed with his foot, and a piece of fruit fell from his bag as he racked his butt across the splintery floor. Scratches and claw marks textured the surface, and the monster's booming voice rattled the frame.

He stood up, walked backward, and stepped on something soft and juicy.

It was the peach, and he watched as the ground absorbed its blood. The fruit disappeared. The walls turned a reddish brown.

James clenched his bag and sat on the bed. He flopped next to a strange man leaning over with his hands relaxed across his knees. The man's shirt torn and bloody, dirty and moldy, his pants ripped, his shoes littered with holes, he was world war one and two all wrapped up in one nasty explosion.

"So you're him?" the man asked and his eyes remained on the floorboards.

"Yeah, you can say that," James said to him and scooted away, closer to the man, as far as possible from the howls of his reflection beating on the door.

"He can't get in you know," the man said. "That mirror is bewitched for people to see themselves as they are. It's an evil trick demons use to torture you. They'll…They'll." The man paused. "They'll put you in a room and leave you there with just your reflection. For days, weeks months, years. Leave you to be tortured by your own hands."

As the creature banged and buckled and the screws came loose from the inside, James swung his head and watched as the screws dinged on the ground.

"I thought you said he can't get in here?" James stood up from the bed.

"He can't," the man said. James covered his ears when he heard a loud scream. The scream shattered the mirror in the room and turned the stations off and on from the radio.

Silence.

The banging left with the scream.

"Told you," the man said and smiled at James.

"So you got a story for me?" James asked and rubbed his hands on his pants.

"Yeah buddy I do," the man said. "He forced you to come here." He stood and went to the desk. He shoved the books that covered the surface onto the floor, picked up an invisible object, and brought it to his mouth. "Ah," the man said and sat back near James. "You know what door it is yet?"

"I'm thinking ten. I keep hearing ten in each story," James said.

"Stop the shenanigans, O'Malley."

"What?"

"It's not." The man scratched his shallow beard.

James slammed his bag on the ground, and a peach fell from the opening. As he stomped on the loose boards in the room, he smashed the peach with his foot. "I give up. I have no idea. If it ain't ten, then well, what is it?"

"I'll tell you," the man said and his words calmed James.

Sitting next to him, James took a deep breath. "Name's—"

"James, I know. I'm Bill Lee, *The Spaceman*," he said.

James shook his hand and noticed all the burn marks and cuts that lay on the guy's arm. He was awfully skinny to be *The Spaceman* and three inches too short.

"The pitcher for the Expose who used to be on Boston?" James narrowed his eyes. *I saw the game with the Spaceman the other day, this isn't him? What's this guy's deal?*

The Spaceman offered James his right hand to shake. "In

the flesh, but don't tell anyone else here. I don't like the attention."

James shook his hand.

The man stood up from the bed, walked to the table, and tapped on the surface as if it were a piano.

"Right…," James said and widened his eyelids.

"I have to say I'm the sanest person in this house," *The Spaceman* said and slid his fingers across the table.

"So, so how does this all work? How'd you get trapped in a place he can't enter?"

"He can enter all the rooms, all except one," *the Spaceman* said.

"Why?"

"Your grandfather cursed it with, some lame assed thing called love."

"So he knew I'd come here?"

"Glory, glory is the sound of the wind." *The Spaceman* turned around to James. "Something I've been working on. What you think?"

James winced and became confused by the question. "Think about what?"

"The arrangement. Here, I'll play some more of it for you." *The Spaceman* turned around to the table and continued smashing his fingers into the wooden top.

But James only heard the tapping noises of the man's fingers making contact with the table and his annoying voice replicating the intonation of a singer in the big band era.

"How long he have you?" James asked as he tried to avoid the question from *The Spaceman*.

"Thirteen months, would you believe that? Thirteen of the worst months of my life, and it wasn't worth it. I would have been better off juicing than taking a deal with him."

"I don't want that life," James said.

"Yeah? Neither did I, but here we are. Two regular guys who sold their souls without knowing, because that fucker placed it in his fine print. We are here today because we were taken advantage of with his sick, sick games. He has a best of forty policy. Did you know that?"

The colors from outside became louder and the smell of lilac seeped through the cracks of the room.

"A best of shit-me-sideways forty. He might give you two or three for good spirits, but he wins them all, and when you reach those forty games, oh, he will make sure your soul's on the betting table," said *The Spaceman*.

This dude's only been here for thirteen months, and he thinks he is The Spaceman.

"I needed you, darling." T*he Spaceman* stopped tapping the table. "Wait, I didn't hit that right." He cleared his throat. "I need you, darling. There, that's right."

As *The Spaceman* continued to banter on about pitching for Boston, in-between his songs, James looked at the floor and noticed a dark red color appear where he smashed the fruit.

Squinting his eyes to focus and zero-in on the change, he studied the color of the wood nearest the door and compared the image to the ones closest to the window. Back and forth he looked. He looked at his shoe and lifted his heel. Then he reached in his bag. "Huh."

He glanced back at his odd companion. "So about this story you have to tell me?"

"Oh, yes." *The Spaceman* stopped his ballet and turned to James. "He told me to tell you a story about a guy I knew," *The Spaceman* said and rubbed his forehead.

"Unfortunate what happened to him. His name was Andrew Carter. Real smart lad. But something happened to him. That's the story he told me to tell you." *The Spaceman* stood up from the table and sat near James.

As he told the story in third person, James observed the liquid on the ground forming together. It spelled out: *You got it in the bag, James.*

CHAPTER 17
NOTYAHS

The Southern Iraq sun burned Andrew's skin as he probed the site outlined with rope and sticks, paper and notes. The desert's blood became his second skin. The wind scraped its sandpaper across his face, and the brightness of the sun left spots in his vision. He stood over the valley of Baten El Ghoul in the Ancient city of Erikidus—a great Sumerian city filled with legend, history, and myth—and looked at the progress his team had made in the last couple of weeks. Now known as Tell Abu Shahrain, its past echoed in the rocks and the air. It held onto your soul and struck a chord with your senses.

Kurds, hired locally, and some pashtunwalis hired from Afghanistan helped with the excavation that his former professor, Vernon Maximillian—whom he called Max—had invited him to.

"We did it, I am so glad you could come out here," Max said to Andrew and shook his hand with as much excitement as a kid who'd fallen head-first into the ball pit at Chucky Cheese.

"You have no idea how happy I was, honored, the Zoroaster's worship site near the mountains. That is a find. How'd you know it would be out here?" Andrew asked him.

"We are using a new spectral graphics, and this ground-penetrating device the Army uses to measure disturbance in the earth. Oh, and I can't lie, someone tipped us," he said and tapped his visor.

"Welcome to 1980," Andrew said to Max, who laughed

with him.

As the two men walked around the site, they shook the hands of the locals who helped with the work.

"Manana," Max said and placed one hand over his heart.

"That's not Arabic. Is that Farsi? Urdu?" Andrew questioned and drank water from his canteen. It fell on his wet chest and his already soaked shirt.

"Oh, this fine lad's from Afghanistan, ah, I want to say Kandahar. Is that right?"

"Yes Mister Vernon," the boy, Agha Jon said and lifted himself from the hole.

"He came with me to help with the dig, and he is an intern for my company in England."

"Is that so? Well nice to meet you…" Andrew held his hand out, and Agha took it.

"Agha Jon," Agha said to Andrew and shook his hand.

After the salutations, Andrew patted his face with a wet rag, removing the dirty sweat.

"Come, to the tent. We must speak in private about something." Max guided Andrew away from the site "Agha, join me later." Max patted Agha's shoulder.

Raising his eyebrow, Andrew shook his head and turned away from them. Max told him the year prior he wasn't taking apprentices. He'd lied.

"*As salaam alaykum*," Agha said.

"*Wa alaykum as salaam*," Andrew said as he nodded and waved in an informal manner.

After they walked across the dig site to the location of their tents, Max looked around, back at Andrew, and then opened his temporary home. Swatting his hand against flies, the size of a quarter, Andrew hurried into the tent behind Max.

"I like the Ritz Carlton you got here," Andrew said and examined some of the artifacts that sat on the table.

"It is the best I can do with this. How is your tent? Any better?" Max asked while he rummaged through his desk drawer.

"Not as big. When'd you fly back here, anyway? I started

assuming you weren't coming back or were gonna come back and tell the others we were out of money." Andrew scooted the items out of the way and leaned on the table.

"Well, I was negotiating funding, and I needed to ensure all the loose strings were tied for something I am going to do in D.C."

"Hey, you mind if I take back something to show my students, or, if it's cool with you, if I take these photos back I took?" Holding onto a clay pot, Andrew blew sand from around the broken edges of the artifact and fixed his square frames that fogged and slid down his face.

"You can take two things. I'll write them off as donations, and you can keep the photos. Send me copies after you develop them."

Max reached for a silver pot that shimmered against the orange and red light of the sunset bleeding through the tent. After he poured a steaming cup for Andrew, he poured one for himself. "Chai tea, it is very tasty. Not as great as the ole Earl Gray but tasty just the same." Max sipped the tea from his silver-plated cup and offered Andrew a seat across from him.

"So, what's got you all secretive and nervous?" Andrew sipped the tea, but allowed most of it to backwash into the cup.

"I need a huge favor from you, one that I have pondered these last few months," Max said. "I need you to take something back to the States. Something I don't want to get into the wrong hands." He reached under the desk, accessing a trick drawer. He pulled a covenant-sized book from the cryptic spot. Max laid it down and removed it from the deerskin casing.

"I am putting on the exhibit next Sunday in D.C. I have been planning it and getting the funding these last few months," Max said as he felt the surface of the book's cover.

Setting the cup on the table, Andrew stood and got a closer view of the book. "What, no?" Andrew took off his glasses.

"Yes, the book Zoroaster wrote himself. I need for you to sneak this back to the States and keep it there for me until I am able to find a place for it in England."

"Why...why me? Can't you sneak it back?" Andrew fell

into his seat.

"If I do, I will have to tag it and put it in the inventory, so giving it to you means it never existed to England." Max slid the book to him.

Touching the leather surface, Andrew felt the brown engraving of Palo-Samaritan symbols. "Stop the shenanigans, O'Malley," he said.

But as he opened the heavy cover, Max sprung from his seat, despite his old age. "You mustn't open it. I am not religious, but something about this book tells me what we find, we may not be prepared for. Someone gave me a tip of where to dig, and they stressed, no matter what, don't open it." After smacking Andrew's hand like a bad toddler, he slumped back into his chair

Andrew closed the book.

"Use that case to keep it safe from the elements, and put it in a messenger bag. No one will know what you have there," Max pointed, "is priceless. They will just assume you are a professor with 'his' books." Max tossed a leather case his way.

Lifting the moleskin cover, Andrew opened it up, slid the book inside, and wrapped the leather threading around the book.

"My plane leaves tomorrow, after we finish clearing out the dig. Are you staying here?" Andrew asked him as he stood up from his seat, tapping the book.

"No, I leave tonight." Max put down his tea. "Oh, and will you be able to build this for me by the end of next week?" He handed Andrew a crude drawing of a peacock with seven feathers.

"Ten days is pushing it, but yeah, I can. Why the rush?" Andrew folded the paper and put it in his pocket.

"It just feels right," Max said and touched a green jewel on his desk.

"Good night," Andrew said and walked out of the tent. As he left for his own, he lifted his shirt and rubbed the tender spots of sunburn he'd developed that scarred his Egyptian tattoos of pharaohs, cats, and pyramids. On his forearm, he had tattoos of passages of Egyptian hieroglyphs, which wrapped around his arm.

The next day, Andrew took a plane to the Qatar Airport, which connected to the U.S. When he landed, he took a taxicab to his house in Arlington County, Virginia.

Three days after Andrew returned from Iraq, he'd begun the project for Max and made great progress. He welded most of the feathers and left the thing to cool until Monday. While putting piece after piece on the statue, Andrew became light headed and took breaks in between his sculpting. He'd done projects bigger than this and never experienced the light-headedness before.

***

Monday night, Andrew went to the university's engineering department and touched the almost finished sculpture. When his eyes fell on a yellow gem rammed into a spot on the feathers, he stopped welding the beard. As he tugged at the object, he was unable to pull it from the hole.

"I must have put that there yesterday," he reasoned with himself and put on his mask that reflected the light from the torch as he polished the surface. Before he sprayed another coat over the figure with golden spray paint, he applied the weld to the feathers again and let the bird cool.

Working into the night, he stopped painting the body after his watch beeped at eleven. He removed the mask and wiped the sweat from his face.

"Wow, already. Well, I will start on this tomorrow," he said and changed back into his clothes.

Walking to the exit, the windows opened and whispers in babel multiplied. Once Andrew opened the door, the windows slammed shut.

"Hello?" Andrew called.

A man appeared at the door with his hands folded across his body. "Hello."

As the stranger spoke, something red glimmered from his neck, blinding Andrew. After fixing the welding mask to his face to shield the light out, he looked up the empty space of the hall.

"What kind of weed did Jake give me? Must have been because of the heat." He took off the mask and left for the train.

Andrew stood at his apartment door thinking of all the excuses he could use on his wife. She loved going out on Sundays and doing things. He liked them, but this Sunday Max was holding his exhibit. He was tired of sleeping on the couch and his sore neck was testament to that. "Becca, I love you and...no... No. How's Paris sound next summer? I guess I can't lie this time." He turned the knob on the door.

"Honey?" he said as he entered the apartment. Parting the dark room, he walked to the kitchen counter and saw an invitation to a catwalk gala at the downtown museum lying on the table. "That looks interesting."

"What does?" his wife asked coming out of the room. She held pillows and covers in her hand.

"This." He held up the paper.

"Oh, that. I am doing a shoot for an exhibit that is opening Sunday. We are doing cultures of the world," She said to him and kissed his cheek, then pulled back and lifted one eyebrow.

"What?" he asked. His eyes were half-open.

"You smell, bad," she said and went into the kitchen.

Andrew sniffed his shirt and rubbed his face. "I've been trying to catch up on the thing Max wanted done by Sunday."

"So you gonna miss my show?" she asked and her playful face turned serious.

"That is impossible. I think this is the same exhibit that Professor Max is hosting."

She tossed the pillow and covers to Andrew and treaded back to the bedroom.

"Honey..." Andrew said then walked to the coach with his head down.

"You make this, and you get back in the bed. Goodnight," she said and blew a kiss to Andrew. After the bedroom door closed, he slumped on the sofa and turned on the television.

No excuse needed. He wouldn't be sleeping on the couch another week.

***

Tuesday, he didn't have classes, and this allowed him to make up some much-needed time on the structure.

Andrew worked hard on it most of the day and stopped anchoring the feathers on the statue, when he noticed a yellow ruby in the hole. He hadn't placed it there, and no one besides him and the engineering director, Professor Clyde, knew he was down there.

"This isn't right…" He lifted his mask and rubbed the ruby cemented into a hole he hadn't constructed.

"Maybe I did it yesterday. I was really tired." He slapped the mask back over his face and continued welding the metal together.

After leaving the university, he headed home and arrived to an empty house.

"Guess Becca's got another shoot," he said as he grabbed a beer from the fridge. The folder he had forgotten about lay on the table near the couch. He picked it up, parsed through the originals, and fell onto the couch. The Sumerian letters turned into Roman text, which scrambled on the paper.

"No, that can't be right." He closed the folder and opened it again. The Sumerian letters returned.

"This is crazy," he said, slipped them back, and as he walked to the bathroom, he lost control of his legs. The ceiling spun above his head, and he became nauseous. He bit back the urge to vomit onto the wooden tile he and his wife had installed that spring. However, the urge overtook him, and the salty liquid that came before the vomit flooded his mouth and drizzled down his face. He sprinted to the bathroom and released the acidic chunks into the toilet.

***

It wasn't until Thursday that Andrew continued fixing the statue. The nauseous feeling he experienced on Tuesday hit him hard on Wednesday, and he canceled his class because of it. Later on Wednesday, Andrew went to Jake's to drag from a joint to ease his nausea, and to go over his ideas of what the documents meant.

Jake created a program that looked at text and found connections between two languages. They found connections with some of the letters to Palo Hebrew, but not enough to translate it to English. Jake suggested asking his father to help with it, and the duo planned a trip to the Jewish side of town the next day.

To add to the stress of completing the structure and translating the documents, Andrew had to deal with Marcus, the head of the history and artifacts department, stealing and running off with the complete Zoroaster book. He trusted it to Marcus for him to keep safe while they prepared for the exhibit, now he felt he let Max down. No wonder he didn't choose him as an apprentice. He was never the dependable type.

The other thing that bothered Andrew was that Marcus and Max wore the same type of necklace around their necks. Although Marcus' jewel was purple, his jewel had similar engravings and artistry to the one Max wore.

On Thursday, Andrew headed for Jake's house, but not before stopping at the local bakery.

"Thanks, John, keep the change," he said to the man behind the counter.

"I love these things!" he said and stopped while eating a steak hoagie. While he ate away at the sandwich, blood splattered on his face. At his feet lay a girl, her arms twisted in multiple directions, and her bloodshot eyes open.

Cars honked, and women screamed and pointed at her body.

Andrew dropped his hoagie. On her hands, he observed six symbols burned into her skin.

The police arrived at the scene, roped the area off with yellow tape, and blockaded the public from seeing the body.

During questioning, Andrew told them all he knew. He'd bought a hoagie. He was eating, girl went splat, and he dropped his sandwich, end of story. There was nothing else to tell.

After he left the stomach-turning scene, he met with Jake.

They ventured to the Jewish side of town, where Jake's father studied.

"So, she just fell?" Jake asked.

"Yes. She just went, splat like a goddamn bug. You know, I think she was smiling," he said.

"I mean she just—" Jake created the motions of the girl falling with his body.

"Enough about it. I don't want to lose more of my food. So your dad is like the high Rabbi in D.C.?"

"Yeah, Torah Rabbi," Jake said.

"Rad," Andrew said to him.

Inside the Jewish sector, they took in the smells of Naan and hummus. They listened to the sounds of Yiddish, Hebrew, and broken English spoken by the old and young. Some signs in the downtown market, written in Hebrew and English, sat close to the subway, and they traveled along the paved sidewalks toward the center of the town, where the Synagogue was. It had seven candles engraved in the center of the building, and the Star of David sat atop the structure.

Andrew pushed open the entrance. They walked into the heavenly opening where four men sat in a circle near a large platform. Once they came within a few feet of them, an older man, with a long curly beard, wearing glasses and a kippah, stood up and kissed Jake on the cheeks.

"*Shalom*, my boy," he said and held his hand.

"*Mamosh Tov*," Jake said, and he embraced his father.

"Andrew, this is my father..."

"Call me Michael," the Rabbi said as he shook Andrew's hand. "Come, come. Jake told me you wanted me to translate something. Ichabod will you join us?"

A smaller man with long curly payots on the sides of his face stood from his chair and skated to them. Around his neck was a ruby jewel that the sun reflected from and blinded Andrew as he watched Ichabod come near them. While beaming at Andrew, Ichabod crossed him and walked alongside Michael. Michael walked them to an office located in the back of the synagogue. The spacious office contained volumes after volume of encyclopedias, religious books, and literary works from the Greeks to the Roman Philosophers.

"Have a seat," Michael said and guided them to a desk with a large lamp in the middle.

"So my son, what am I to look at."

"These," Andrew revealed the copies of translations they created the previous day. Lowering his glasses to his nose, Michael squinted at the letters, pulled the paper in, and pushed it further away from his face as he read the words.

"This says, *tbya ly shb'e mh'erb, az any t'elh shvb*—Bring me seven from Eve, so I shall rise again," he read and scrunched his eyebrows.

"And something about a traitor." Andrew put his hand on a line of translations he and Jake had deciphered.

"Ichabod, Ichabod, take a look." Michael handed the paper to Ichabod.

"Where's this come from?" Ichabod asked.

"This." Andrew handed him the copy from the book.

Ichabod's face became pale, and he tossed the paper on the desk, then he chanted in Hebrew and rocked back and forth, holding his Star of David.

Jake turned to his father. "Dad, what's wrong?"

"What is it, Ichabod?" Michael asked and placed his hand on his shoulder.

"Those are the words of the evil, the words of Ta'us Melek. Don't read any more. Don't look at the face of the book, don't turn the pages, and don't touch its surface. It is calling for a sacrifice of seven, from Eve," Ichabod said to them.

"Why? What does that mean? I know the Yezedis are the outcast of the sematic religions, but that doesn't mean their book is evil." Andrew looked at the Rabi with his arms folded.

"Tell me, what area of archeology do you study?" Michael asked.

Ichabod continued to hyperventilate, and Andrew saw his eyes beam at the paper that he held in his hand. He slid it back in the folder.

"Egyptian, and some Judah, some Hindu, but this is all new

to me. Why?"

"Come, let me tell you a story of Zoroaster," Michael said and took the two to the table in the room.

Sitting at the study, Andrew and Jake leaned in and listened to the deepness in Michael's voice as he began the tale. "They believe we are the spawn of Eve, and the Yezedi are from Adam and not Eve."

"Sick," Jake said.

"They believe in the seven pillars of the peacock, seven colors, and that Ta'us Melek is the Almighty Angel," he said and sipped the tea he made for them.

"I heard Professor talking about that, but I mean some things are legends and made up. You can't believe everything you hear or read," Andrew said and sat back in his chair.

Andrew and Jake left the synagogue with the new information about the papers they had that caused more confusion than clarity.

Seven from Eve. What did it all mean? When Andrew thought he had it figured out, Michael provided him with information that sent him back to the drawing board. His original assumptions about the text were that they were ancient burial rituals and calls to prayer. Maybe even recipes for wine but nothing about human sacrifice.

***

After taking a nap, Andrew went to the university and worked on the peacock for most of the night. While he installed brand new lights on the figure, he stopped when he saw an additional gem in the fourth feather of the peacock.

"Here is the yellow one, then the orange...purple?" Andrew took off his protective eyewear. "This was not here." He reached for the gem that appeared loose and shook and wiggled it, but before his eyes, the gem melded with the brass feathers.

"Someone has to be fucking with me," he said and turned on the power to the lights. Along with the Christmas lights, the yellow, red, purple, and orange gems shot out light like a laser and bounced off every shiny object in the room.

"Wow."

The lights danced on the mirrored surfaces and sparkled on the brass of the gold painted peacock. "Damn it, no prism. Back to the drawing board," he said after he powered it down. The gems he didn't install powered down, too.

Andrew packed up and headed out the door, but stopped and turned to his creation in the corner of the shop. "So surreal," he said and turned the light off and locked the lab. The gems turned on, and a gust of wind flew in the room.

Walking into the dark hall, Andrew turned to Max who walked in a trance state to the door of the shop.

"Ma-max, what are you doing here?" he asked.

"I, I don't know," Max said, bewildered and sweaty. He held on to his green necklace.

Andrew walked him to the train station and the two sat waiting for its arrival.

"What's the last thing you remember?"

"I was in the hotel drinking coffee, watching TV. There was a large gust and the window opened, and well then, I saw your face." Max wiped his face and looked at Andrew.

"I think I am stressed because of the show, I am so stressed. I did things too fast. I should have waited. Longer! I only planned this the last two months, before we got back and this month. It's too soon." Vernon messed with his hair and looked to Andrew for an answer.

"We all get nervous. Hell I don't know how great the peacock's gonna look. Go back to the hotel and get some sleep and tomorrow when you wake up, remember you are Professor Maximillian, one who has had more discoveries of ancient civilizations than any archeologist alive," Andrew said and comforted him until the train arrived.

***

Andrew came home to the phone ringing. Marcus was on the other end of the line. He sounded panicked and frightened.

Andrew agreed to meet him in the local café not far from his house early in the morning.

In the cool morning breeze, Andrew sat in the café twirling the butter knife in his hand and checking the time. It was now nine thirty, and Marcus hadn't shown.

"Something isn't right," he said and left the café.

He took the train to a suburb part of Virginia, twenty minutes south of DC. He went to a stylish townhome toward the back of the property. As he came to door 1010, he stopped before an open door.

After stepping back and looking around, he moved forward, pushed the door open, and called to Marcus.

No answer.

Papers swarmed and scattered around him, and he pushed them aside.

"Marcus," he called, and his voice wavered when he saw a trail of blood near the window. Following it led him to the bathroom, and as he opened the door, he pulled back at the sight of a scarlet red handprint on the door. After turning on the lights, he covered his mouth. A man sat against the tub, wearing only his underwear. Andrew vomited in the sink.

While over the sink ridding his stomach of his breakfast and dinner, blood hit his ear, and above his head, he glared at the word *Notyahs*.

On top of Marcus' head were engravings similar to the letters from the book. The necklace around his neck hung, without the emblem.

"My God, my God, Marcus, what have you done?" Andrew picked himself off the bloody floor. When he rushed to the phone, he stopped turning the dials after he saw a note on the desk.

I regret what I have done. I killed those women, and for that, I am sorry. I couldn't take the pain and decided that death was the only option.

Andrew swallowed and held back his tears. He placed the paper back on the table and continued dialing the police.

They arrived to the mess of it all and sectioned off the apartment. Andrew sat on the couch, staring at the bathroom, watching the paramedics haul away Marcus' body in a black plastic bag.

"Hey, hey, I saw you when that woman jumped," a young detective said and sat next to Andrew on the couch.

"Yea, that's me." Andrew didn't make eye contact with the officer.

"I'm afraid to say, we need your statement."

"Okay, hey, there's one thing I would like to see, the body of the girl from the other day," Andrew asked.

"You can't see the body," the man said and raised his eyebrow.

"I'm an archeologist, I have a PHD, and I can do autopsies. Plus, I might be able to help with the engravings on the body. I-I recognize them." Andrew stood up from the couch.

The paramedics rolled Marcus' body out of the home through the back door.

"Okay, meet me at the hospital around noon," the officer said to him and handed him a witness form.

***

Andrew made it a habit to go to the university and work on the structure after six each night. Entering the engineering department, he dropped his equipment when he saw a new ruby welded in the feathers of the peacock: indigo.

"What the hell?" Andrew scratched his head. He went to the structure and examined the jewels. He touched the red-crusted substance dried on the indigo jewel and flinched. After rubbing it between his fingers, he placed his hands to his nose.

"Gross," he said and wiped it on his pants. Snapping a Polaroid of the structure, he waved the white surface against the air and walked around the room. The sound of someone in the hall called his attention, and he dropped the picture and grabbed a board that sat against the wall.

He crept into the dark. "Who the hell's there?"

An older man in all black with a salt and pepper beard rushed past him, pushing his elbow into Andrew's stomach. He fell on the floor, holding his stomach and catching his breath. He yelled at the man, but it was too late, he'd left the building.

***

The next morning, Andrew turned on the radio and chugged orange juice from the carton.

"Another woman found dead with unknown markings the other day near an abandoned warehouse. Police are looking for an ID on the woman and would not commit whether they were connected to serial killer, Marcus Vicenti, whom police found dead in his home on Friday. They need help from anyone who may have information on the perpetrator," a woman announced over the radio.

As promised, Andrew left his home and met up with Jake. They accompanied Max and Agha to help the detectives identify the markings on the woman killed, presumably by Marcus. With the newfound information he obtained from the corpse he and Jake examined, he decided to pay Jake's father a visit.

Buried in his study when they arrived, Jake's dad lifted his head behind his book as they entered.

"Dad, we need your help," Jake said

Andrew pulled out the pages from the translations. "We used this key to figure out what was on their hands, but we only got *Melk Mikcal* and *Cebral* and *Daus*."

"Melk? Mikcal?"

"Sounds like Melek and Michael. What was the other one?"

"Cebral, Kebral, Gabrerial?" Andrew shrugged.

"So if we are wrong about the C's and G's what if we were wrong about the D's?"

"Ta'us Melek, ugh."

"How much have you translated?"

"Almost all of it."

Michael spun around on this desk and looked at some of his papers. He took the paper with the key and the missing pages from Andrew, and the three of them modified the translations with their new discoveries.

"The seven angels and Ta'us Melek shall raise again?" Michael said and removed his glasses. "We have been looking at the wrong things. Grab me the New Testament."

Jake put the book on his desk, and his father flipped to Revelations.

"Wait why do you have this? I don't -"

Jake's father raised his hand and used his other to flip through the Bible.

"I am a Theologist. I read them all." He smiled at Andrew. Pointing to the words, Michael read the passage under the lamp's light. Jake and Andrew came closer to him.

"The mystery of the seven stars that you saw in my right hand and of the seven golden lampstands is this: The seven stars are the angels of the seven churches, and the seven lampstands are the seven churches." Michael looked up to them. "Ta'us Melek is another name for Djinn, who the Christians call Satan. This is to revive an evil spirit. Someone is trying to summon a demon," Michael said and sat in his chair. "This is scary stuff. I have to call the other Rabbis. This is not to be taken lightly."

Andrew squinted at a man's face as it passed by the blinders of the study, then it vanished thereafter. He walked to the door, opened it, and scanned the area. He saw no one. "Hey Mike, is anyone here today besides you and us?" He continued to scan the perimeter.

"No, just me. Why?"

"Thought I saw your friend Rabbi Ichabod," he said and closed the door.

Later that day, Andrew took Jake to the engineering department to discuss the events that had taken place the previous nights.

"Okay look—there on the floor is the picture I took yesterday, and look at the peacock. Five jewels." Andrew pointed.

Jake stopped over the picture on the ground and scanned the photo. "Who was in the room with you?"

"No one. Let me see," he said and snatched it from Jake.

"What the hell," he said and covered his mouth. He paced the room and stared down at the object. In the corner near the statue, stood a man illuminated with a light blue aura. Andrew was unable to identify his complexion; it seemed to reflect all colors at once and no colors at all.

"Every time someone dies, there is another jewel. This shit is freaking me out big time. And this," Andrew flicked the picture and turned to Jake, "There was no one there when I worked on the damn thing."

"It looks like a rainbow to me. You're just missing green and blue," Jake said. Andrew looked at his creation as if someone else's hands constructed and molded it. He pushed it down and kicked it. Grabbing his foot, he hobbled and danced the pain away.

"I don't think that was a good idea, but it was funny." Jake stood with his hand on his head, laughing at Andrew.

The room went cold.

"You turn the a/c down?" Jake asked and rubbed his arms with goose bumps.

"No I don't have the controls to do that, Jake," Andrew said as his teeth chattered. Their breathing produced white fog.

"We should get out of here, I'll destroy this tomorrow, bring blow torch in hand," Andrew said, and as he went to lock the door, he saw the peacock sitting up as it was before he knocked it down.

"Stop the Shenanigans O'Malley," Andrew said.

"What?" Jake peeked through the windows on the door to the lab and stepped back from the door.

"Let's go," Andrew said, and they continued out of the university and away to his home.

***

Andrew woke in the middle of the night with the feeling of a hangover. Since his wife went on a trip to Baltimore, he got to sleep in his bed that night. He walked to the sink, looked in the mirror, and saw the word *Shayton* on his bathroom wall.

"What the fuck?" he said and hugged the sink. He ran to his phone and dialed the cops.

"Yes, yes, someone has broken into my home and vandalized my bathroom. They wrote *Shayton* on the wall in red marker, maybe, I'm not sure," he said.

"The police are on their way," the operator said

Andrew hung up the phone. To pass the time, he sat on the couch looking at the translations and the new evidence from the corpse.

The cops arrived, and he tossed the folder to the side and opened the door. Five or so men came to his door.

After searching his home, they discovered large foot prints trailing to the open window then vanishing. The police searched outside and inside his apartment for the person that broke into his apartment.

"We need your statement, sir. We looked for the guy, but the trail went cold. Do you know if anything is missing?"

"No." Andrew shook his head and kept his gaze on the trail of footsteps at his window. "I just wish whoever is playing this joke on me comes out and says gotcha, cause I can't take this anymore."

"So you said it said *Shayton*? We see *N-o-t-yahs* on the wall."

Andrew ran into the bathroom to confirm. "I could have sworn," he said and looked into his mirror. In the reflection of the mirror, the words reflected Shayton.

The cop watched his eyes. "I see," he said and called for more help with the area.

"This, this was the same thing I saw in Marcus' place. Shayton...Shayton?" Andrew asked and walked into his living room.

"Shayton? Sataan? Satan!" he said eyes wide. "Satan," he whispered.

His wife returned home from her trip to Baltimore before midnight, and Andrew sat in the bathroom scrubbing the words from the wall and painting over what remained. The bag in her hand dropped to the floor when she got to the entrance of the bedroom.

"Not bad, can barely see it," Andrew said and scrubbed harder.

"See what?" she said as she continued walking into the room.

"Some creep broke into our house and wrote *Shayton* on the wall. Satan is what I think it means."

"Oh my goodness," she said and placed her hands over her mouth. Andrew dropped his scrubbers and walked to her.

"Did they take anything?" she said. She stretched her eyes and rubbed Andrew's arm.

"No, just vandalized the wall. They think it may be an accomplice of Marcus or a copycat killer that came here last night." Andrew held onto her.

"I can't believe it," she said. He felt her heart beat. She wasn't here when it happened, yet she appeared more frazzled than he was.

"Should I not do the show today?" she asked and looked into his eyes.

"No, you should go."

After nodding her head, she picked up the bag she dropped by the door. Walking into the bathroom, Andrew dumped his bucket into the toilet. Reddish white liquid that smelled like dish detergent, spilled into the bowel.

"Flush," he said and pulled the lever.

"Promise you'll be there?" she asked.

"I promise," he said over his shoulder. Then he smacked the palm of his hand on his forehead.

"Oh, honey, I'm gonna leave and go down to the university." As Andrew walked into the room, his wife removed a rectangle purple box and hid it under the pillow.

"At this time?" she asked. "What if they come back?" she asked and looked at the window in the living room as if expecting a lunatic to jump through the curtains.

"There's a cop walking around, waiting for the guy to come back," Andrew said and kissed her forehead.

"I have to destroy what I created for Max's presentation and break the bad news to him."

"Why are you destroying it?" she said and undressed.

"Because the things freaks me the hell out, and someone has been fucking with me since I started building the damn thing."

"I think you are stressed. I'm sorry I made you sleep on the coach this past week. Tonight you can sleep in here *with* me in it." She laughed and patted the mattress.

"That sounds like a plan. And honey, call this number if something happens again. It goes straight to the detective's office, which means you won't have to wait thirty minutes for the cops to arrive. Plus, the guy patrolling outside can come in immediately."

After giving her the paper, Andrew kissed his wife and went to the university with his blowtorch and welding equipment in his Red Sox bag.

As he walked down the dark hall to the engineering lab, he shielded his face from the flames that battered the door. Andrew heard pops and zings from the room. After dropping his equipment on the ground, he sped inside.

"*Max!*" He ran to him.

Walking with his hand around his necklace, *Max*'s eyes fixated on the colors that danced and swirled around the structure. He snapped off the jewel around his neck.

Andrew skidded away from a frightening looking man who stood in the corner. He had sky blue eyes and long thick hair. The same as the one from his picture. The man kept his chin pressed in his chest and brought his gaze to Andrew. He gave Andrew a skin-peeling smile. With tattoos of the world racing and circling around his body, Andrew could not figure out the skin tone of the man. Andrew's feet cemented to the floor, and he remained watching Max near the object that sparked and blazed.

"So wonderful," Max said.

"No." Andrew reached out to Max, but his feet stayed pressed into the ground.

After Max slid the green jewel in the slot on the sixth feather, a gray aura ignited around it, and the same aura formed into a glove that scooped up his body.

The structure developed brass fingers and wrapped them around the jewel. After the jewel melded with the statue, a bright light beamed from it and loud buzzing sounds shook the foundation of the room. With his hands over his ears, Andrew dropped to the ground, and then laid down completely.

Andrew observed from his slanted view as an older man dismounted the statue and walked to the horrible man with the unknown skin tone. He watched until the two were no longer in the shop.

When he rose to an unconscious Max laying on the floor, he slid across the pavement and tapped on Max's face

"Max, Max hang in there," he said and sat up from the ground. He ran to the pay phone in the hall and dialed 911.

When the police arrived, the detective from the other crime scenes showed up and approached Andrew.

"What did you tell me the other day? Two's a coincidence and three's a pattern. You are a pattern, Andrew." The detective laughed.

"Don't get me started," he said and wiped the blood from his nose.

"So who stole the statue or peacock?"

"I don't know. This burly, large, son of bitch, tattoos, rings, long hair, blue eyes, the works. A real scary fucker," Andrew said and held his head back.

"So I am looking for a linebacker or a Minotaur?"

Andrew smacked his gums at the officer's comments. "It's not funny. Shit, maybe I hit my head hard when I fell." Andrew leveled with the officer.

"Yeah, I think it is just some sick cocksucker pulling pranks before this guy's exhibit. People try to emulate folklore or do crazy things to protest or get your attention when these things come to town. So you said someone wrote Satan on your walls last night?" the officer said and curled the sides of his mouth up.

"Could you take it a little seriously?"

"I'm sorry, really I am. Just let me know if there are any goats being killed." He slapped Andrew's arm.

Andrew looked away. "Is he going to be okay?" He pointed to Max as the paramedics carried him out of the room.

"Yeah. Small concussion is all, bruised rib. Won't be able to put on the show though. The medics have to see to you outside."

* * *

Andrew's feet dangled from the back of the ambulance as the medic treated the cuts on his forehead and tended to his bloody nose. When they finished, he joined Max before they placed him in the back of the vehicle. Opening his eyes, Max looked around, bewildered.

"What, what happened? Andrew?" he said and grabbed his hand.

"The thing around your neck—you put it in the statue I had, and the thing went weird and we passed out," Andrew said over the sound of the truck's engine.

"Well, tell them to release me for the show," Max said and lifted his neck.

"Sorry no-go. You have broken ribs and a possible concussion."

"I have to let Agha know then. He has to make sure it goes on. The statue—where is it now?" He settled back into his stretcher.

"If I knew, I'd toast that piece of shit," Andrew said.

Max looked to the ground, frowned, and lifted his head to Andrew. "Please make sure the show goes on, and Agha will do the rest."

"Okay. Wait, how do I reach him?"

"He's staying in my room," Max said as the medics loaded his body into the back of the truck and drove away.

Looking to the sky as the sun rose, Andrew placed his hands in his pockets, and remembered it was still winter in D.C. "What am I going to do?" he said as he walked to the train station to get home.

* * *

Eying the phone in his house, Andrew took out a piece of paper with the word 'Max' written on it and spun the wheel of his phone.

"Room two forty two please."

"Hello?" a tired voice said.

"Agha? Hey buddy it's me Andrew. Yeah the professor is in the hospital. The main one by the university."

"Oh no. What happened?"

"I'll explain it all later or Max can tell you himself. He needs you to do something for him."

"What did he need me to do?"

"Go to the museum and make sure they set up everything the way Max wanted it." Andrew pulled on the cord to the phone.

"Okay, I'll make sure the show is set up the way Vernon wanted. But I'm going to the hospital first. Thanks, Andrew."

"Okay, bye," Andrew said and slammed the phone on the hook. "Okay take a piss then off to Jake's," he said and ran into the bathroom. On top of the toilet sat a white stick with a pink plus sign in a white paper in the stick. "Oh wow, I'm gonna be a daddy," Andrew said, jumping off the floor. After he took a piss, he rushed out of the house to meet up with Jake.

For hours, they sat around stringing up clippings in the room from newspapers, pictures from the morgue, and reviewing the translations. Comparing the translations to the events that occurred, they figured out the murders happened after each jewel appeared in the Peacock, and that each woman killed wore a religious emblem around their necks. Six Eves dead and only one remained.

"The thing just went puff," Andrew said and animated the actions with his arms. He tried his best to demonstrate to Jake how the being disappeared before his eyes the other night in the lab. "I don't get it. Really, we've been at this for what, three, four, five hours and how much weed? Okay so, we know these pages are like the Bible's revelation. We know that this demon man wants to kill seven chicks or 'Eves'. We know that the chicks are all Christian, Muslim, or Jewish. We know that there are colors of the rainbow, and this has happened in seven days. Blue's the last one, and I have no idea where the statue's at or where to find the jewel. I don't even think I want to find the thing."

"Yeah, who would believe us if we called the cops anyway—yeah we may know where Satan's at, and he wants your daughter." Jake laughed.

The two choked on the smoke of the weed as it burned their lungs.

"So we know the next woman is gonna be, Muslim, Jewish, or Christian. There isn't a pattern. There are more Jews killed, but why? What the hell does the traitor mean?"

"Maybe it's Agha?" Jake said and sucked the paper from the cigarette before passing it Andrew.

"Agha? That guy couldn't fight his way out of a wet napkin." Andrew yawned.

"Think about it. He's close to Max. He wants the fame. He may be a traitor in his country. What better way to get rid of him and take the glory?" Jake said and uncrossed his legs.

"Yeah, but if he was the traitor, wouldn't he be the one targeted? Plus, he isn't what I would classify as an 'Eve.'" Andrew rubbed the sand from his eyes.

"I guess you're right, maybe all those girls are traitors or maybe it's a Yezedi traitor." Jake sat up from his beanbag and raised his hands.

Andrew looked at the clock on Jake's wall that sat behind his five-foot lava lamp and rubbed his eyes. "Is that right, is it really six?" Andrew asked.

Jake turned and walked to the clock. "No, this clock is an hour slow. I set it that way because I figured time would slow down for me, but it hasn't worked."

"Oh, hell. I am supposed to meet Becca at the museum before her show at seven thirty. She has her lucky blue jewel."

"Isn't she from the Middle East, Becca?" Jake asked as he met Andrew in the frame of the door.

As Andrew's feet slid over the floor, he braced himself at the door. "Wait, stop the shenanigans, O'Malley. Becca is from Turkey, and her family was banished." He ran his hands through his hair. "It has been in my face this whole time. Call the cops. Tell them to go to the museum that the killer will be there."

Andrew forced his one hundred seventy-pound frame down

the stairs as if he weighed ninety. He ran down the hall and skipped down the steps. He darted away from traffic and down the subway tunnel. He jumped the hurdles of the turnstile and shot his change into the machine. Lucky for him, the train that stopped at downtown had just pulled in for boarding.

"Come on! Come on," he bartered with time.

Once the train screeched to a halt, he pushed out first, knocking old women and children aside. Continuing his marathon to the museum, he reached into his bag. His special pass was not there.

"I forgot I didn't pack it. Goddamn it." He headed toward the back door where there wasn't security. "She said this room." He banged his hand against the doorframe in the back of the museum. No one answered, and he sprang from the area.

"Shit," he said and ran around the corner to the sounds of disgruntled models and the snapping of photos. As he ran in, he batted through fashion designers and models walking around him naked or changing into a new outfit. Bumping into a clothing rack, he wheeled it into a girl with the waist the size of a toddler's and explored more of the changing area.

"Oh no, oh no." He stopped every model that crossed him to drill them about his wife. They either smiled, shook their heads, or gave no answer.

As he looked around, under the mask of clothes and makeup, behind bright lights and stage craft, for any clue that would lead to his wife, he saw Agha on the other side of the room.

"You!" Andrew said and jacked Agha up off his feet. "What have you done? Answer me!"

"I don't know what you are talking about," Agha said and his eyes shifted to the security guard that removed Andrew from Agha's trembling body. Before another word fell from his lips, Andrew's gaze followed a figure that lit up the hallway as it glided into the open area.

"That burly son of a bitch," he said and ran after the man with a thousand tattoos, into the hall, downstairs, around the corner and into a drippy corridor. At the end of the path, lights magnified and gleamed through the crack of a door.

"Lizzie!" he said and pushed himself inside. There in the middle of the room, stood a woman with her hand on her chest, walking to the captivating lights from the peacock statue.

"The traitor," a small man in the corner whispered as she neared the structure.

"Ichabod, help me. Help me with my wife," Andrew said to him

Ichabod smiled to Andrew and walked next to the statue. "You don't get it do you? She is the traitor, the last sacrifice for Ta'us to rise. The blue jewel of the sky. The jewel of Shayton." Ichabod stared at Andrew's wife, Becca, hungering for her death

Crying as she willingly approached the peacock structure, she tightened her hands around her necklace. "So, so beautiful," she said as she ripped the necklace from around her neck.

"No." Andrew ran to his wife.

The gray aura grabbed her, floated her to the middle peacock feather, and she placed the stone in the center feather. Voices howled from it and the aura around the bird dissolved all light from the room and grew beyond the center of the room.

"She's with child." Ichabod clapped and circled to watch her body levitate in the room.

As Andrew continued trucking to his wife, his feet stiffened, and his body became rigorous and stiff. "Let her go...let her go." But the more Andrew begged, the more the gray aura set fire to her skin.

She turned to him and smiled. Tears fell down her face like a waterfall. "It's okay," she said and moved her head back to the statue that held her captive and continued to raise her body until she dangled over twenty feet in the air.

Once the jewel became one with the structure, the aura let go of its shackles around her body, and she fell, flat on the cement, her eyes open, her brains spilling onto the floor, a peaceful expression on her face.

Blue light, the colors of the sky, sparked from the statue and over the tattooed villain that stood in the corner. As his skin cracked, the tattoos on his body swirled into a cyclone, and the room became a wind tunnel.

Andrew shielded his eyes and shook his head at his wife's dead body bleeding out on the floor. As the light show progressed, the eyes of the creature shot beams of radiation that burned Andrew's skin a deep purple.

"I am Ta'us Melek, the divine, the alpha and omega." His voice rumbled the foundation of the building.

Ta'us walked to Ichabod sitting in the corner, and placed his hands on either side of his bearded face.

"My lord," Ichabod said

Ta'us brought his lips to Ichabod's lips. It was not a romantic kiss; it was the kiss of death. As he pulled away from Ichabod's face, his hands traveled down to his neck. "Your job is done," he said and twisted the bone like a bottle top.

The body thudded to the ground.

When he looked at Andrew, Andrew dug down deep to keep his nerves from causing his body to tremble.

"Sleep," Ta'us said in English.

Falling to the cold cement, Andrew watched the image of the structure leave with the man when the smoky cloud that surrounded them disappeared. Everything went dark.

***

Lifting his head from the floor, Andrew put his hands in the air as the cops surrounded him like a campfire.

"Freeze. Don't move."

"What?" He turned to his corpse of a wife, still with that smile on her face.

The officer from the other crime scenes, Officer Daniels, stood over him, gleefully banging a flashlight in his hands as he knelt down. Two other officers snapped the cuffs on Andrew's hands as he gazed up at Officer Daniels.

"So, like you say, two's a coincidence, three's a pattern. What's four? Proof?" the officer said to him, and the cops took him away.

Andrew tugged and pulled his body toward his wife, but the cops overpowered him and pushed him out of the room. On the ground from his bag, the picture he'd taken the other night fell to the floor. It contained an image of a blurred ghost.

"No, Becca!"

"Don't feel guilty now. You'll have plenty of time to think about it where you're going."

The cops stuffed him into the back of the car, and he leaned his head against the glass, peering out the window at the swarms of lights that drove around and the thousands of people that wandered outside. Unable to think or form a logical explanation for what happened, he didn't hear the sirens blast. He only could conjure the thoughts of his wife. Dead and bleeding out on the floor. And her smile. Why had she smiled?

***

Although he couldn't recount when he arrived at the police station, as soon as a cop shoved him into a small cell, his conscience kicked in, and he realized the seriousness of his situation. Pleading with the officers that tossed him into his jail cell, Andrew slid down the steel bars as the officer locked the door.

"I didn't do it. Some sick freak did this!" he said and slid his arms through the bars.

"Knock it off! I'm trying to watch the Phillies game," a large cop with a mustache, chewing gum, said to him and smacked the bars. Metal to metal sound rang in the cell, and Andrew covered his ears.

After fifteen minutes of dripping snot from his mouth and yelling, "I need to speak to my attorney," Andrew retired from his fight and sat on his bed with his head in his hands.

"What is happening? This can't be real," he cried in his palms.

The bed weighed down and squeaked and not from his weight. He peeked through his hands at an image of a man, intimidating in every way, who smelled of lilac and wore a grimacing smile.

"I see you are in a bind. Demon killed your wife and pinned you to the murders."

"How…the?" Andrew asked and scrunched his nose.

"We can talk about that later. Question is, do you want to make a deal that would clear you of all this?"

"I told the cops I didn't do it. I didn't do it."

"I am not talking about cops." The man snapped his fingers, and the cell opened

"I'm talking about killing a spoiled brat, who is mad Daddy loves Adam more than him. I am talking about getting your name cleared, erased."

Andrew stood up from the bed, walked to the bars, and touched the surface. He searched for anything electronic that might open the door. "How'd you do that? This isn't real. You had to have had some electrical device or something."

"Of all you have seen? Have a seat," the man said.

Andrew continued to search for copper wire or a trigger. Then his feet slid backward, without his doing, and he plummeted onto the bed.

"Who are you?" Andrew said, frightened. He fell from the bed and scooted into the corner of the cell. His heart beat loud enough to hear in the neighboring cells, and the weight of his clenched teeth chipped his molars.

"Call me The Gentleman."

Chapter 18
Run

James sat up on the bed and looked out of the dreary window filled with shadows and clouds of green and purple, while he waited for *The Spaceman* to conclude his story. The clock outside the room chimed, sending shock waves of sound into the room, shaking James' insides.

The Spaceman rubbed the Egyptian tattoos on his arm, and for a second, James recognized them and realized who he really was.

"Andrew," James said as he massaged his stomach and ignored The Gentleman's voice over the fictitious intercom.

"It is now five fifty, James…I'll be waiting."

"Who you speaking to?" Andrew jetted from the bed and stood by the window.

"You're not *The Spaceman.* Never was. Your name's Andrew Carter."

"Stop saying that. That's what he says. That's what he calls me." Andrew sobbed, walked around James, and paraded to the door. "If I wasn't *The Spaceman,* how would I know he was from California or how he felt in the World Series when he pitched those amazing games and still lost?" Andrew pulled at his hair as he walked back toward the window.

"Encyclopedia and sports channels." James shrugged his shoulders. "He explained how he felt in an interview before he left the team." James stood up from the bed and walked to Andrew. He felt bad for the guy. His intense experience caused him to create his own safe place to block out what had happened to his wife. "I'm sorry for what happened, but you are not the—"

"I am!" Andrew pointed to his chest and turned to the window.

James saw the reflection of Andrew's face, and he appeared as if he had seen his face for the first time.

"I'm Andrew Carter." Andrew lifted his shaking hand and touched the reflection of himself.

Opening his mouth to say something, James remembered what his father had said, 'If you got nothing to say, keep your trap shut'. He backed away and picked up his bag. On the floor, the words from before disappeared.

Looking back at Andrew, he saw him trace the outline of his face that reflected on the window and then touch his own.

"She's gone. Becca. My Becca's dead…our baby…"

As James shook his head, he slung his bag over his shoulder and walked to the door.

"Four," Andrew said.

"Four?" James continued facing the door. While his hand hovered over the handle, he heard Andrew's feet as they moved backward. He heard the speed at which he ran, and then James heard the shattering of the window and smelled the musk of lilac that seeped into the room.

Before the fog could strangle him, he forced the door open and ran out into the hall. As he closed the door, he caught a glimpse of the whirlwind of glass and fog circling in the room and Andrew floating outside into the storm.

Walking away from the door James spun around and looked at the Norse letters that shone brighter on the doors than when he'd first started his journey.

"Where do I go? Four, he said four." James picked up a light jog down the hall as he added the numbers on the doors. Around corner after corner, he ran, and not one door equaled four. One mile of running caused him to lean over and catch his breath, and then he continued.

"Where is it? He asked as he scanned the doors, which he

passed. While he turned his head, James ran into something solid that knocked him to the ground.

"You!" he said as he looked into Roberto's face.

"Me."

"I don't need your help anymore. I know where to go. There were no clues in those fuckin' rooms," James said and pushed past Roberto.

"Oh. Then where is the room?" Roberto said and remained standing in the middle of the hall.

James stopped and turned to him. "I'm guessing you know?"

Roberto faded and reappeared next to him.

"I don't need your help," James said as he walked away backward.

"Oh. How long have you been looking?" Roberto said and stared into James' face. Roberto was right. James had walked around, down, up, and across halls in this great mansion, and he hadn't come close to finding the magic door. The further he wandered into the maze, the more he lost his bearings.

"The ring first, then I tell you." Roberto held his hand out to James.

James reached into his pocket, pulled out the ring, and bounced it in his hand.

"No, you tell me. You take me there. Then I give you this." He held the jewel up between his thumb and index finger.

Roberto smiled and began to walk down the hall.

"Okay," James said and followed behind Roberto as they walked through the maze. The dungeon-style lanterns flickered as they passed. And the numbers on the doors rotated and began to change, confusing James as he added them up. "The numbers are changing." James sprung to the doors and touched the flames for the numbers as they switch from nine to two, and then back again. "Again and again." James faced Roberto and went to him. "You're doing this? I knew you were working with him. I knew this was a ploy to get me to go along with this crap. I'm not giving you shit. The deal is over," James said.

"Oh, you think I am doing this? How? You think I am

working with him? He took away all of *me*." Roberto moved with James as they stood in the middle of the hallway.

"Then why did you only show up after something fucked up happens to me, huh?" James asked as he neared Roberto.

Roberto remained silent and watched as James walked past him and further into the blackness of the hall.

"Silence speaks volumes." James stopped and pulled the ring out and lifted it up for Roberto to see.

"I guess you aren't as smart as I thought," Roberto said.

James could feel him as he came closer, brought his hand down, and placed the jewel in the palm.

Twisting to Roberto, James held his ground and pulled out his knife. "You wanna go again?"

Roberto snapped his teeth and retreated from James.

"Humilis, oh humilis, the boy cheated, he knows the room now." Roberto smirked at James.

"You son-of-a-slut," James whispered as he shook his head.

"I really was going to help you out, but now it appears I should only help myself." As Roberto folded his hands over one another, the entire place started to swirl and shift.

The Gentleman came to collect his debt.

"What? No. No." James turned around and began to run down the hall, but once it became too unsteady, he braced himself on the wall to prevent from stumbling to the ground.

"Are you able find it now?" Roberto laughed and the volume of his voice rose over the shattering sounds of the walls cracking.

"Fuck you, you son of a slut."

"Ha-ha." Roberto continued to walk down the hall, unwearied by the shaking underneath them.

The shaking became more unsteady as the clock in the hall struck six. It roared, and the windows opened and snapped shut. The doors in the hall flung open then smashed closed, breaking pieces of wood. The lavender-colored flames in the lanterns flickered and cracked from the air that whished in the hallway. When the ceiling trembled, the crystal pieces to the chandeliers broke off and hit James in the face. While he batted the shards from his eyes, the ground shuddered, and he dropped the ring.

The ring rolled to Roberto who knelt down, without a sense of urgency, and picked it up.

"No," James said while holding out his hand. He levered himself against the wall as the earthquake rattled the foundation of the house. Roberto remained unmoved by the tremors and strolled to James as he caressed the ring in his finger. He marveled at the gem.

The shaking stopped.

"It has been fun, James, really, but now I shall become who I once was," Roberto said and turned away from him. "It's been a long time." He slid the silver-plated ring onto his pinky finger.

"No," James said and peeled himself from the wall. He skirted away from Roberto before hell burst from his fingers.

Nevertheless, hell didn't come, and the ring remained dull.

Roberto removed it, blew on it as if it were dice at a craps table, and then slipped it back on his pinky.

Nothing.

The ring was as normal as any other was and didn't glint or produce any supernatural power.

"Shit in a box..." James saw the face of The Gentleman materialize in the blackness of the hall next to Roberto as he tinkered with his dull ring.

"I should have figured this much from you, Van Herr," Roberto said without looking up at him. A smile spread across his face. "Post Mortem."

"After death? Is that supposed to scare me?" The Gentleman waved to James then brought his attention to Roberto.

"It's in your blood, James. In the peaches. The same blood," Roberto called over his shoulder.

The Gentleman smacked Roberto's face. After Roberto retracted from it, he walked to him.

"You think I would allow you to get back your powers? Oh no, I ate them." The Gentleman licked his lips.

"*Si*, the humilis is shown that he can be clever." Roberto spat on The Gentleman's coat.

"James. Run," Roberto said and ran into The Gentleman.

James did as Roberto told him and ran in the opposite direction. He heard Roberto's screams and shook. He almost vomited from the sounds of The Gentleman's hellish laughter and the sounds of The Gentleman's teeth sinking into Roberto's flesh.

James ran down the hall, no, he glided down the hall. He fled past each door and added the numbers he saw.

"Uhm...four plus five. No." The hall behind him brightened, and the shadows of black orbs with holes for eyes stretched around every curve. They stretched until they touched him.

"Shit," he said, and pushed them away from his hand.

"Six...plus..." he said and patted each door he passed. To James, one plus one was as difficult as adding 45689 to 9865.

The spirits reached for him. They ripped his clothes and tore his hair. They scratched his skin and called his name, *"Jamesss."*

After ramming his hand into his duffel bag, he smeared a peach on the orbs and chucked it at the wall where the faces imprinted. It reduced their rampage and helped him progress to room four.

Without looking at the number on the room, he charged to the closest room he could find to escape the horrors.

"I can make it." He lunged to the handle and twisted the knob. A seal fell and sparked from it, and bright red and golden light shimmered around the door. The shimmery light fell to ash. After the blood rained down the edges and the foundation of the frame, it evaporated into the air.

The gong of the grandfather clock shook loose and plummeted to the ground. The numbers floated around the hall and roped round his neck.

He bit off the black ghost and frayed the black ink from their threading. Once the door gave way, he forced himself inside.

"My God," James said, panting as he lifted himself from the floor.

"James," a man called.

He elevated his head and saw those green eyes peeking through the dark. The eyes capable enough to take a soul, to stop time and collapse a country. Green eyes with the opposite of meaning and feeling of green, covered with hate, envy, and F and evil - a pure evil. James recoiled. "Leave me alone, I got it right."

The Gentleman stepped into the room and left behind his shadowy appearance, his solid body returned. After looking around the frame of the door, he stepped further inside the room.

"I'm in," The Gentleman said low. "You had help, you cheated. Before we came in here, I gave you the clue on the steps." The Gentleman stepped further inside, "I told you to look for a constant occurrence. I gave you two clues inside of the clues, I appeared four times, the numbers on the doors added to four. The hotel room I gave you, what was the number?" The Gentleman snarled and puffed from his pipe.

James looked at his hand, and his fright faded into desperation. He stood up, grabbed his bag, and pulled out the fruit.

"I got it in the bag, in my blood," he muttered and launched one near the frame of the doorframe, missing The Gentleman within inches.

"Oh, oh, was that supposed to hit me?" The Gentleman tapped his cheek. "Go ahead. Try it again."

James rounded up and hit the same spot on the wall. One after one, he launched the fruit and they collided in the same spot. One by one, they absorbed into the wall. He threw the blood orange fruit until he was out and braced himself against the wall from exhaustion. Turning to James, The Gentleman broke into a frenzy of laughter, even slapping his knees at times and wiping tears that formed in his eyes. It rumbled the house and broke the glass of the picture frames on the wall into microscopic pieces.

"Pitcher, in high school?" The Gentleman mocked.

James peered at the broken frame as the blood fell to the ground and soaked into the boards. It connected to the floor and spread on the walls. The red and orange from its flesh tinted the room's green and purple one.

"That wasn't to hit you; it was to let him in." James smiled.

The smile on The Gentleman's face morphed from confusion to surprise and then anger and he turned around. The blood from the peach continued to spread around the door's frame. Motioning to the door, The Gentleman held out his hands. The wood rose from the floor and separated into different directions, and some floorboards folded in. Soon, the walls looked as though an earthquake shook the place. Heaps of wood toppled to the ground and the foundation under James shook, causing him to hold onto the wall behind him. The more wood the Gentleman cracked and destroyed, the faster the blood spread in the room.

"Stop this. No. Stop," The Gentleman said as the blood stayed one-step ahead of him and spread across the wall.

He raced to it, a lunatic attempting to exhaust a flame. A man anxious to survive spading away any chance of peril to beat the odds. The surface of his skin transformed. Rigid, it resembled the color of clay and appeared rough as sand. His green eyes deepened, and his canines elongated in his mouth.

"Stop this!" he insisted, his suit rippled and muscles inflated.

When the boards under James moaned, The Gentleman retired his campaign against the blood and stomped to James. His body transformed to his normal appearance.

Once there was no more room for James to back into, he stopped on the broken glass that sat under the window.

"You promised to give me what I wanted, but here we are in the room. You broke your deal now, you will obey," he said and raised his hand.

Pain fizzled up James' spine and he contorted on the ground. James released howls from his mouth as if he were giving birth.

"Scream out, scream out to me! You will find it, you will find it. His blood's needed to break the curse. That's what broke this door, James. And to find the missing pages, I need it. You are his blood." The Gentleman stood James up puppeteer style. He forced James' arms and moved James' head.

A feather floated out of James' pocket and landed on the ground near his feet, it flapped into the blood that trickled from his fingers. James' eyes widened when he saw something forming behind The Gentleman. But the pain from The Gentleman's torture didn't allow him to make heads or tails of it.

When he tired of torturing James from afar, The Gentleman decided to do it manually and jackknifed his fingers into James' arm. The Gentleman slid his fingers from the wound and blood gushed to the ground. It geysered and sprayed on the walls. It seeped into the boards and traveled around The Gentleman's barrow. James' blood mixed with the strange fruit, and the feather that fluttered on the ground. Then, all these ingredients ignited.

The Gentleman's hand burned after James' blood poured over his skin, and he spit the lava fire from his mouth, which reversed the damage. "Look at that, Theodore. I can counter your god damn blood *skit*." The Gentleman held his hands up for anyone to see and laughed as if he was in disbelief

James' eyes rolled backward. He opened his mouth and released the agony that ran through his body. "Why-y?" he asked.

"I need those pages." The Gentleman moved back to James.

As James' arm lifted, pressure marks appeared on his arm. His blood trickled down on the floor and soaked into his bag.

Once The Gentleman spat on the liquid, the redness became as golden as a phoenix's wing, and it smelled of burning flesh. The plasma traveled to James' bag and absorbed at the bottom. The Gentleman's face contoured to anger as the blob of blood gathered around James' duffle bag. "This entire time!" he said and lifted and his hands.

The Gentleman snapped his fingers, and James' arm snapped. Purple and violet bruises spread on James' arm and large knots poked through his flesh.

Tossing him to the wall, James passed out from the pain.

But The Gentleman forced him back to consciousness.

"I want you to feel it all. I am going to torture you for years. I won't let you die like Andrew, and Roberto. I want you to become so corrupt you won't recognize who you were, are, or ever was."

"I'm done, I'm done with it all," James said and kneeled before the Gentleman with his head bowed, holding his arm together.

As James raised his eyes, behind The Gentleman, he saw the lavender aura The Gentleman created turn into a deep red. A figure shadowed the demon.

"Kneel to me!" The Gentleman said.

"Now that's enough," a man said and touched The Gentleman's shoulder with his bronze hands. The Gentleman turned and spat in the man's direction.

"You, you!" he said.

"Nice to see you too," the man said and blew a metallic gray powder in his face.

CHAPTER 19
THEODORE

The Gentleman froze into a mannequin of himself. He stood with his sinister smile and his hands extending out.

James fell to the ground. He let out a breath of relief and curled into a ball.

Then, when quiet filled the room, the man reached for him.

"Dad." James looked up through his tears, but as his tears dried, he noticed it was not his father and scooted from him.

"No. You're, you're Theodore," James said as he nursed his wounds.

"I needed my blood to break the seal. Let me heal your arm, son." He touched James' arm, snapping it back into place. After the man sealed the wound on James arm, he touched James' belly. The feeling was warm. And on his arm, it felt as though more than a thousand hands were sewing up his wound.

"That should make you feel a lot betta," Theodore said and helped James up from the ground.

As James began rushing fully cocked at the freeze-framed Gentleman, Theodore pressed his hand on James' chest and stopped him.

"No! You have no idea what he'd done to me!" James ate his snot as he spit out his words.

"I do, but if you rush him, you'll mess with the spell. It'll be all for nothing. When the time is right, we will kill him." Theodore let go of James.

After walking to the bed, James pressed his head on the

palms of his hand.

"I need you to focus for me. You gonna help me get rid of im." Theodore rubbed James' shoulder.

"How?" James turned to the man. "No more fuckin' riddles. I don't want to play these games. I don't want to be some hero. I thought I could do it. I thought, *I got this, I was in Vietnam, and I can do this.* Then he killed a demon in the hallway and took his soul. That boy was seventeen when he took his soul. He made two guys crazy as bats, and what he did to you." James faced Theodore. "You didn't even sign a contract. He killed her, in front of you. He killed my dad." James put his mouth to his hands and wiped away the snot.

"He did, and I've planned this for over a century. How to kill him and how to use him in his own game. I thought if I sealed off the room and kept the papers from him somewhere else, it would keep him guessing. But he wouldn't stop messing with my family. He wouldn't stop. So I turned to your granddad, then he gave into him. I turned to your dad. He didn't want to help, and the demon forced him to have a heart attack. He never made a deal, your dad." Theodore's voice cracked. "I had to watch y'all suffer, wanting to help but forced on this property with my only outreach as a tree, the papers, and in this room. I knew if anyone from my line broke the seal, he'd have it. Your granddad broke it the first time, and when he couldn't find what the demon was looking for, he drove your granddad crazy."

James gawked at the dimples in Theodore's cheek and raised the corners of his mouth.

"I had to seal the room off again, and it almost killed me. I tried keeping y'all away. I tried destroying this place."

"Why you didn't give him what he wanted?" James looked into Theodore's familiar eyes and gave a subtle shake of the head.

"The papers never had words on them. He found them, and when he saw what they were, he became real nasty." Theodore settled next to James on the bed. "My biggest mistake was leaving that book. He learned loads from it. I took away some of his powers when he touched the door. Believe it or not, this ain't him at full."

James peeked at The Gentleman, anticipating him coming back to life and tearing holes into their chests.

Theodore faded the image of The Gentleman away and the two appeared outside in a sunny Georgian summer, filled with the sounds of birds and nature.

The wind wheezed through the trees, blowing leaves into James' face. He pulled one off his lip and crushed the leaf in his hand. "I like this better," James said.

"I know you do. I figured this way I can talk to you without him being there," Theodore said and the two sat on the porch.

"I was born a slave, James. I was born Napoleon Smith. I ran away from Alabama after I got in a fight with the slave master's slaver. They used him to break in the toughest slaves. He upset me one day after I cleaned the stable. He dirtied it up again and told me to clean it. I told him, no, you do it. He pushed me, and I fought him. I socked him good in the face." Theodore laughed and slapped his knee. "I still can picture his face. He was scared of me. Scared that I fought back. He was a hair taller than I was, but I managed to stand up to him. I knew then I had to leave. My travels to where I ended up are a tale for another day."

James leaned back against the stoop and placed his elbows on the step. The air smelled of sweet grass and peaches.

"An Indian tribe adopted me. They found me in a river. I was gonna die. I stayed with them a while. I learned a lot about the Shaman magic and would've become one, if not for all the wars. When I was 'bout fifteen, I had a dream I was an owl, and I soared high into the clouds. I ran to the Shaman the next day and told 'im my dream."

As Theodore spoke, an owl landed on the branch and rotated its head one hundred eighty degrees. The brown spotted raptor blinked its yellow eyes at James as he stood up from the porch and walked with Theodore into the yard.

"He said, 'it's time.' He taught me all there was to know, using metals, nature, plants and how they act on each other." Theodore led James to the tall tree and the two walked casually around it.

"The tribe was forced out of the area in Florida, so I ran north. That was the second time they came to remove them from their home. I think I have traveled on all sorts of transport, James. I did it alone for years until I meet this hoodoo man in South Carolina, and he taught me about stuff I could never've imagined. He was a Gullah. I taught him about the Indian ways. We combined all of it—Chemistry, Alchemy, Voodoo, Indian Shamanism. We came up with methods to kill demons, and we got damn good at it, too. But when it drew too much attention, I had to hide. I let the white folks catch me. I ended up on one plantation after the next, changed my name to Theodore, and it worked, for a spell. I went to Mister Greene's place where I planned my final escape, and then I saw his daughter Lizzy. I saw those baby blue eyes, brown hair, and a smile that I couldn't get ova'. We were inseparable." Theodore smiled as an attractive woman with brown hair walked onto the porch and waved to him.

"One by one, the demons sniffed me out. They found where I was, but I couldn't leave her." Theodore looked away from James.

As they continued walking around the tree, James stared up at its impossible height that provided shade for over twenty meters. "This is amazing," James said.

"This sweet grass used to surround the property until that demon stained it, and it turned into devil's weed. The tree grew larger when I melded my blood with it. My spirit went into the owl. My heart went into those papers. You brought the three together, James."

"Why didn't you fly to my father and stop this demon?" James asked and touched the rough bark.

"I can't leave his world." Theodore took a deep breath and progressed with his tale. "Next thing I know, he kept lurking. I could feel him around. Didn't see at first because they like to test the water before they show their faces. Then, he got real bold and started coming by. Threatening me. Month after month. Then he just snapped when he got word I was gonna kill im."

"Were you?" James asked.

"Yeah," Theodore said, and the imaginary world faded into the green evil room where The Gentleman stood. The lilac smell turned into sulfur.

"He got to your granddad before I could. He had your granddad tear down the tree. The fruit kept falling on him." Theodore laughed and James joined in.

"That tree ain't in the livin' world any more, only in the land of the dead. He separated my link by cutting it down. All but them papers stayed." Theodore walked in front of The Gentleman.

Although James' feet shook, he walked with him.

"I kept my knowledge of how to kill a demon away from everyone." Theodore tapped his temple three times and winked at James. "There ain't no words on them papers."

"Dad... I'm sorry, I mean Theo?"

Turning to face him, Theodore returned James' mistaken identity with a merry smile.

"Why didn't The Gentleman ever notice?"

"I masked them, made 'em look like a news clipping of whatever you wanted it to be. Only my blood could see what they really was. I tried to send your dad messages. I tried everything," Theodore said and coaxed James next to him.

"I don't think I can help you," James said.

"Why, because he overpowered you? Because you don't believe in yourself? You fought in Vietnam. You didn't let your mom's leaving and your father's death stop you from living. You dealt with Jeff's death. You are my blood. You can do this."

He nodded at The Gentleman. "That demon, he like all demons, holds onto something from their life. This one, it's lilacs, that's why I created something for 'im." Theodore smiled. "With weeds, you gotta rot their roots, using alkaline. And I got something that will rot those things faster than Sunday."

"I just need you to read. Get the bag." James walked around

the demon's body and picked up the blood-soaked bag. As more blood soaked into the boards, James held it up and handed it to Theodore.

Theodore pulled out the papers and they shimmered. After placing his hands on their surface, the blood evaporated from them.

"What, that's what he wanted?" James asked.

"Yeah, that's what I made him chase."

Sitting his back against the wall, James smoothed his hair and rested his eyes on Theodore. "I never met my granddad. He died before I was born. Dad told me stories of how he was before he went crazy."

"I just don't know how I let him get that damn book. I knew I should've burned it." Theodore shook his head, disappointment reflected in his face and displayed in his actions.

James reached his scared hand out and rubbed Theodore's face. He snapped his hand back once he realized what he was doing. "Sorry about that. You look like... I mean... you're darker, but my dad looks so much like you. It's like he's standing right in front of me. He called me Jimmy." James laughed and rubbed his head. "I hated when anyone else did, but when he did it, it was okay."

"Is that right? I never met 'im. I felt 'im because of the papers but never met 'im."

"You look like my dad when I was a kid, the face I remember the most. He raised me when my hippie momma ran out. I remember that day because he made us oatmeal for dinner and he said, 'Son, your mama don' run off with them scallywags, so it's you and me, Jimmy. You and your ole pop.' What the hell, man." James laughed and his confidence returned.

"I like this James, not the one he created," Theodore said and squeezed James' shoulder. "Jimmy."

Theodore tilted his head and James nodded.

"It's time. Do as I say and when I say run, you run."

"What...what about you? I mean you can—"

"I'm afraid this is where I belong. I allowed myself to be

killed. I couldn't live in a world without her. My Lizzy."
Theodore held James' hand. Theodore's touch warmed his
heart. It broke away the chains The Gentleman had secured
around his ankles and feet. It threw oceans of sand into the pit in
his stomach. His father was there with him through it all.

James nodded and exhaled.

"Take these pages and read what I put on 'em. Don't be
scared." Theodore walked behind The Gentleman.

Facing The Gentleman, James took the mound and waited
for the catcher to give him the signal for the pitch to throw.

"Now!" Theodore said and grabbed The Gentleman's arms.

When he defrosted, the demon snarled and hollered. "What
are you doing?"

"You made of lilac, and I drank alkaline before you had me
killed," Theodore said.

Roots formed out of the boards and wrapped around The
Gentleman's feet. They melded him with the room and
prevented him from moving. He pulled hard and away from
Theodore. He closed the doors and flickered the lights on and
off. His aura, purple, protruded and his feet slid over the floor,
breaking wood chippings, as he moved towards the door.

"Now, James," Theodore said and tightened his grip around
the demon's body.

As James' nightmare vibrated in front of his eyes, James'
feet and hands refused to move. The horror in The Gentleman's
face peeled and foamed.

"Look at you. Can you do it? You were always a coward.
Left your daughter, Jeff's sister, your father. A coward. Just like
your mother," The Gentleman said and sent camel spit in James'
direction.

"Don't listen to him James. Read!" Theodore said.

But Theodore's words didn't match the volume of The
Gentleman's voice.

"I-I-didn't! I'm not a coward," James said.

"Oh, but you are. Even your deadbeat mother saw it, and
left. When this is over, I'll show you what I do to cowards."

Standing with crumpled papers in his hand, James remained

and didn't flinch to the clashing and burning wood or the sparks and fires around him.

Theodore held on to the demon. *Read!*

James trembled where he stood and held on to the words of the demon, coward. A skipped tape played in his head.

Coward.

Coward.

Coward.

The Gentleman, more confident than the previous minute, played the cards dealt.

"Jeff, you couldn't even tell his family what happened. You reacted too late, and the enemy was about to shoot down your plane. Your fault, James. Jeff died because of you."

Jeff stood next to The Gentleman. "Why James," he said as he coughed up blood. Blood drizzled from the large gash on the side of Jeff's body, causing his army greens to turn purple. "You let me die."

"No, it wasn't my fault. You saw them before me," James said as he backed further toward the open door.

"Jessica, your daughter, you'll never see her face again. But I'll let you see me be her first. I'll let you see me destroy her soul. You'll miss our first child. You'll miss her first hit of crack. You'll miss her becoming mine."

James took steps backward.

His daughter appeared, the way she did when James was in the hall. Another image of The Gentleman manifested near her, and he pulled her into his arms and graced her with a sloppy kiss.

James charged toward their image, but it disappeared before he could reach them. Treading to the doorway, James turned his head from The Gentleman who stood enjoying torturing James.

"Your wife!" The Gentleman laughed and shook off the root that traced his lips.

"Don't listen. Look at me!" Theodore said.

"Your wife - you beat her. She stayed with you after the war. *Oh*, did she deal with your flashbacks, nightmares, and gambling problem. And you beat her. So bad once, her eye closed for a week. How many stitches?"

The image of James' wife appeared to the left of The Gentleman. She wore a loose nightgown and she pulled up the sides of the dress that fell from her shoulder. Her eyes were the size of a golf ball and blacker than the hall behind James.

"No, no you drove me to it," James said and took another step back as he took his eyes off his wife.

"I see it runs in your family. Your grandfather was the same way after the first great war." The Gentleman looked into the black hallway.

Shuffling his feet to the sounds of a rope swinging, James looked at a man swinging in midair in the hallway.

"No," he said to the palc and lifeless body dressed in business casual attire. "No."

"Oh, yes. The man that raised your father was a coward like you." The Gentleman smirked.

James backed from the body and turned to The Gentleman. He held the papers in his hand tight, crumbling the fabric of the cotton paper.

"You give me those, and you get your soul back, and you go on with no worry in the world, James."

"James the coward," the image of Jeff said as he coughed more blood.

"No."

"James the horrible dad." The image of his daughter smacked her gum.

"Jenni," James cried.

"The wife beater. The wife beater," his wife said through her swollen lips.

"James the coward." They all chanted.

The Gentleman laughed at James' shaking, ready to run out of the room.

As James stood baffled at the images of his loved ones pointing and laughing, feathers swirled next to him, and the figure of his father materialized from them.

"Jimmy," his father said.

James raised his gaze to him and almost dropped the papers

from his hands. "D-Dad?"

"Read, son," he said and grasped James' shoulder. After the feathers returned and circled his body, he became an afterimage.

James blinked at the papers and sweat from his brow splashed on them. Magically, cursive letters scribbled on the surface.

"*Jimmy, think of the place we left.*"

James closed his eyes and saw the swaying of the trees. He smelled the sweet nectar of peaches, and felt the swift breeze play in his hair. He heard the voice of his father call him "Jimmy." He opened his eyes and focused on Theodore's face—and the face resembled his father.

At last, the voice of The Gentleman turned down fifty notches.

"That's it, look at me. Don't look at him anymore. Now read the words on the paper, James. Now."

James held the paper with both hands and started from the top. "Know the demon's name. You know his name, and you have his attention."

"His name is, Von Aka Herr."

James looked at The Gentleman and the demon's grotesque form deflated to his usual appearance.

"Know his house, The Norse House, and know his elements."

The Gentleman snarled, "Stop this James! I can give you your soul back. You keep this up and there is no return."

James looked away from The Gentleman and placed his gaze back on Theodore.

"Know his elements. Know what his elements are and you will know how to destroy him from the inside out." The word *alkaline* appeared. "The chant of the spirits binds the dead with the living. They become one, and they become light. They meld into the infinite and burst into energy."

When James looked at Theodore, an aura appeared around his body, and banished the purple ooze from The Gentleman. Then, Theodore chanted.

James looked at the paper and joined in with him.

"Two become one, two become one," James said.

Theodore's body fused with The Gentleman. His limbs lined up with the arms of the beast, and his face smashed into the dreadful demon's bone structure. His chest imprinted on The Gentleman's Roman breastplate and his hazel eyes swirled away the green light from The Gentleman's pupils. A fire show erupted and bonded with everything within arm's reach of the nucleus of the reaction.

Within the mixture between good and evil, James saw Theodore.

Gleaming at James, Theodore spoke, "Jimmy, run."

When The Gentleman pushed away, trying to break the fusion, he retracted to his prison like a rubber band.

"We are bonded like the elements of hydrogen and oxygen. This is Alchemy," Theodore said.

"Alchemy? Alchemy?"

"Yes, this whole time, you thought I was doing voodoo, oh no," Theodore said. "A demon can't beat no alchemy and that paper, that paper ain't got any words on it. All I know is right here. I just told him what to say."

The Gentleman ran his body away, lashing out with his magic, which flickered in the room. The wood kindled, and a purple green flame burst into a roaring fire.

The sulfur smell became grotesque, and James vomited on his way out the door, grabbing his bag before he stumbled into the hall.

CHAPTER 20
AND THE HOUSE COMES TUMBLING DOWN

The body in the hall swung and hit him in the face. He fell onto the cold floor. As the shadow of the body enlarged, James stood and faced his grandfather. James saw the rope around his neck left burn marks.

"Hello, James," his grandfather said and reached for him.

James pushed him away, but his grandfather grabbed his tattered white shirt. He smashed James' body into the third door, and James inhaled the dead man's breath.

"Let me go."

"Where's the fun in that?" his grandfather said as he crushed James' body against the door.

After James turned the knob, the two fell inside to see Eric sitting at the piano. Eric jolted to the corner of the room, and James and his grandfather danced for dominance around the floor. Their actions backed Eric against the window where the green storm battered and cracked the glass.

"I am your grandfather!"

"My grandfather died," James said and gained advantage over him. The window shattered, and the fog entered. It spiraled into a small tornado and helped Eric run away into the corner.

James held his grandfather's head to the ledge, nearing his neck to the razor sharp edges of the jagged broken glass. He used all his energy to puncture the corpse's neck.

Then the old man stopped struggling. James' force became as still as water, and a wicked grin streaked across his grandfather's face. Once he overpowered James, he forced them to switch places.

"Eric, help!" James said as his grandfather pressed his cold forearm into James' throat.

Closing his eyes, Eric raced to them with his hands up, and pushed James' grandfather into the suction of the storm. James pulled on Eric's shirt before the wind took him and pulled him away from the window.

James watched the ghost of his grandfather swirl then disappeared with the wind.

Soon the wind stopped and they were able to walk to the center. The sounds of death from room four turned his attention to the struggle between his kindred and the demon.

"Eric, you're alive," James said and put his hands on Eric's shoulder. "If you are alive, then the others must be, too," he said and hustled Eric to the exit. James recoiled once Eric stopped running with him.

"I can't step out of this room. He cursed it." Eric held his arm and stared at the ground.

James furrowed his eyebrows and pulled out his knife.

Stumbling as he backed up, Eric lifted his hands over his face.

"I'm not going to hurt you, Eric. You're a good kid and a better man than I ever was," James said and faced the door.

"Let's hope this works." He walked to the exit of the room and cut his finger. Blood trickled on the frame, and it traced the seal around the door.

"I don't know," Eric said as he came behind James.

"You stay, you die," James said and held out his hand. "Let's go," James said and ran into the hall.

After testing the water with his foot, Eric stepped all the way out of the room.

When James' hand hit the flames from door four, James pulled back and put his finger in his mouth.

"That is not good, it's getting bigger," James said and they

battled around it and away into the other side. His finger
continued to throb and the tips began to change to purple.

"Okay, I think this is it," James said and began to reverse
his steps when he saw the straw man sitting in the corner
brushing the hair of one of the dolls from the attic.

"Oh shit." He slammed the door shut.

"James the beater," he squawked from the other side. They
sprinted down the hall searching for the room where Frank
resided.

"This is it," James said as he hit the surface of the door. He
turned the handle and went to Frank leaning on the table.

"Come on, Frank. Let's go!"

"Why? What for?"

James grabbed him.

Frank vanished and reappeared on the opposite side of the
room. "I'm not going," he cried.

"You don't want to stay when this all comes down," James
said. "We don't know what's on the other side. If there is a
chance, even a fraction of a chance you'll make it, why not take
it?" James shook his hand out to Frank who stood slumped over
with his finger to his lip.

Frank looked into James' eyes, sat on the bed, and placed
his head in his hands.

"She could be right outside that door, waiting," James said.

The boom of a jet's engine shook the floor and sent James
and Eric to the ground. The ceiling crumbled around them, and
the boards on the walls bent inwards.

After picking himself up, James retreated to the door,
facing Frank.

"How do you know?" Frank said from behind his sloppy
hair.

"I –I don't."

"But we don't have time and if we're gonna die, let's die
knowing we did all we could."

After severing one of his fingers again with his knife, James
spread his blood on the seal of the door, and the blood destroyed
it.

"Just in case." He stepped into the hallway. "Eric, is there anyone else here we can save?"

"No, Andy's gone." Eric lifted his saddened face to James.

"Well, then let's get out of here."

James stopped when something tugged at his shirt. He turned to the tug with his fist ready to release his angst, but stopped when he saw the tattered image of Frank in the corner of his eye. The two men nodded, and James coaxed the group down the hallway.

As they ran down the hall, the shape of the walls morphed and changed. The lavender flames set fire to the wood and the hellish smells of lilac became mustard gas to James and his crew. The lilac watered their eyes, and James found it difficult to breathe. The gas burned his chest and caused warm liquid to gather in his mouth. They held on to the sides of the hall, as they lurched down it, no longer running.

Once the lilac gas decreased, they picked up the pace and trotted faster.

James blinked and the halls shifted. The corridors stretched and corners appeared and disappeared. The doors to either side of them vanished or materialized. The simple maze James started traveling through became a complex labyrinth.

It felt like twenty minutes since Frank accompanied them to find the exit to the house. James hadn't the slightest idea where the exit lay and led them down one dead end after the other.

"Okay, I'm lost...," James said and slowed their progress. He used his shirt to remove the dried tears from his cheek

"How do we get out of here?"

James looked to Frank and Eric, and they looked at one another unable to answer James' question.

"He changes the rooms too often for us to know, all but the fourth one," Frank said.

"That's by the stairs." Eric added.

"You know where that's at?" James asked.

Frank shook his head. "Was hoping you knew, since you found me."

"Shit. Shit..." James walked around them looking down

each direction of the hall for a sign of the room where The Gentleman was. At least the lilac gas dispersed.

Feathers, the same from the ones that crept into the house, bounced from wall to wall and swirled near James.

"Wow," he said, and the feathers brushed past him and sailed down behind him, turning the corner.

"Let's follow them. Theo hasn't let me down yet," James said and led them down the trail the feathers laid out.

Once the feathers came close to the explosion in room four, they scattered and turned into amber.

Down the way, James saw the start of the staircase. "If we run fast, we can pass that. Luckily, we got some room between the flames. But don't let it touch you," James said and showed them the scar from the fire on his hand. His fingers turned green, and the tips deteriorated before their eyes.

They forged past the ball of energy collecting in room four and halted at the opening of the stairs that spiraled downward to a fog of ghosts, demons, and howlers.

"Where did these come from?" James asked and peered down into the darkness.

"He ain't controlling them anymo' now. Now they wanna show who the head of the pack is," Eric said as he gazed down into the mosh pit.

"I bet." James took one-step on the board and it gave way.

It fell to the yells of ghouls and cackling hyenas in the basement.

"How are we supposed to leave?" James asked and searched for anything they could use to pass the crowds of spirits. His eyes met the chandelier above their heads.

"James, I'll distract them. Leave, leave me behind. It's the only way you gonna get out of here," Eric said.

"I can't do that. You will go down with the house." James paced the hall.

The sparks from the room punched the walls of the rooms out and caused fragments to swirl in the air, defying laws of physics. The roof at the end of the hall folded like soft wood. The windows shattered, and the glass spread to their faces.

"Get down!" James covered Eric as the glass jetted into the air.

Some of the spirits climbed the stairs. They slid up the boards and crept to the top. James looked at them and back at the atomic bomb that imploded in real time. As the roof fell apart, each room folded into room four, and they were next.

Eric walked to the edge of the steps and looked back at James. He reached into his pocket and handed him a handkerchief with a metal object inside. "If you see my momma, tell her, tell her I love her," Eric said to him.

"Eric, no." James reached for Eric's body, and some of the claws ripped the skin from Eric's chest.

"I have his blood. Let's see if it works again." James slit his wrist down to the bone and let the blood fall on the banister. It rolled down and evaporated anything it touched. The ghouls and ghosts screamed, and then shattered into a puff of black smoke.

"Okay, it works," James said and swayed as he looked up to Eric and Frank.

"Take it easy there." Frank removed his shirt and wrapped it around James' arm.

"We have to jump down the side of the stairs," James said and leaned to the right. Forgetting about his fatigue, he hurried backward, but not far enough to mix with the catastrophe behind him. He ran and leaped over the rail.

After landing onto the ground, he rolled into a crowd of ghouls, unwrapped his cloth Band-Aid, and spewed blood on their transparent bodies.

"Now." He motioned for Eric and Frank to join him.

They jumped into a pool of black and gray fog and fell hard on the unsteady ground.

"Agh," Eric said as James helped him up.

James turned his head to the disaster that imploded down the stairs as the light from the flames banished the steps nail by nail. From his view, none of the rooms remained. The debris from above tumbled to the ground and the dust and ash from the fire covered their skin and the areas of the grand room.

"Let's get to the door before the ghosts know what

happened." As they ran to the door, James fell to the ground.

"What's wrong?" Eric asked.

"He lost tons of blood." Frank pulled James up, assisting him to the door.

"I should be okay. The door isn't too far, and I can do it," James said. A force drew them back and he turned to it.

"Well, well, if it isn't James," a voice called.

He stood and faced a slender man with a complexion James couldn't figure out. On his skin, tattoos with strange lettering circled and continued over his body. And around his massive frame was an aura with a sky blue color. This was Shayton, the one Andrew had told him about. James looked down at his bleeding arm that dripped on the floor and dissolved pieces of wood after it fell, and then his eyes visited the thing that stood before him. God's spoiled brat.

When James rubbed the blood from his wound on the boards, they liquefied and crumbled into an abyss. The ghost fell in and James finished the job by putting more of his blood inside the vast hole. The more blood he added, the bigger the whirlpool in the sinkhole became, and it vacuumed the souls away. James fought the current and put his arm to his face as he searched for Eric and Frank.

"James!" Eric called.

One of the demons halfway in the hole clawed at his leg, and James ripped it to shreds with his hands. He threw blood in its eye, sending it to Hell. He held on to Eric, pulled him up, and pulled Frank from the ledge before the tornado captured him as well.

"Hold on to me," James said over the wind as they pushed away from the perimeter.

"We have to go now."

As they lifted their feet, the suction stole the boards underneath them. The explosion from upstairs traveled faster down the stairs and board after board floated and zapped into the bright light.

"That is crazy." Eric captured his hat before it flew into the storm. The light from the battle reflected in his eyes.

"Don't look into that, it is all bad news. Let's go." James turned them to the door. Near the exit, two teenage girls with a box in their hands stood, swaying their bodies.

"Hello," they said.

"Whoa, these girls were the twins he brought. That box, that box," Frank said and reached into his pocket. Presumably for a cigarette, but none was there. His hand came back empty.

With each step the twins took, James and his friends took two backward steps. The magnitude of the destruction behind them expanded and heat rose.

The twins stepped, they backed up, and the explosion enlarged.

The hole behind them intensified.

"We have to choose. We have to do something," Eric said, picked up a board and threw it at the twins.

They faded in-between reality and fiction, becoming a static projection of their solid bodies. The board collided with the door and didn't hit them. The twins looked back as the wood broke apart then looked back at the group.

The storm upstairs claimed the steps and was victorious over the sinkhole.

James squeezed together the slit in his wrist into his hand and launched blood in the twins' direction. They faded, and when their image returned, Anna opened the box with her cracked hands. The dance of the ballerina took stage.

"I gotta have another fruit one?" James asked and reached into his bag.

"No!" James shouted and frantically searched.

"Wait." His hand ran across his short-barreled shotgun. He snatched it from the bag, cocked it, and aimed at their heads.

"Let's see how you do against this." He squeezed the trigger and hit Maria between the eyes. Smoke from the rifle drifted. The shell bounced onto the wood and quivered on the ground near Anna's foot.

Eric and Frank held on to James. They dug their feet in to resist the surge of energy pulling them further away from the door.

Anna turned to her sister and shrilled at her sister's mangled face. Soon, her chin grew back and Anna focused on James, revealing her black teeth through her grin.

He placed his finger on the trigger again, steadying his hands as best he could.

After he lifted his rifle, he repositioned his aim, and hit the box. A high-pitched frequency escaped their mouths and shattered the glass from the window. The life from outside fluttered in and fought against the men's attempt to leave. The images of the twins became ashes that flew into the destruction.

"Let's go!" James called.

The trio ran through the dematerialized bodies of Mengele's experiment. The wind at the window blew their faces and dried their eyes. It choked them and cut their skin. They pulled each other along, fighting the forces working against them from all directions.

James turned the knob. It burned three layers of his skin. But he held on. He held on as his blood fell from his hand, searing the door as he completed the rotation.

He held on to Eric with his free hand, and Eric grabbed on to Frank. The fog broke into the house and traveled with the storm behind them, which pulled in gallons of it.

"What do we do?" Frank asked, and his hair blew all around his face.

"Jump!" James looked back one last time at the chaos inside the home: the green spiraling flame that took the upstairs and claimed a majority of the downstairs, the sinkhole that he created, and the tumbling of the home's foundation.

"Thank you," he whispered and turned his attention to the fog outside the house.

James searched Eric's and Frank's gazes. Then, they both nodded. Together they faced the green thunder outside and yelled with all they could, and threw themselves into the cold flames.

They rolled onto green grass and embedded their fingers into the soil.

The house ate itself, piece by piece.

James, watched as the house enclosed on its structure. Without warning, the sounds of destruction resided and the house was no more.

CHAPTER 21
POSTHUMOUS

L ooking to his left, James found the sweet grass that pushed its aroma to his nose. When he took in a deep breath, it smelled of heaven. The sun hugged his skin and touched his soul. No more gashes scraped his bone. No more blood fell from the valley-sized cuts, no more reminders of The Gentleman's tirade on his arm. He brought up his shirt and discovered the scar on the side of his body had disappeared.

Along with the healed wounds, the lightheadedness vanished. James lifted himself off the ground and helped up Eric. Frank helped himself.

"Where are we?" Eric walked down the path of the tall grass.

"I don't know, but we aren't in there." James looked where the house once stood.

They walked around the premise of the property, looking for any sign of it. However, there was none.

As the sun departed from the sky, it cast ribbons of red and orange that torched the blue mist and mixed with the gray clouds. Flaring his nostrils, James searched for a hint of lilac, a hint of that God-awful musk. To his relief, the only aroma he inhaled was sweet grass and peaches. The scent resembled a lazy day in a hemic near the river on the fourth of July.

In the distance, James saw a road sign with three arrows pointing in different directions.

"Maybe we'll know where we're at if we go to the road

sign." James led the two north.

"Y'all I can't think of what he looked like," Eric said and pulled out his harmonica from his pocket.

"I don't think I could ever forget his face," Frank said.

"I can. You must have hit your head real hard when we came out that house," James said over his shoulder to Eric. "No, I don't think so. I can remember how to play this." Eric blew through his horn. "I still can count cards. I remember my best friend Jerry. I remember…"

"Eric, Eric," a woman sang.

"Mom?" Eric poked his head over the fields. "Mom!" He held onto his hat as he galloped in the direction of the voice.

"Hey, Eric," James called. Eric looked at him, tipped his hat, and continued jumping through the grass. He ran to a woman who stood where the path to the grass cut off. James watched as the out of breath Eric held onto his mother. She tiptoed to clean off his cheek. Then, Eric and his mother left with the wind.

"I'll be," James said and headed in the opposite direction with Frank.

"Good for him," Frank said and lit a cigarette that he'd carried in his breast pocket.

"Where did you come from," he said to the cigarette as he rotated it between his fingers. It ignited on its own and Frank brought it to his lips, no longer scared, and inhaled it deeply.

"I'm surprised. This wasn't there in the house when I needed it. I'm surprised *we* came out of the house to be honest," he said and examined the cigarette. "How'd you know that we'd make it, anyway?"

"I didn't. I figured if the blood made the spell it had to break it or we'd die trying." James followed the grass and allowed the blades to weave between his five fingers.

"You know Eric, Andrew, and I, were the only souls he hadn't broken yet. I was terribly close. I would have given in if you hadn't come. Eric… Eric never gave in," Frank said to James and pulled on his cigarette.

"You were the first person he had spoken to, since I got

here anyway."

James walked alongside Frank and exchanged stories from their past without The Gentleman. It seemed to James, the memories of The Gentleman began to fade with the fading of the sun in the distance.

"Can you remember much of him?" James kicked a rock near his foot as they passed more and more sweet grass. Besides trees, it was the only vegetation in the area.

"Not much. I remember his eyes when we landed but now it doesn't ring a bell anymore." Frank sniffed the air. "I don't even remember his scent." Frank laughed and exhaled from his cigarette that he didn't hurry to smoke.

"What was his name?" Even though James laughed, there was a bit of honesty in his words. "I'm kidding...," James added. "I can't even remember his smile anymore. I don't even know what he smelled like." James placed his hands in his pocket and stopped near a fork in the road. At the corner sat three signs pointing in different directions. As he came closer to it, he gawked as the sign at the bottom, pointing north, dissipated.

James read the remaining signs on the wooden post, *Frank, James*.

"Look at that." James pointed to it.

Frank went in closer. The sign for James pointed in the opposite direction where he stood, and the sign for Frank pointed left.

"Says I should go to the east." Frank chuckled and drug from his cigarette.

The smoke from it didn't carry the nastiness of nicotine. It smelled of apricots to James. "Smells like fruit," James beamed at the cherry that blazed on the end of the cigarette.

"Yeah, yeah, it does." Frank raised his eyebrows.

"I think Eric was onto something, James. What's the last thing you remember before we got here, James?" Frank said and placed his back against the post of the road sign as he puffed from his cigarette.

James shrugged his shoulders. "I have glints of The

Gentleman. But nothing really clear." James walked over to where Frank stood.

"I guess I remember my dad more. Him and me working on the truck. Jeff and me bar hopping the night before we had to report for a PT test. My wife telling me she was pregnant. Not in that order, but kind of lumped into one large memory, I guess."

"What's the last thing you remember?" James asked Frank as he scratched his head.

"Adela." Frank looked into the falling sun.

"Frankie, Frankie!" a woman's voice called.

"Adela?" Frank dropped the cigarette from his mouth. He smiled to James.

"Seems this is my stop. I hope yours is as wonderful as mine, James." Frank saluted James, and then he circled in the direction of the voice. His afterimage swirled into the dusk. Frank disappeared the same way James met him.

James scratched his head and stood looking at what was left of Frank.

"Wow." After glaring at the sign with his name one it, Frank's sign became transparent. And James headed south. He walked close to the spot where they started before he stopped to admire the beauty in the unknown world. Shielding his eyes from the brightness of the sunset, the rays from the orange glare hit an object at James' feet. The silver object sparkled and glimmered.

"No..." Something shiny sparkled under James' foot. He reached to retrieve the necklace buried in the Georgia clay—his bones no longer popped like firecrackers.

"Jeff, I got 'im," James said and squeezed the chrome from the surface of the dog tags.

Once he flopped into the sweet grass, he took off his bag that appeared attached to his side since he came to the house. Falling, he felt every fiber of his body relax for the first time in years. He enjoyed the cool breeze wash over his face, the pleasant noise of the birds' hymns, and the speed of his heartbeat—normal. His smile felt twenty-two again. Twenty-two, a year where he'd had it all. He was married, he had his best friend, his dad was still with him, and the hurt of the evil thing was not there. This feeling returned to James, the feeling of true happiness. While he kicked the grass against his shoe, he kicked a ball at his feet and he reached to pick it up. But it got away from him.

"No way." James chased the ball to the dirt path and grasped it before it rolled into the other stalk of sweet grass. Then, he held it in his hand. As he ran his left hand over the red inseam, he placed three fingers on the top. He was now capable of throwing his changeup. The game wining pitch. He did more laughing than crying as he inhaled the memories stitched into it. Then he dropped to his knees, kissing the ball as he rotated.

Reaching into his pocket, he found the picture of him and his old man still there and held it up to the light of the fading sun.

DAD AND JIMMY'S FIRST DEER.

Looking at his hands, he noticed his complexion had returned. When the roar of a truck sounded and broke the hypnotic music of birds chirping, after slowly standing up, he searched above the tall grass.

"That's, that's...," James said and he walked north in the direction of the sounds of the truck's engine.

His walk became a run, and his chest burned. He lifted his legs and pounded his feet to the ground. He swung his arms as the wind forced back his hair. "I can't... believe it," he said, out of breath. The truck, cherry apple red, revved its engine and opened the door to the passenger side as James came within a few feet of it.

"Jimmy?"

James decreased his momentum, sliding on his heels, and motioned to the familiar voice. He smiled. Not the perfunctory smiles from the previous years, but a smile to a welcoming face he hadn't seen in a long time.

"If you're here, then I'm..." James words trailed, and he bounced the dog tags in his hand.

"This whole time?" James lifted his hands and ran his hand

through his untangled hair. "This whole time." He lowered his voice.

"It's been a long time, huh?" the familiar voice said.

The engine of the truck continued to roar as it blew smoke from the exhaust. After glaring at it, James pocketed the dog tags and walked in the direction of his long lost friend.

Once James shielded his eyes to the sky, he saw the sun was gone. All the memories of The Gentleman, even his name, departed with it.

ABOUT THE AUTHOR

Natasha Powell is an avid gamer, anime and manga junky, comic artist, sci/fi nut, in other words, a well-rounded nerd. When she isn't busy fighting pirates for booty on the high seas, Natasha resides in her home in Tampa, Florida, where she continues to write horror, thriller, and sci/fi.

www.ingramcontent.com/pod-product-compliance
Lightning Source LLC
Chambersburg PA
CBHW071456170626
46811CB00007B/2599

* 9 7 8 0 6 1 5 9 9 0 3 7 8 *